GIDEON FALLS WICKED WORLDS

LAYOUT & PRODUCTION BY RYAN BREWER

IMAGE COMICS, INC. • **Todd McFarlane:** President • **Jim Valentino:** Vice President • **Marc Silvestri:** Chief Executive Officer • **Erik Larsen:** Chief Financial Officer • **Robert Kirkman:** Chief Operating Officer • **Eric Stephenson:** Publisher / Chief Creative Officer • **Nicole Lapalme:** Controller • **Leanna Caunter:** Accounting Analyst • **Sue Korpela:** Accounting & HR Manager • **Marla Eizik:** Talent Liaison • **Jeff Boison:** Director of Sales & Publishing Planning • **Dirk Wood:** Director of International Sales & Licensing • **Alex Cox:** Director of Direct Market Sales • **Chloe Ramos:** Book Market & Library Sales Manager • **Emilio Bautista:** Digital Sales Coordinator • **Jon Schlaffman:** Specialty Sales Coordinator • **Kat Salazar:** Director of PR & Marketing • **Drew Fitzgerald:** Marketing Content Associate • **Heather Doornink:** Production Director • **Drew Gill:** Art Director • **Hilary DiLoreto:** Print Manager • **Tricia Ramos:** Traffic Manager • **Melissa Gifford:** Content Manager • **Erika Schnatz:** Senior Production Artist • **Ryan Brewer:** Production Artist • **Deanna Phelps:** Production Artist • **IMAGECOMICS.COM**

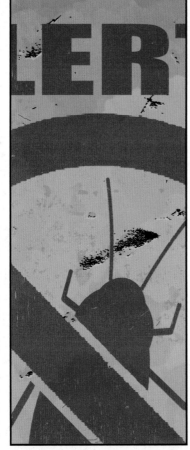
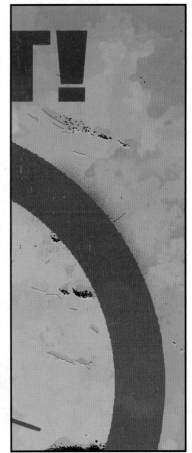

ALERT!

if you see any of these
in a nearby area, leave
IMMEDIATELY and call
the police

888-333-111111111

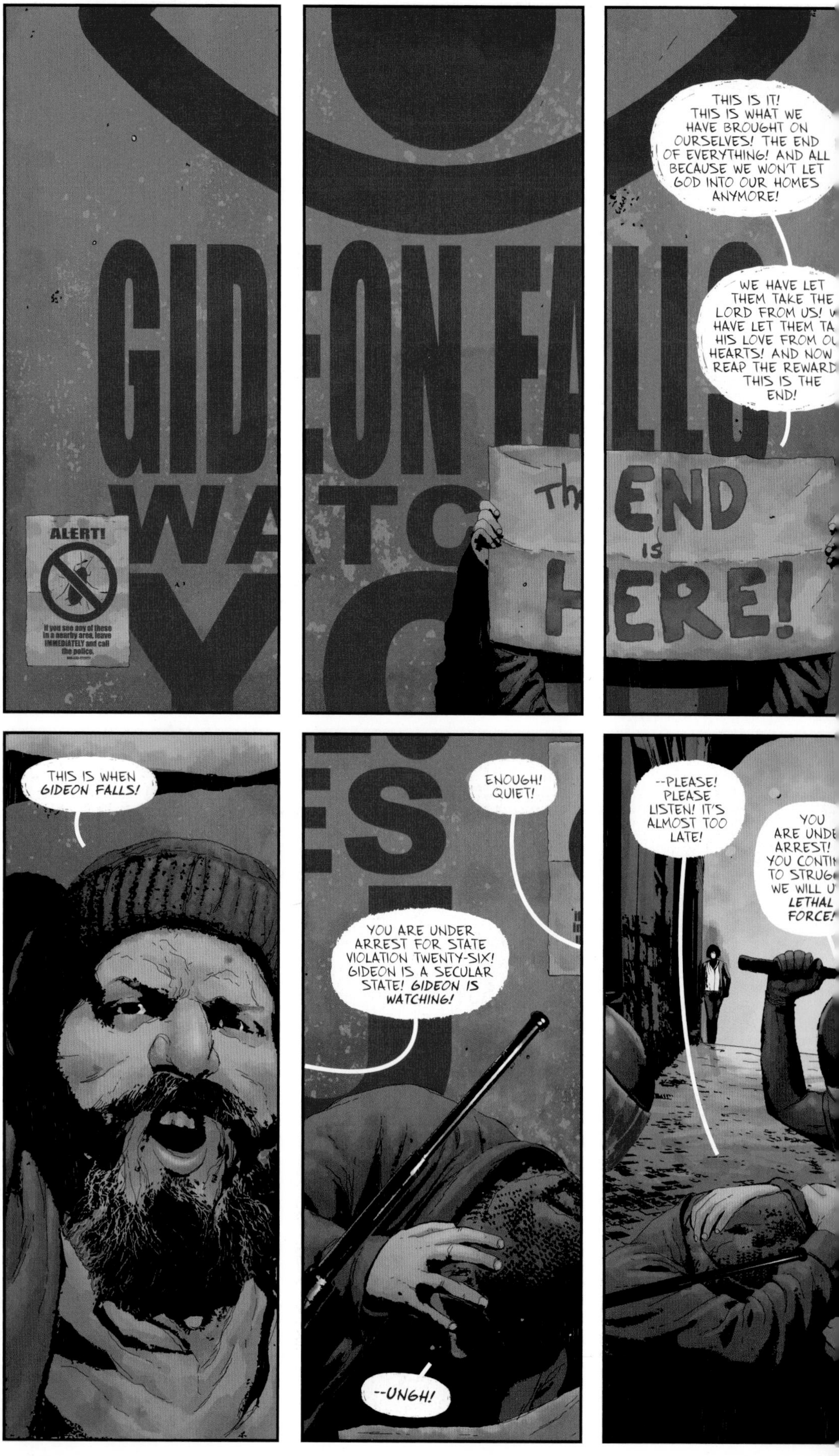
ALERT!
If you see any of these in a nearby area, leave IMMEDIATELY and call the police.
THIS IS IT! THIS IS WHAT WE HAVE BROUGHT ON OURSELVES! THE END OF EVERYTHING! AND ALL BECAUSE WE WON'T LET GOD INTO OUR HOMES ANYMORE!
WE HAVE LET THEM TAKE THE LORD FROM US! W HAVE LET THEM TA HIS LOVE FROM OU HEARTS! AND NOW REAP THE REWARD THIS IS THE END!
THIS IS WHEN GIDEON FALLS!
ENOUGH! QUIET!
YOU ARE UNDER ARREST FOR STATE VIOLATION TWENTY-SIX! GIDEON IS A SECULAR STATE! GIDEON IS WATCHING!
--UNGH!
--PLEASE! PLEASE LISTEN! IT'S ALMOST TOO LATE!
YOU ARE UNDE ARREST! YOU CONTI TO STRUG WE WILL U LETHAL FORCE!

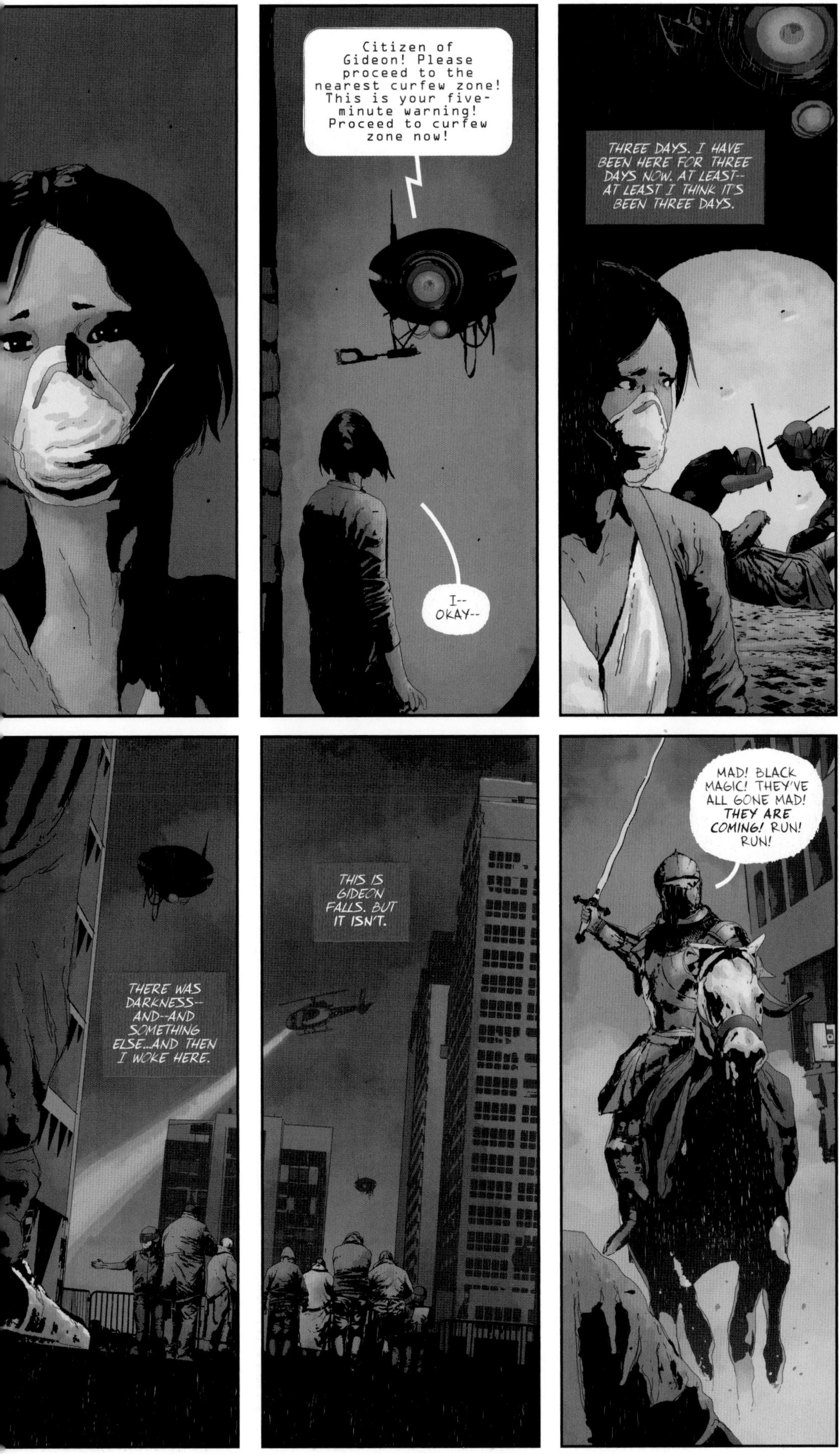
Citizen of Gideon! Please proceed to the nearest curfew zone! This is your five-minute warning! Proceed to curfew zone now!
I-- OKAY--
THREE DAYS. I HAVE BEEN HERE FOR THREE DAYS NOW. AT LEAST-- AT LEAST I THINK IT'S BEEN THREE DAYS.
THERE WAS DARKNESS-- AND--AND SOMETHING ELSE...AND THEN I WOKE HERE.
THIS IS GIDEON FALLS. BUT IT ISN'T.
MAD! BLACK MAGIC! THEY'VE ALL GONE MAD! THEY ARE COMING! RUN! RUN!

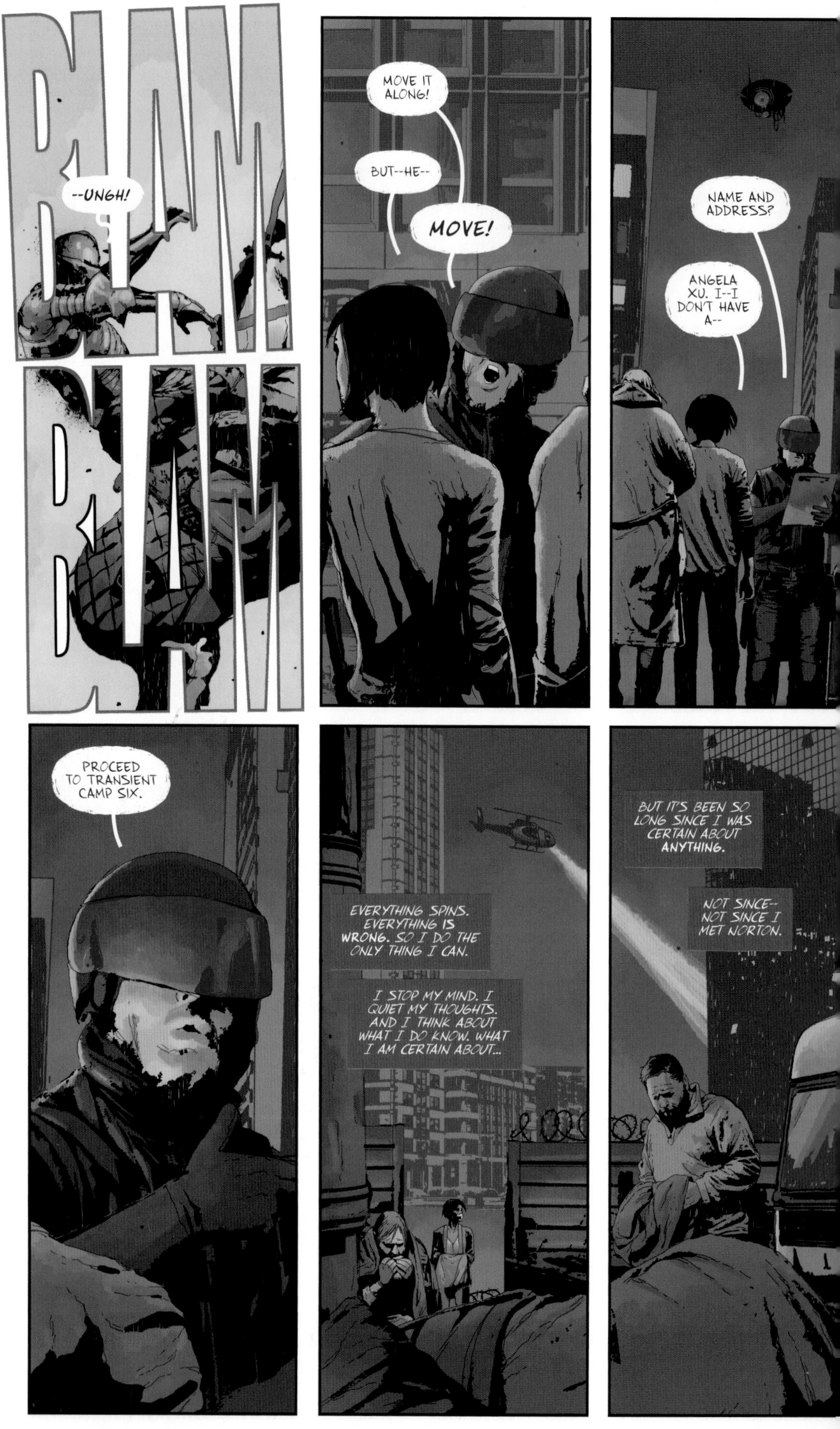
BLAM
--UNGH!
BLAM
MOVE IT ALONG!
BUT--HE--
MOVE!
NAME AND ADDRESS?
ANGELA XU. I--I DON'T HAVE A--
PROCEED TO TRANSIENT CAMP SIX.
EVERYTHING SPINS. EVERYTHING IS WRONG. SO I DO THE ONLY THING I CAN.
I STOP MY MIND. I QUIET MY THOUGHTS. AND I THINK ABOUT WHAT I DO KNOW. WHAT I AM CERTAIN ABOUT...
BUT IT'S BEEN SO LONG SINCE I WAS CERTAIN ABOUT ANYTHING.
NOT SINCE-- NOT SINCE I MET NORTON.

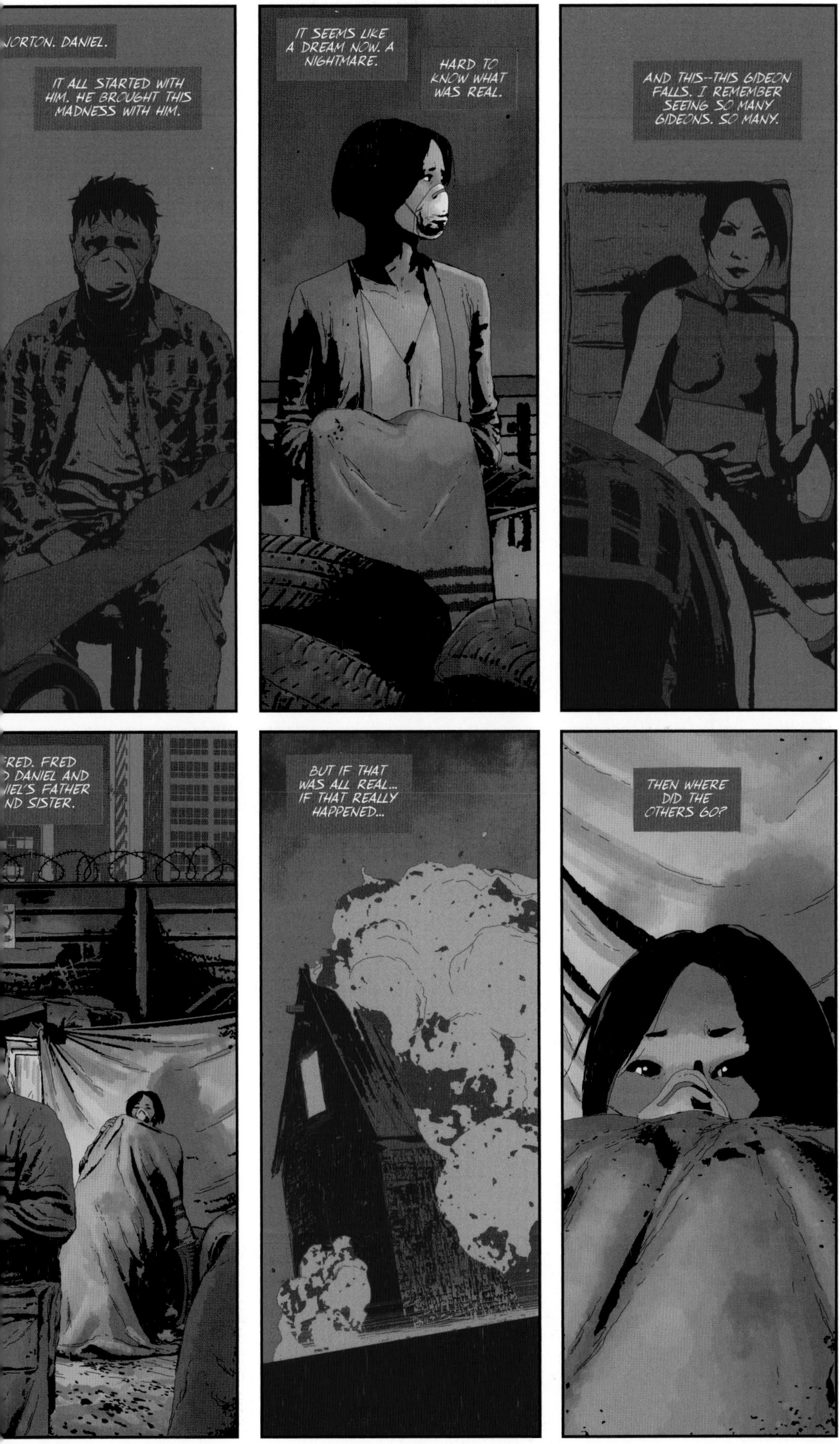
NORTON. DANIEL.
IT ALL STARTED WITH HIM. HE BROUGHT THIS MADNESS WITH HIM.
IT SEEMS LIKE A DREAM NOW. A NIGHTMARE.
HARD TO KNOW WHAT WAS REAL.
AND THIS--THIS GIDEON FALLS. I REMEMBER SEEING SO MANY GIDEONS. SO MANY.
FRED. FRED
DANIEL AND
IEL'S FATHER
ND SISTER.
BUT IF THAT WAS ALL REAL... IF THAT REALLY HAPPENED...
THEN WHERE DID THE OTHERS GO?

Jeff Lemire
Andrea Sorrentino

original colors by:
Dave Stewart

lettering and design by:
Steve Wands

and edited by:
Will Dennis

GIDEON

FALLS

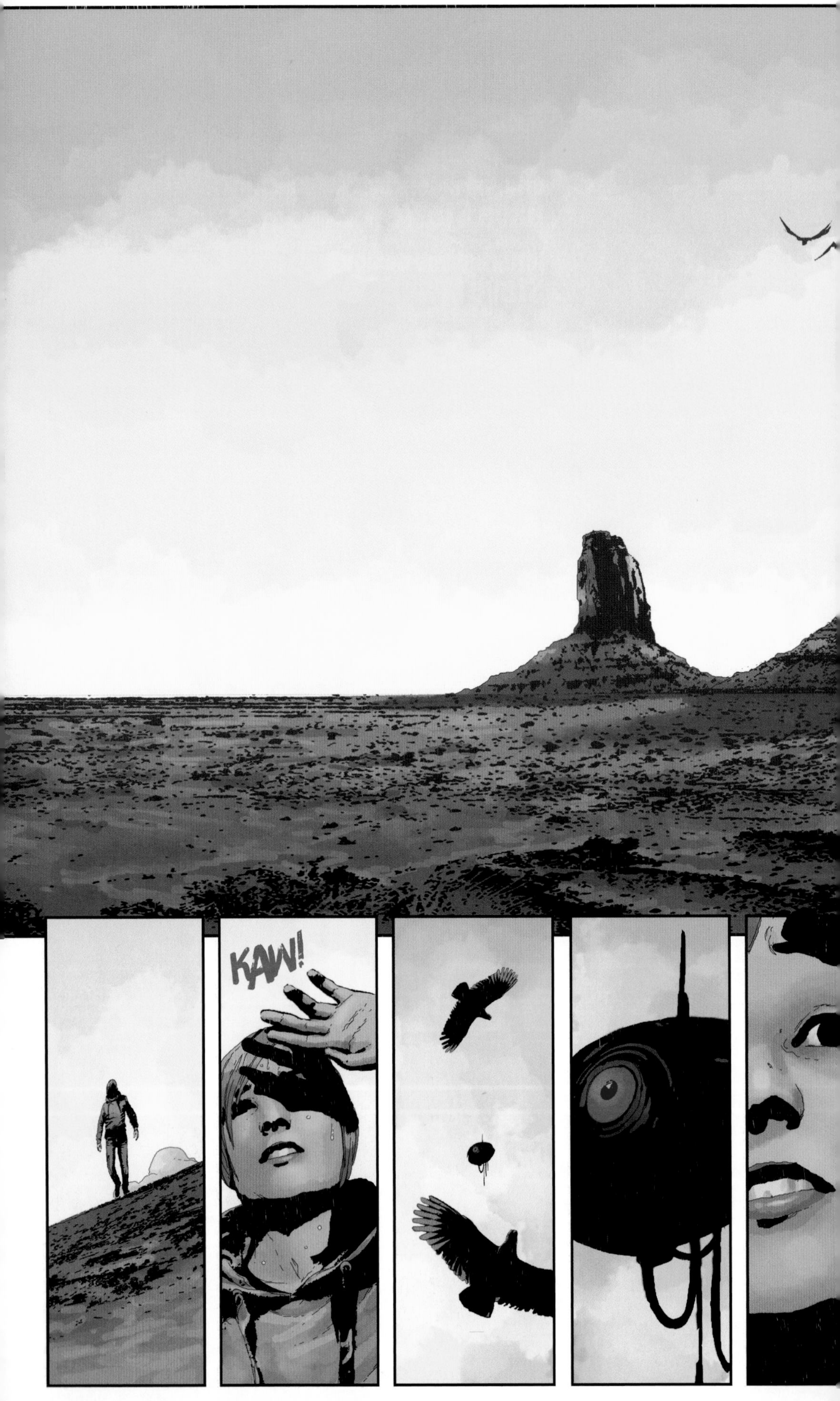
KAW!

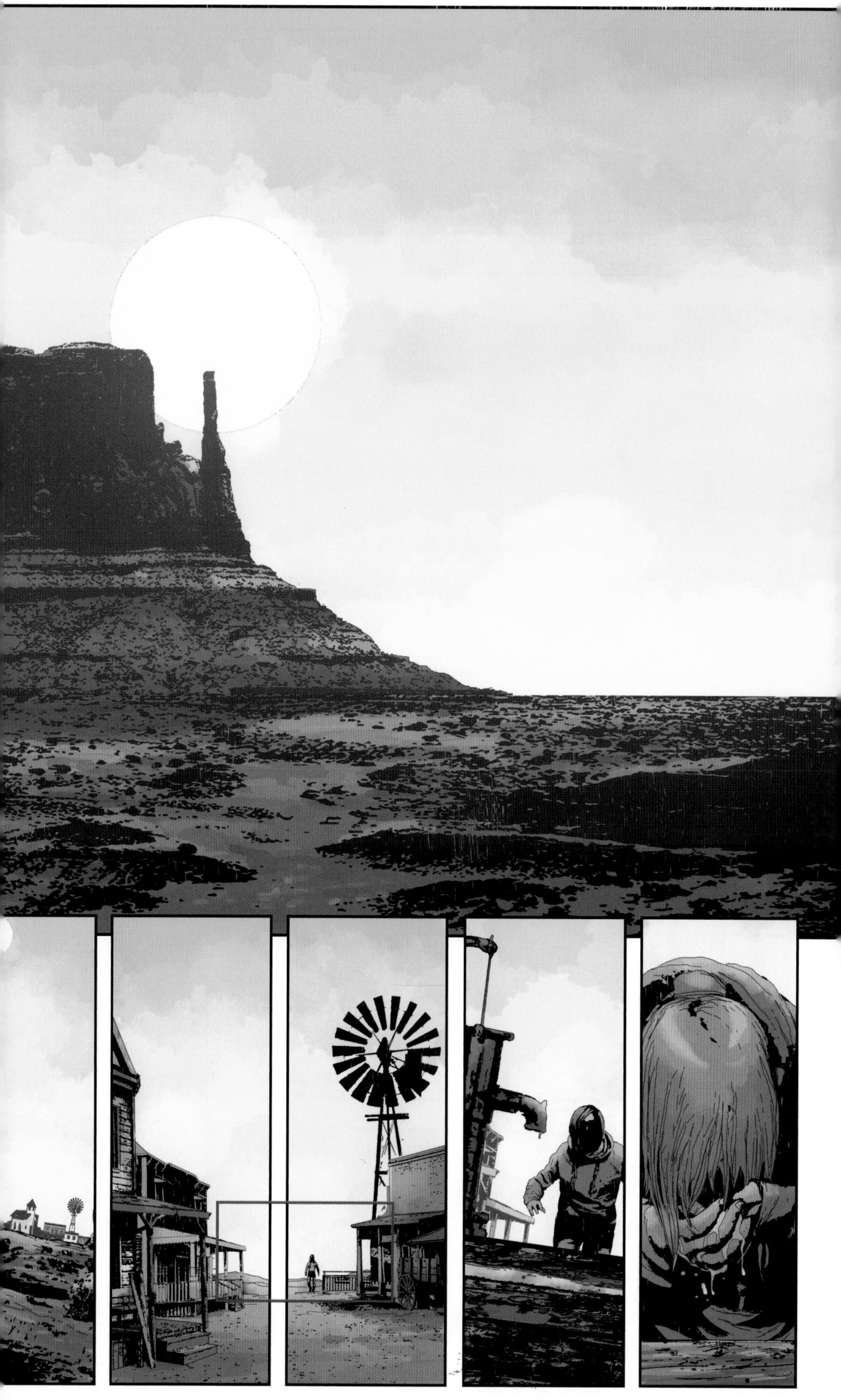

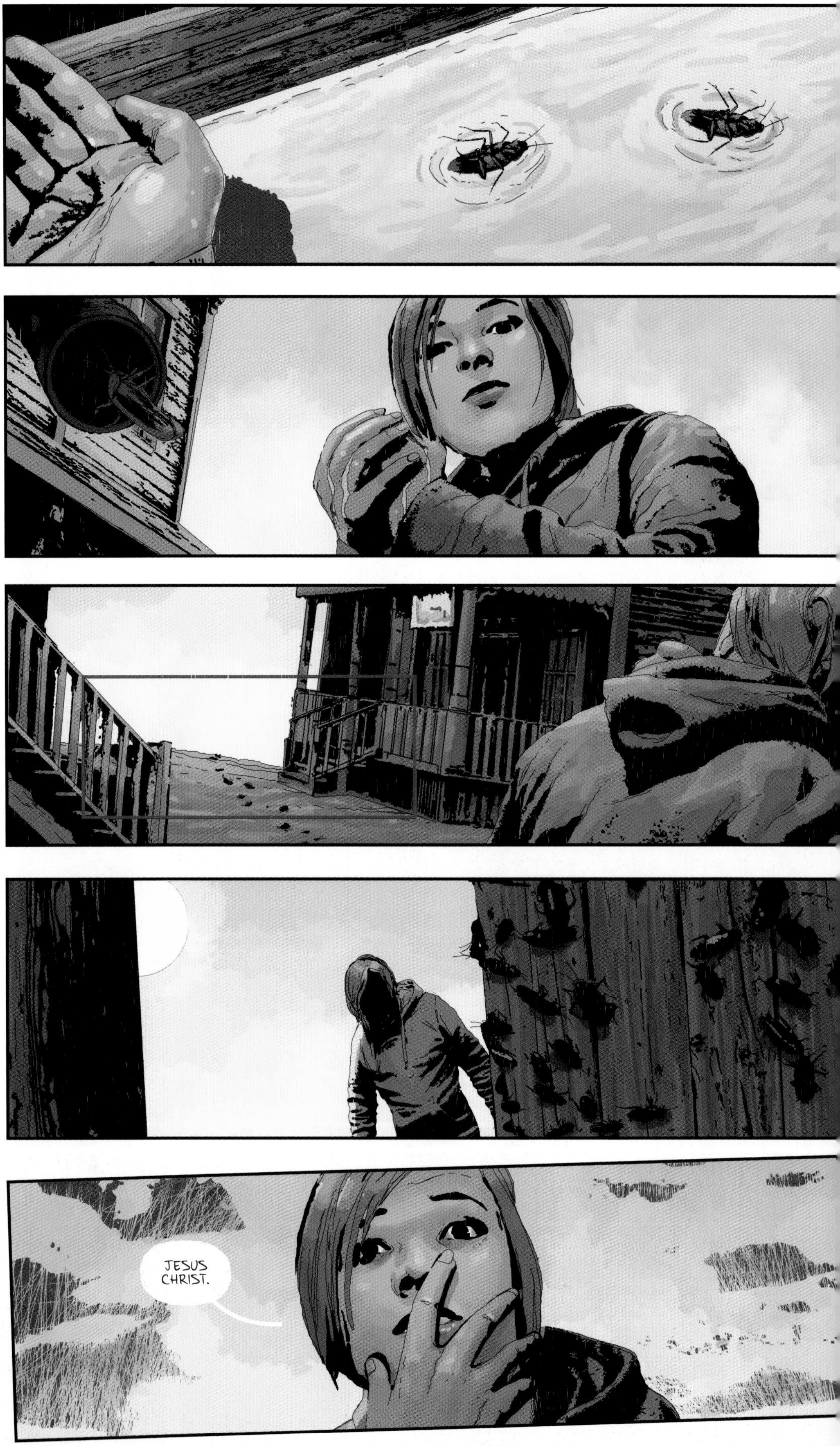
JESUS CHRIST.

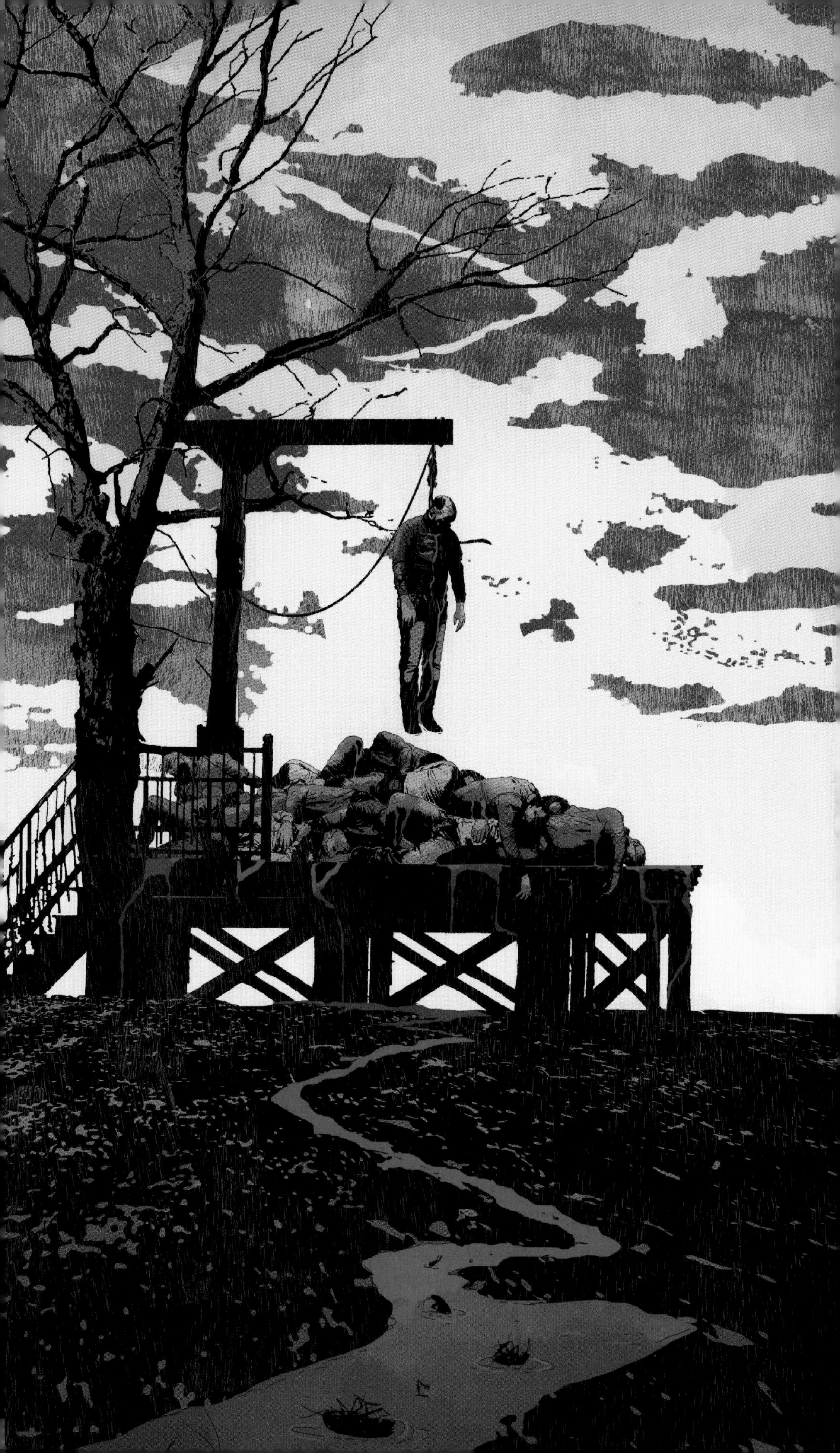

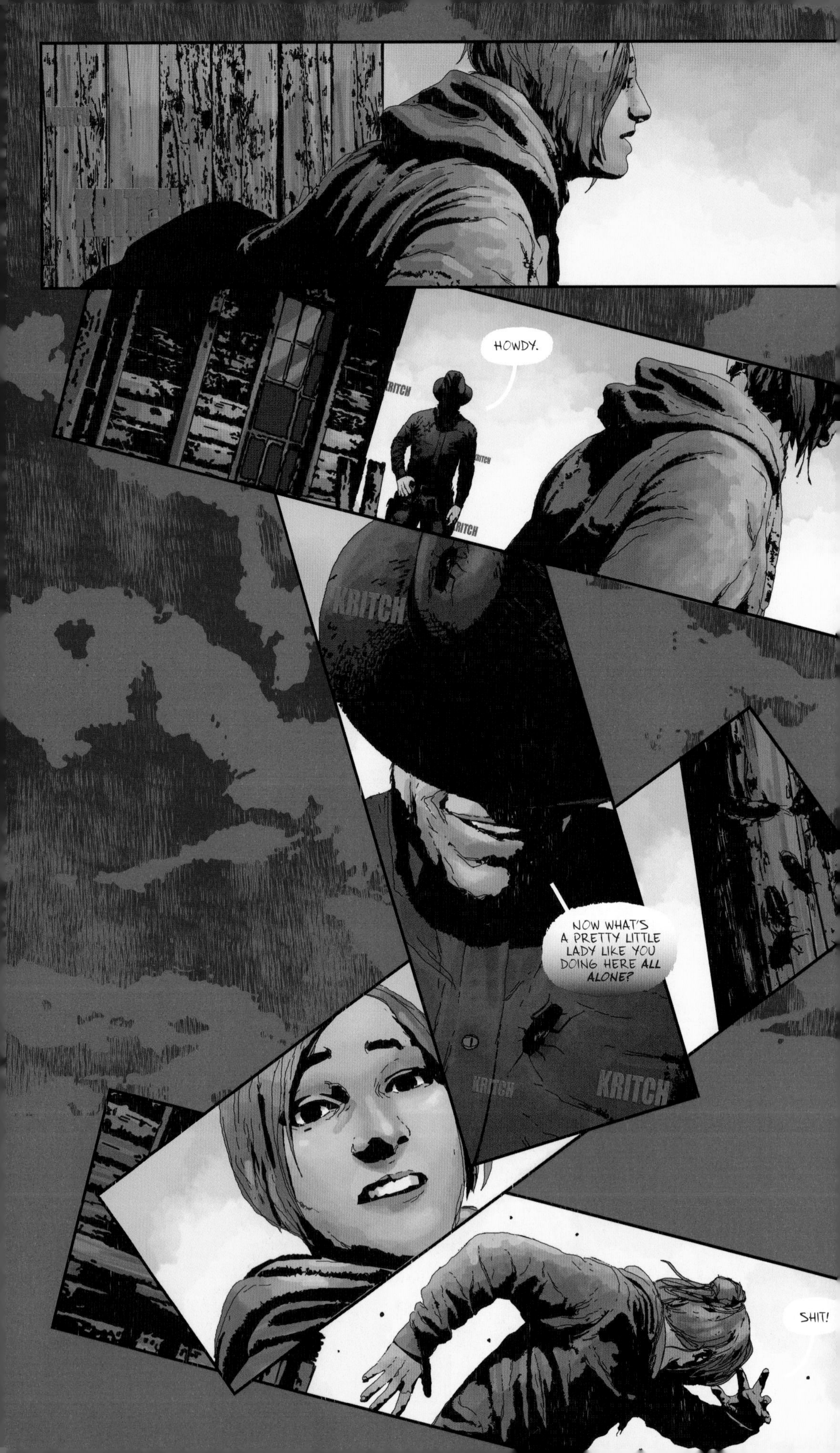
KRITCH
KRITCH
HOWDY.
KRITCH
KRITCH
KRITCH
KRITCH
NOW WHAT'S A PRETTY LITTLE LADY LIKE YOU DOING HERE ALL ALONE?
KRITCH
KRITCH
SHIT!

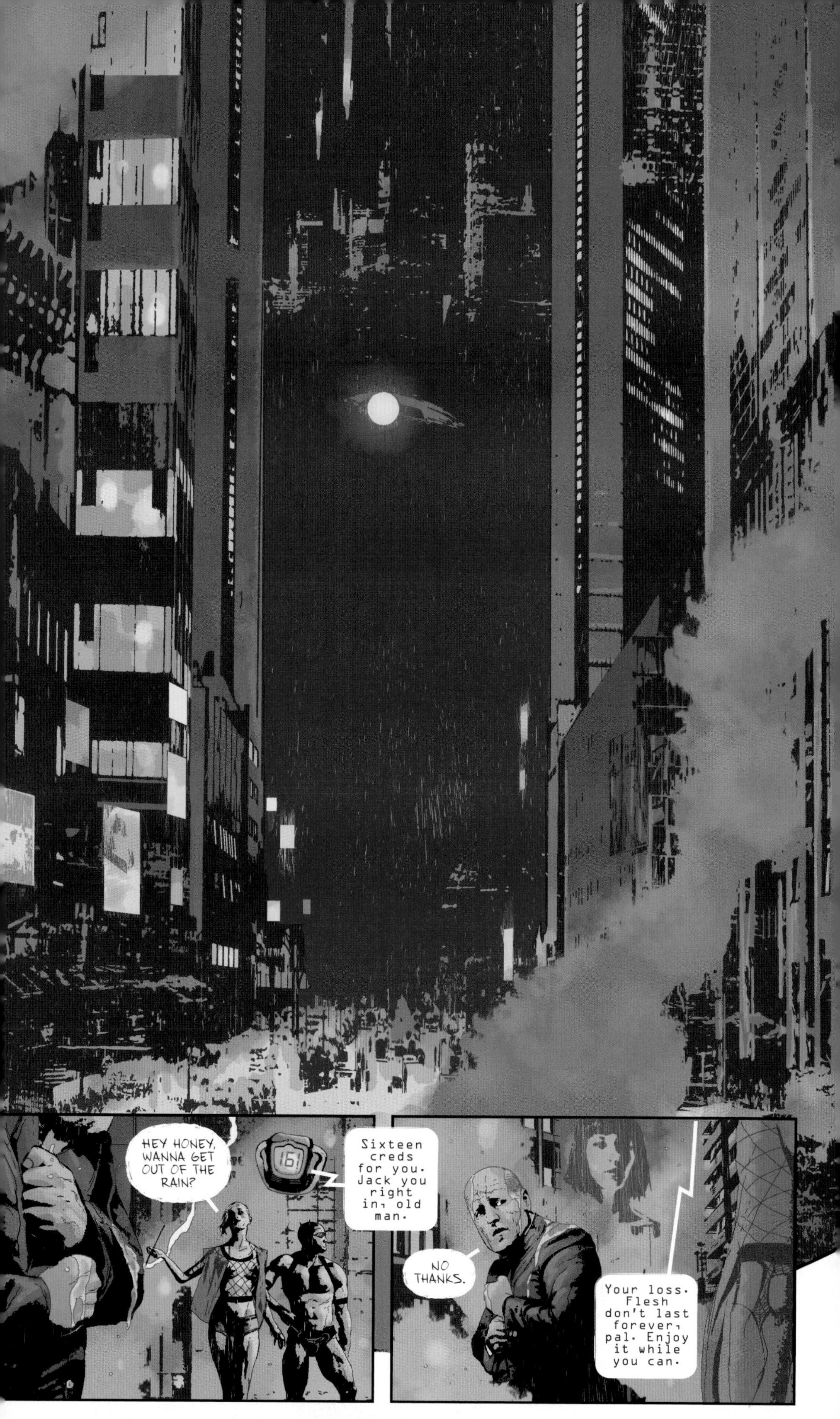
HEY HONEY, WANNA GET OUT OF THE RAIN?
16!
Sixteen creds for you. Jack you right in, old man.
NO THANKS.
Your loss. Flesh don't last forever, pal. Enjoy it while you can.

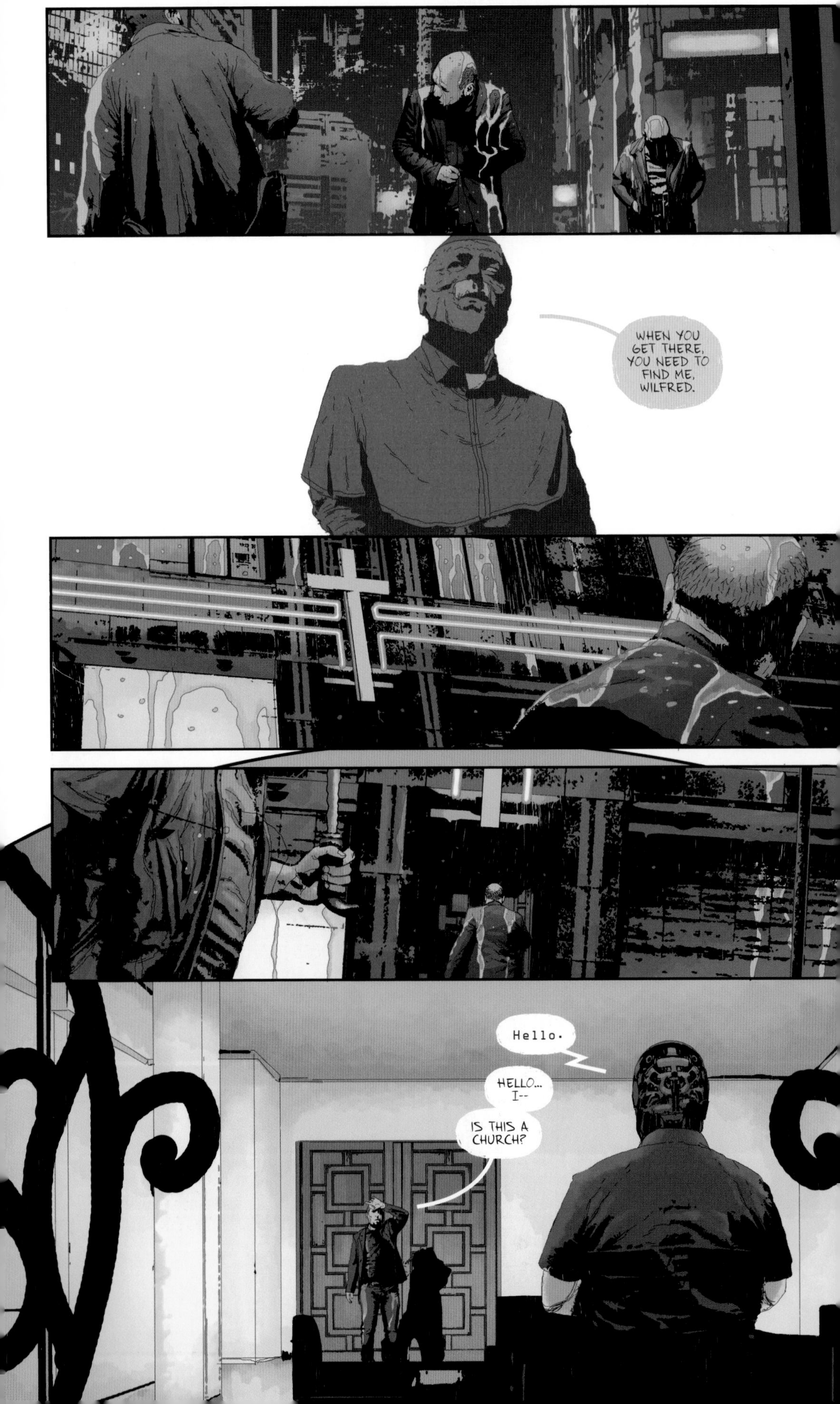
WHEN YOU GET THERE, YOU NEED TO FIND ME, WILFRED.
Hello.
HELLO... I--
IS THIS A CHURCH?

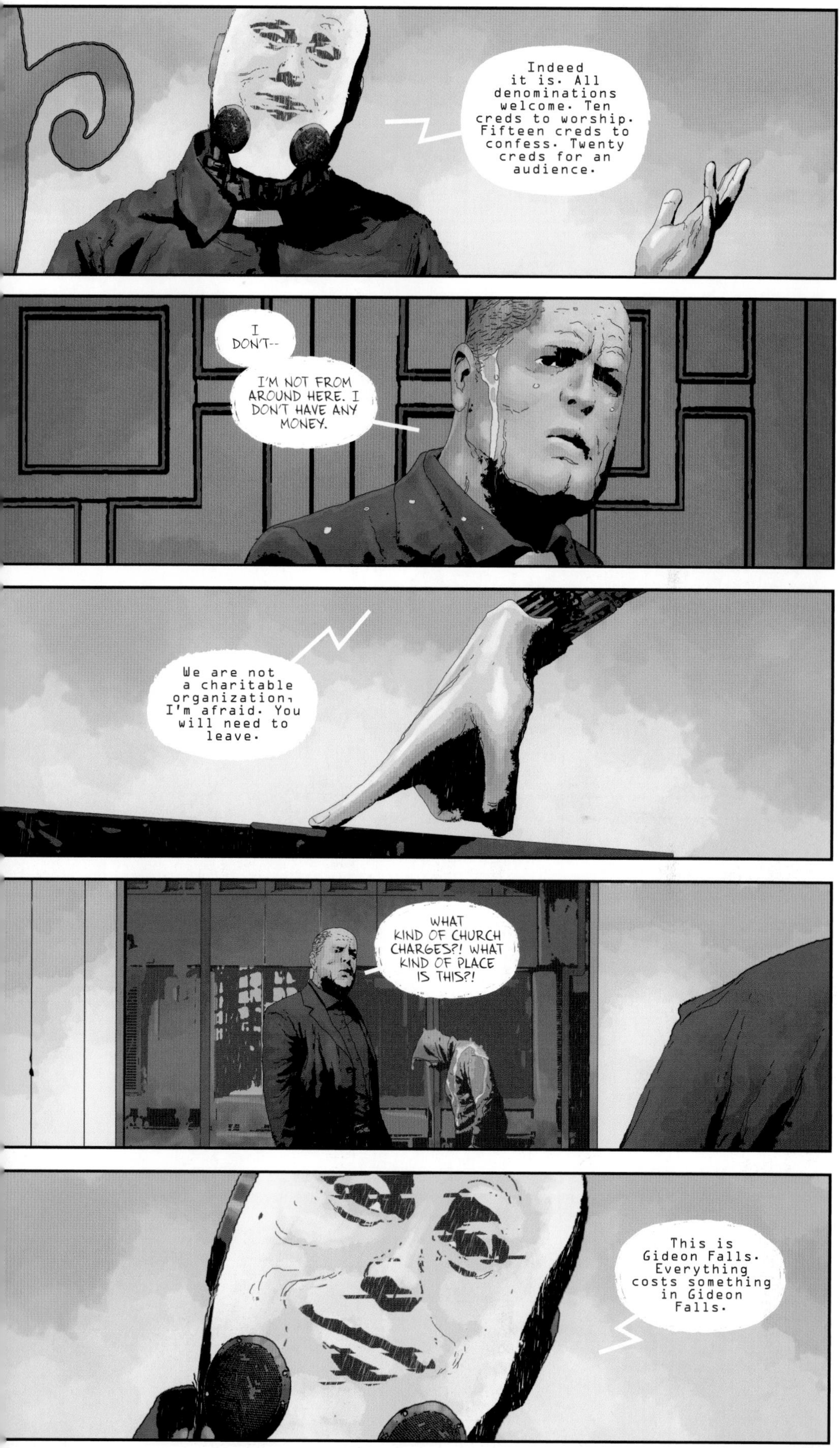

Indeed it is. All denominations welcome. Ten creds to worship. Fifteen creds to confess. Twenty creds for an audience.
I DON'T--
I'M NOT FROM AROUND HERE. I DON'T HAVE ANY MONEY.
We are not a charitable organization, I'm afraid. You will need to leave.
WHAT KIND OF CHURCH CHARGES?! WHAT KIND OF PLACE IS THIS?!
This is Gideon Falls. Everything costs something in Gideon Falls.

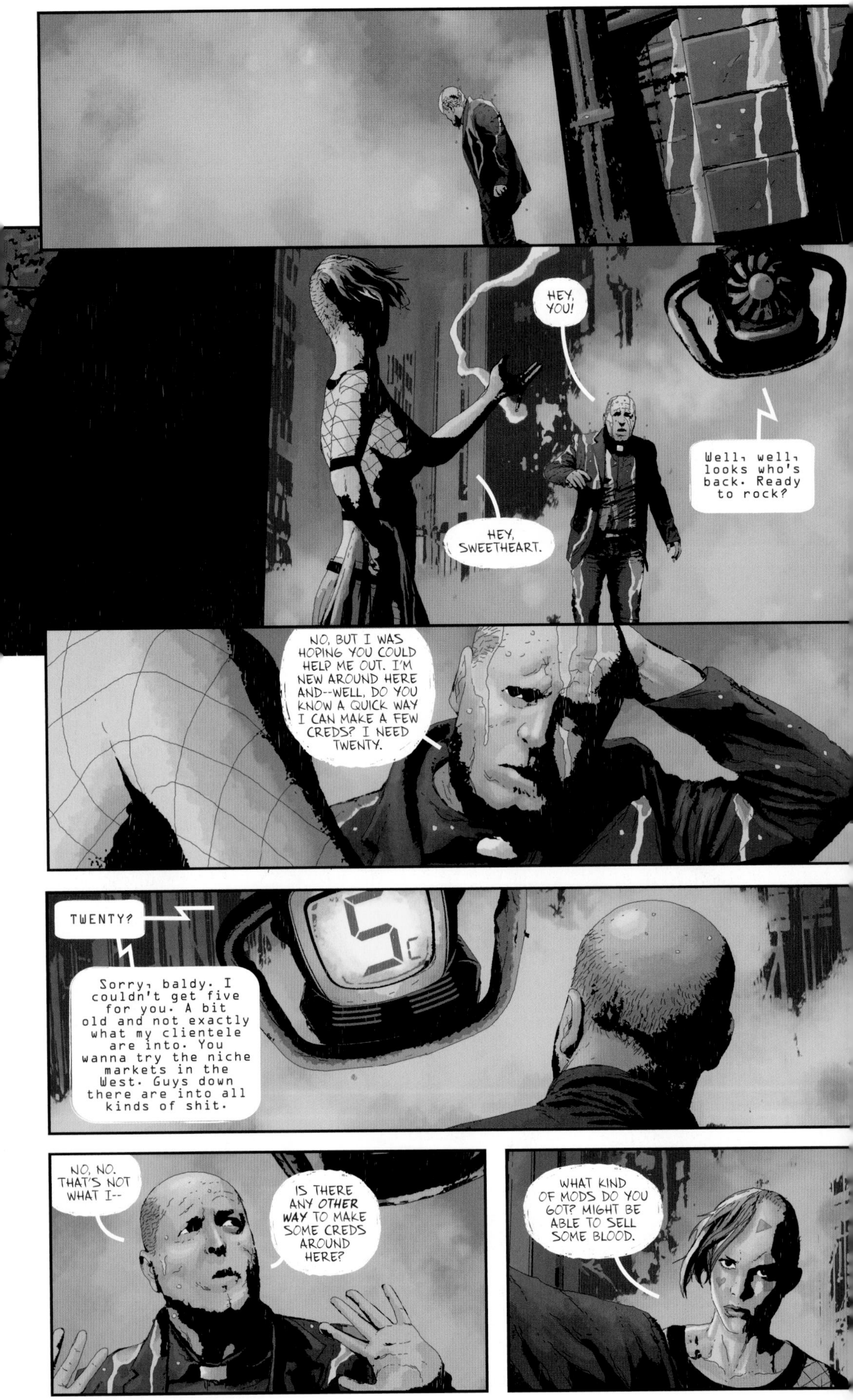
HEY, YOU!
Well, well, looks who's back. Ready to rock?
HEY, SWEETHEART.
NO, BUT I WAS HOPING YOU COULD HELP ME OUT. I'M NEW AROUND HERE AND--WELL, DO YOU KNOW A QUICK WAY I CAN MAKE A FEW CREDS? I NEED TWENTY.
5c
TWENTY?
Sorry, baldy. I couldn't get five for you. A bit old and not exactly what my clientele are into. You wanna try the niche markets in the West. Guys down there are into all kinds of shit.
NO, NO. THAT'S NOT WHAT I--
IS THERE ANY *OTHER WAY* TO MAKE SOME CREDS AROUND HERE?
WHAT KIND OF MODS DO YOU GOT? MIGHT BE ABLE TO SELL SOME BLOOD.

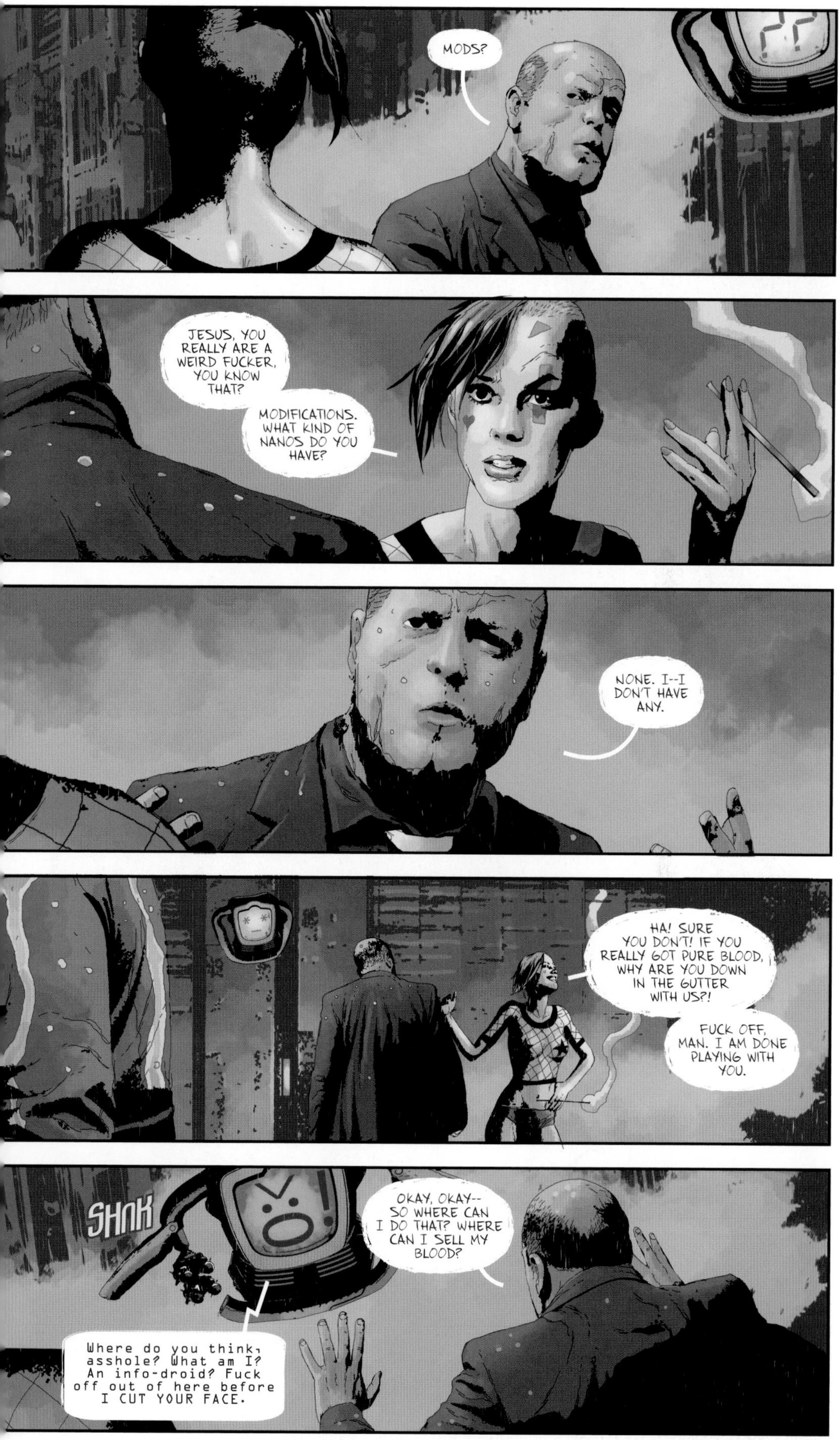
MODS?
JESUS, YOU REALLY ARE A WEIRD FUCKER, YOU KNOW THAT?
MODIFICATIONS. WHAT KIND OF NANOS DO YOU HAVE?
NONE. I--I DON'T HAVE ANY.
HA! SURE YOU DON'T! IF YOU REALLY GOT PURE BLOOD, WHY ARE YOU DOWN IN THE GUTTER WITH US?!
FUCK OFF, MAN. I AM DONE PLAYING WITH YOU.
SHNK
OKAY, OKAY-- SO WHERE CAN I DO THAT? WHERE CAN I SELL MY BLOOD?
Where do you think, asshole? What am I? An info-droid? Fuck off out of here before I CUT YOUR FACE.

WHOA! OKAY, OKAY!

WHAT AM I SUPPOSED TO DO? WHAT DO YOU WANT FROM ME?

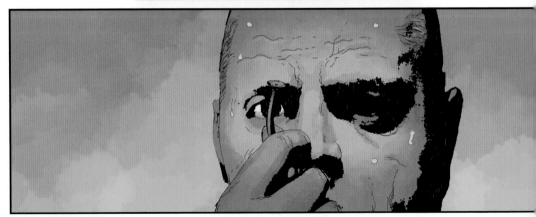

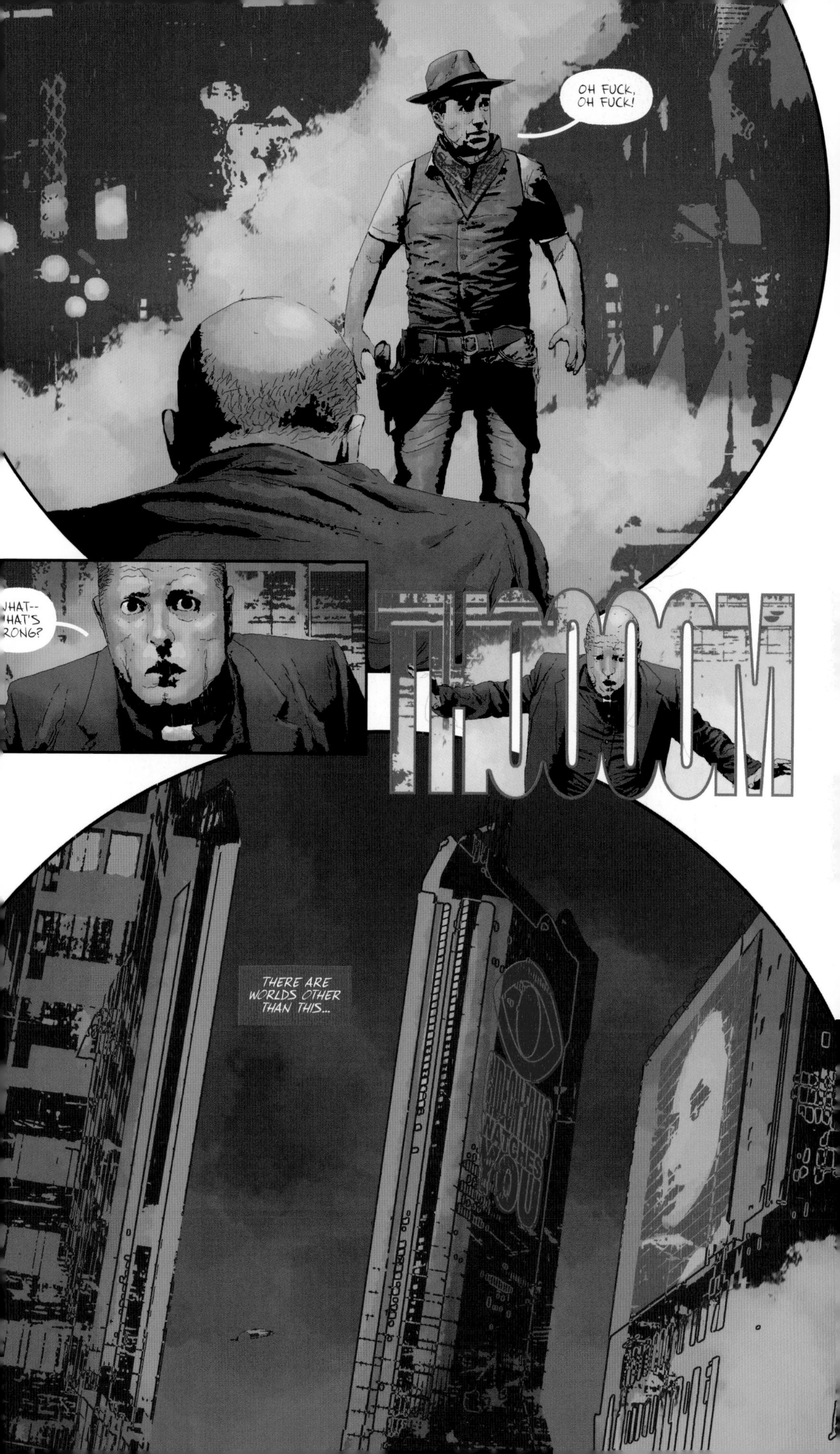
OH FUCK,
OH FUCK!
WHAT--
WHAT'S
WRONG?
THOOOM
THERE ARE
WORLDS OTHER
THAN THIS...
WATCHES
YOU

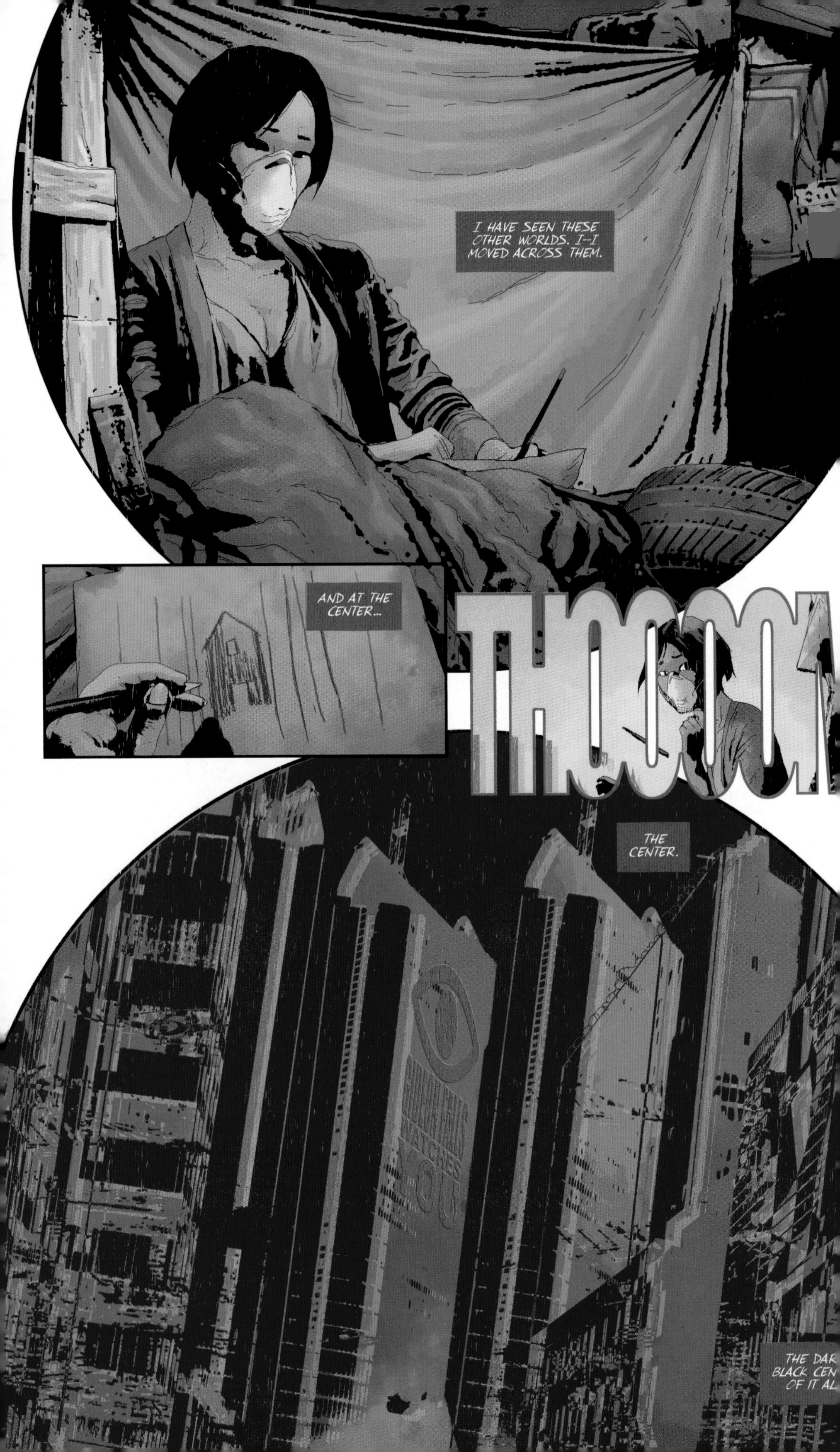

I HAVE SEEN THESE OTHER WORLDS. I--I MOVED ACROSS THEM.
AND AT THE CENTER...
THE CENTER.
THE DAR BLACK CEN OF IT AL

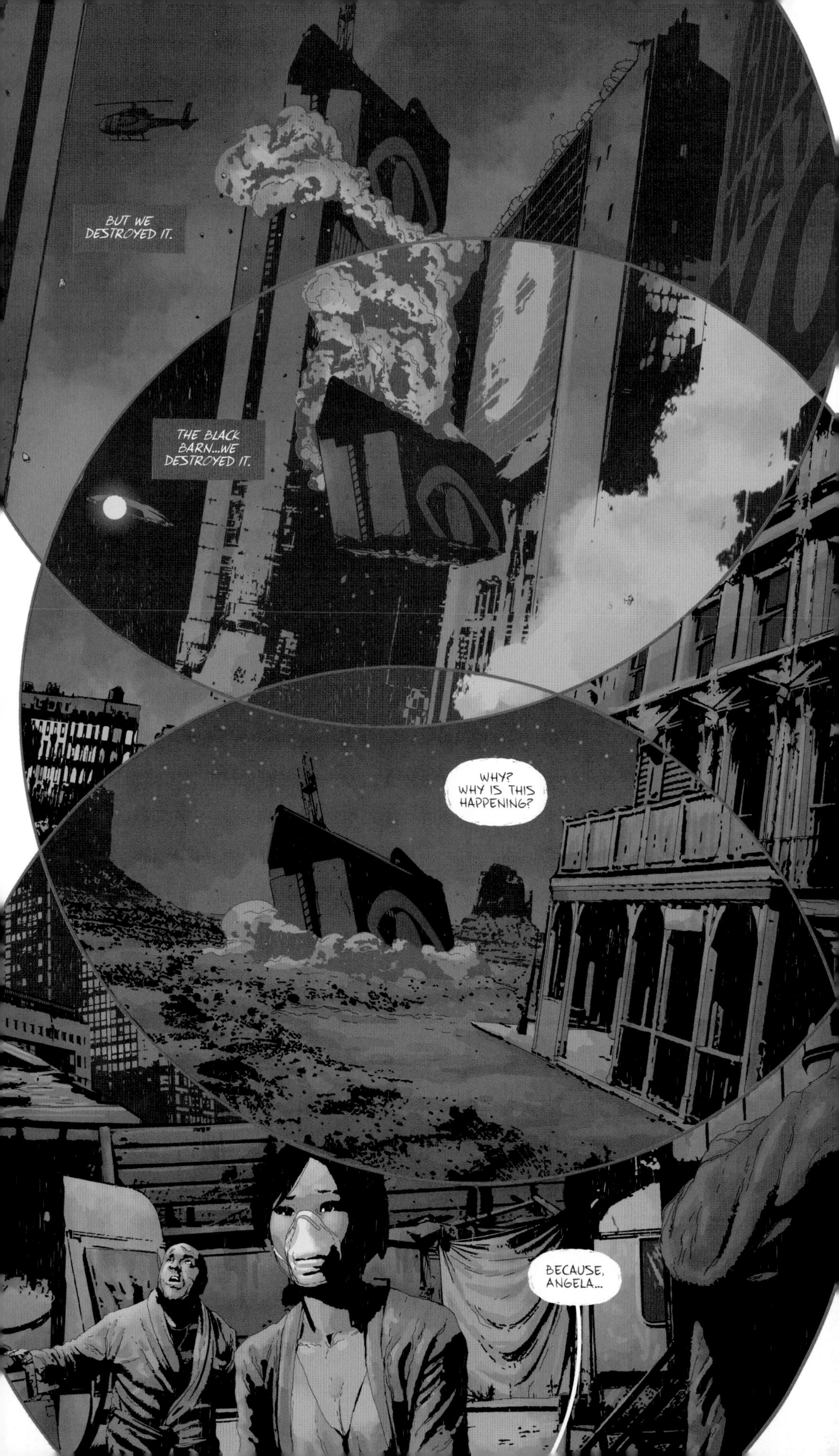
BUT WE DESTROYED IT.
THE BLACK BARN...WE DESTROYED IT.
WHY? WHY IS THIS HAPPENING?
BECAUSE, ANGELA...

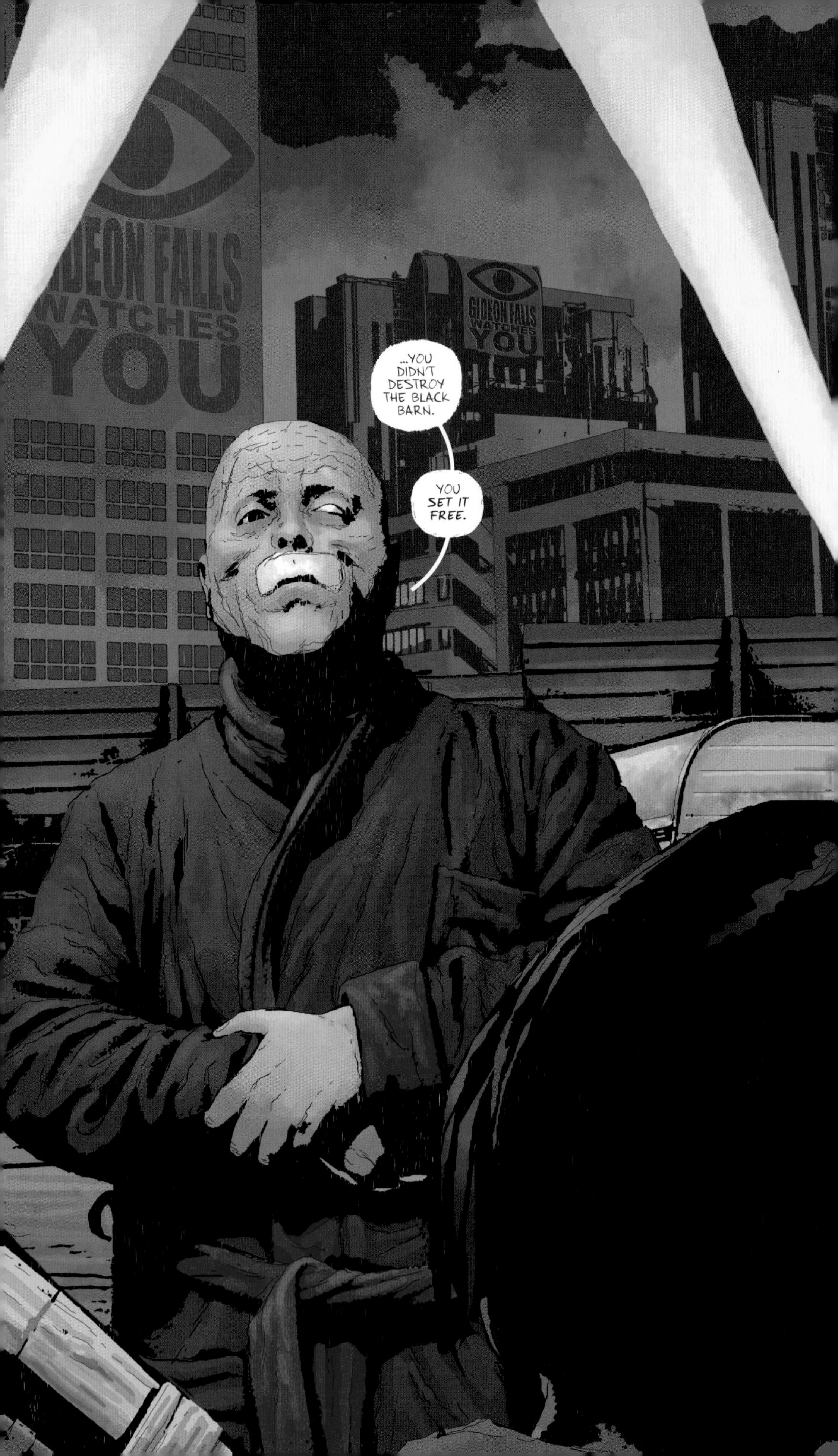
GIDEON FALLS WATCHES YOU
...YOU DIDN'T DESTROY THE BLACK BARN.
YOU SET IT FREE.

GIDEON
FALLS

Twenty-Three

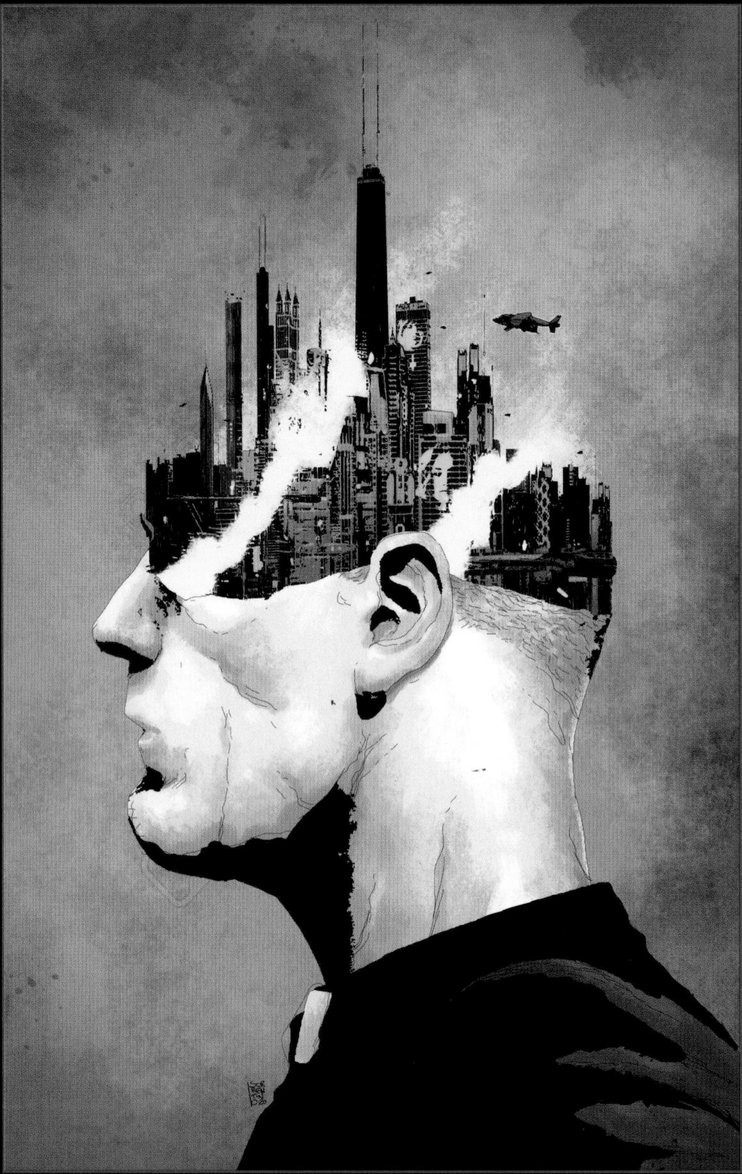

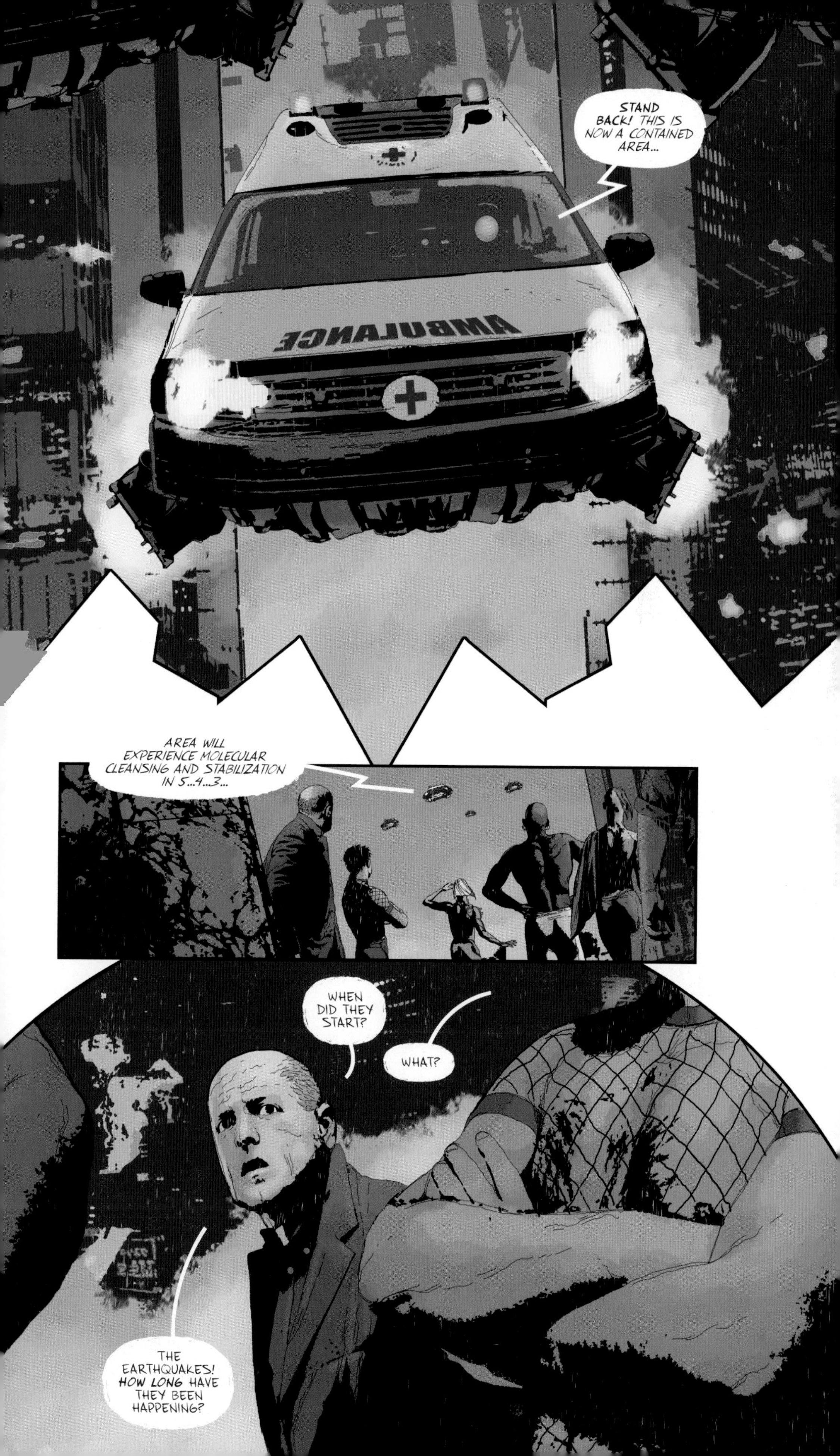
STAND BACK! THIS IS NOW A CONTAINED AREA...
AMBULANCE
AREA WILL EXPERIENCE MOLECULAR CLEANSING AND STABILIZATION IN 5...4...3...
WHEN DID THEY START?
WHAT?
THE EARTHQUAKES! **HOW LONG** HAVE THEY BEEN HAPPENING?

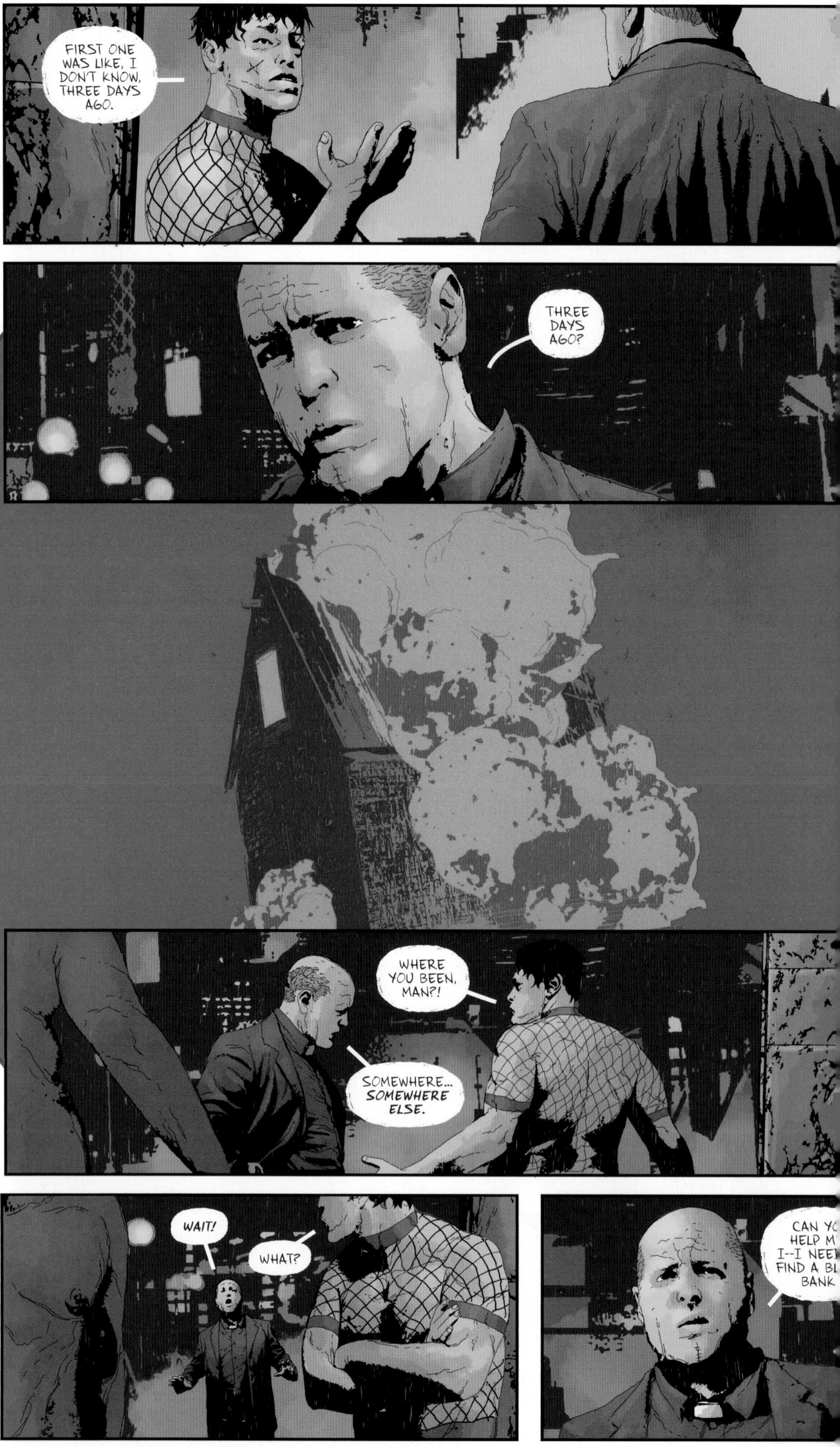
FIRST ONE WAS LIKE, I DON'T KNOW, THREE DAYS AGO.
THREE DAYS AGO?
WHERE YOU BEEN, MAN?!
SOMEWHERE... SOMEWHERE ELSE.
WAIT!
WHAT?

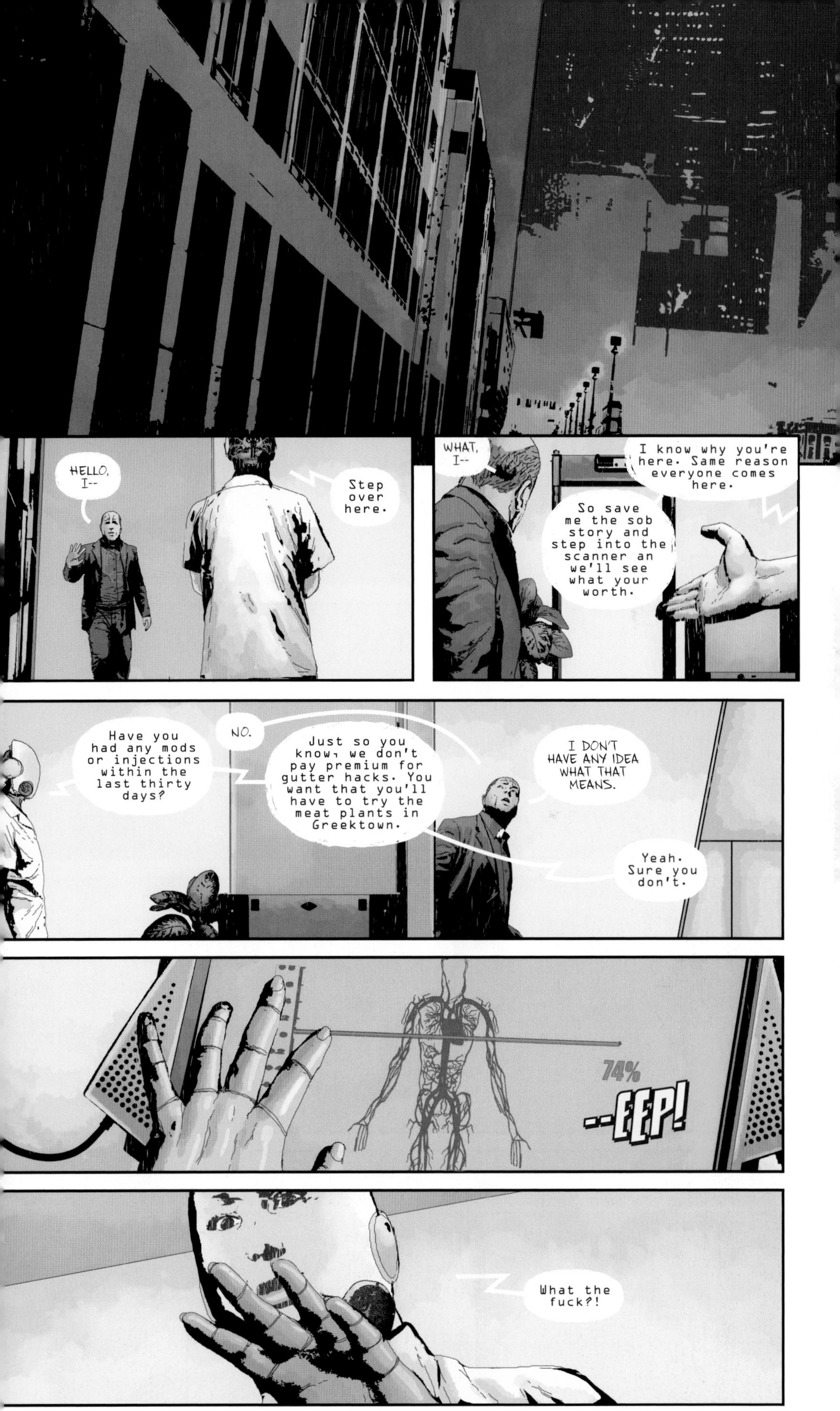

HELLO, I--
Step over here.
WHAT, I--
I know why you're here. Same reason everyone comes here.
So save me the sob story and step into the scanner an we'll see what your worth.
Have you had any mods or injections within the last thirty days?
NO.
Just so you know, we don't pay premium for gutter hacks. You want that you'll have to try the meat plants in Greektown.
I DON'T HAVE ANY IDEA WHAT THAT MEANS.
Yeah. Sure you don't.
74%
--EEP!
What the fuck?!

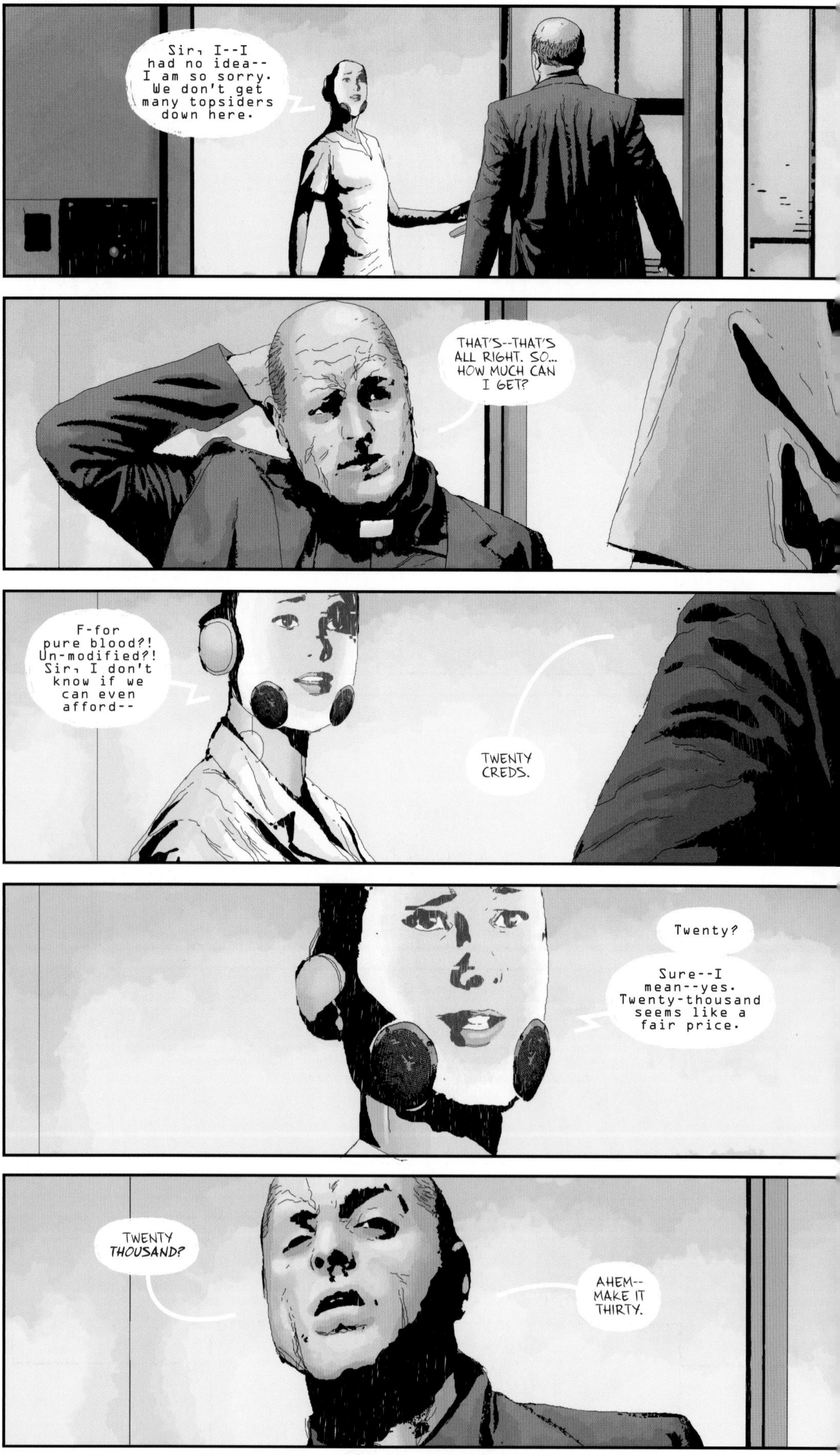
Sir, I--I had no idea-- I am so sorry. We don't get many topsiders down here.
THAT'S--THAT'S ALL RIGHT. SO... HOW MUCH CAN I GET?
F-for pure blood?! Un-modified?! Sir, I don't know if we can even afford--
TWENTY CREDS.
Twenty?
Sure--I mean--yes. Twenty-thousand seems like a fair price.
TWENTY THOUSAND?
AHEM-- MAKE IT THIRTY.

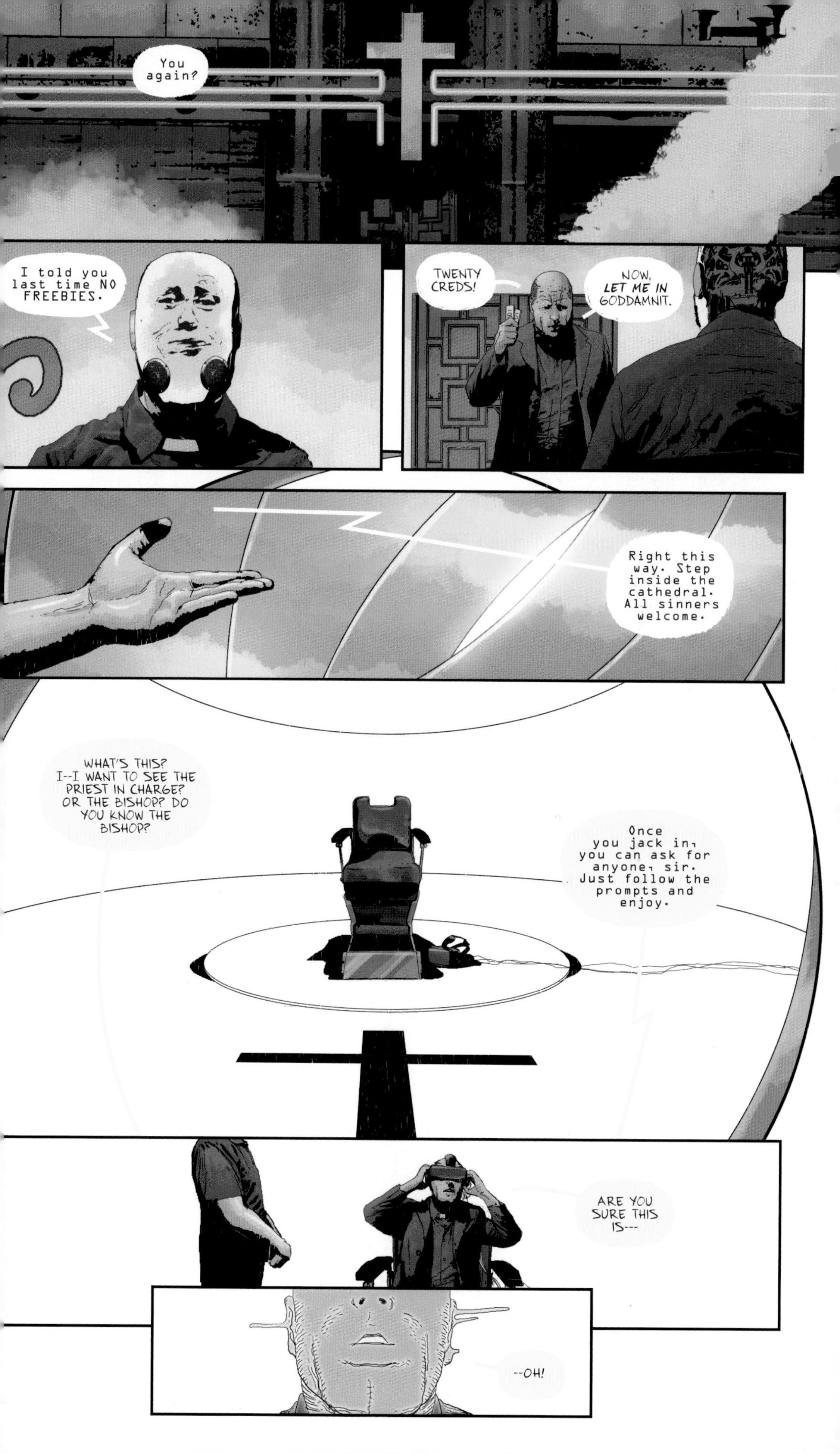
You again?
I told you last time NO FREEBIES.
TWENTY CREDS!
NOW, LET ME IN GODDAMNIT.
Right this way. Step inside the cathedral. All sinners welcome.
WHAT'S THIS? I--I WANT TO SEE THE PRIEST IN CHARGE? OR THE BISHOP? DO YOU KNOW THE BISHOP?
Once you jack in, you can ask for anyone, sir. Just follow the prompts and enjoy.
ARE YOU SURE THIS IS---
--OH!

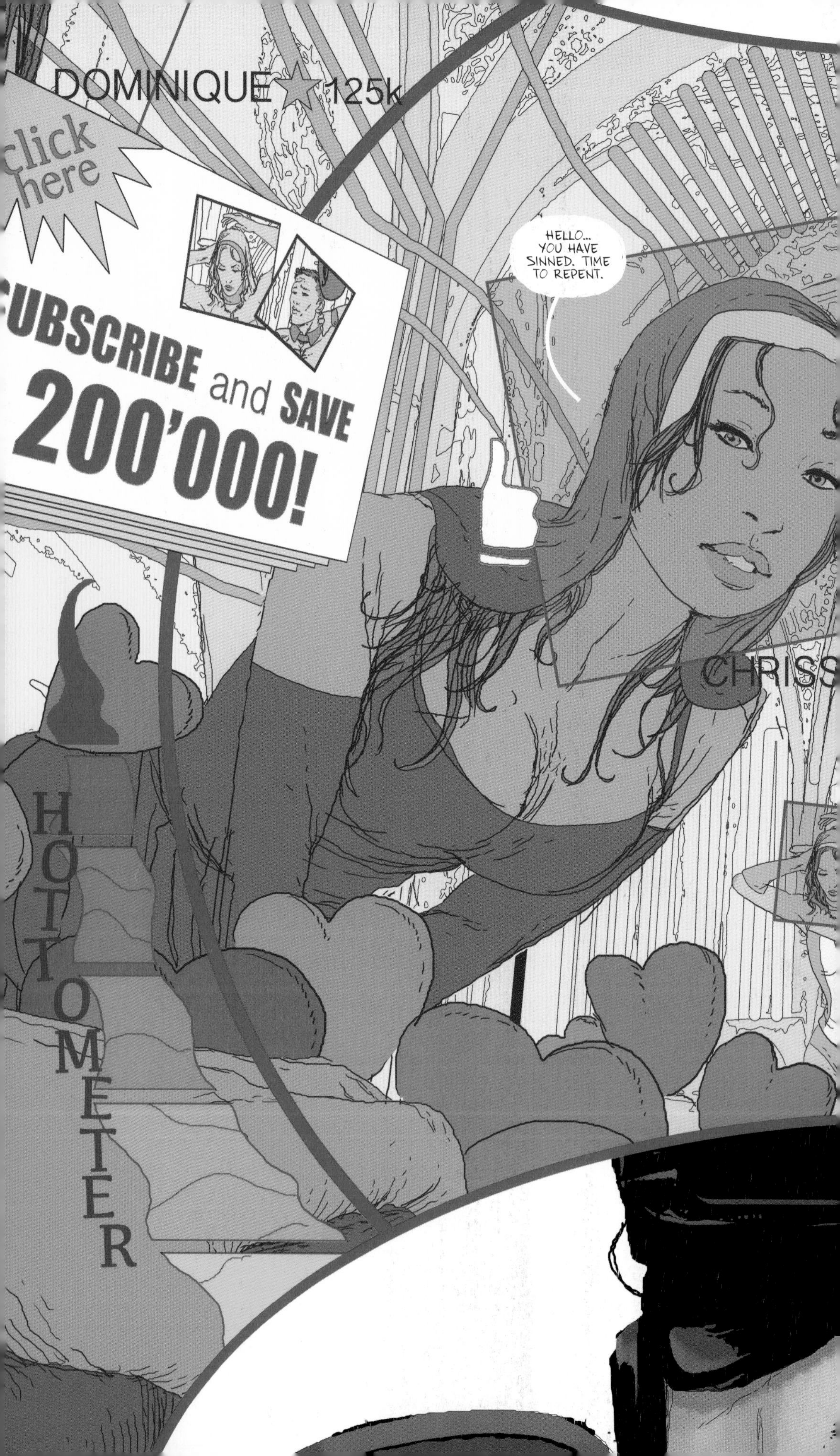
DOMINIQUE 125k
click here
SUBSCRIBE and SAVE 200'000!
HELLO... YOU HAVE SINNED. TIME TO REPENT.
CHRISS
HOTTOMETER

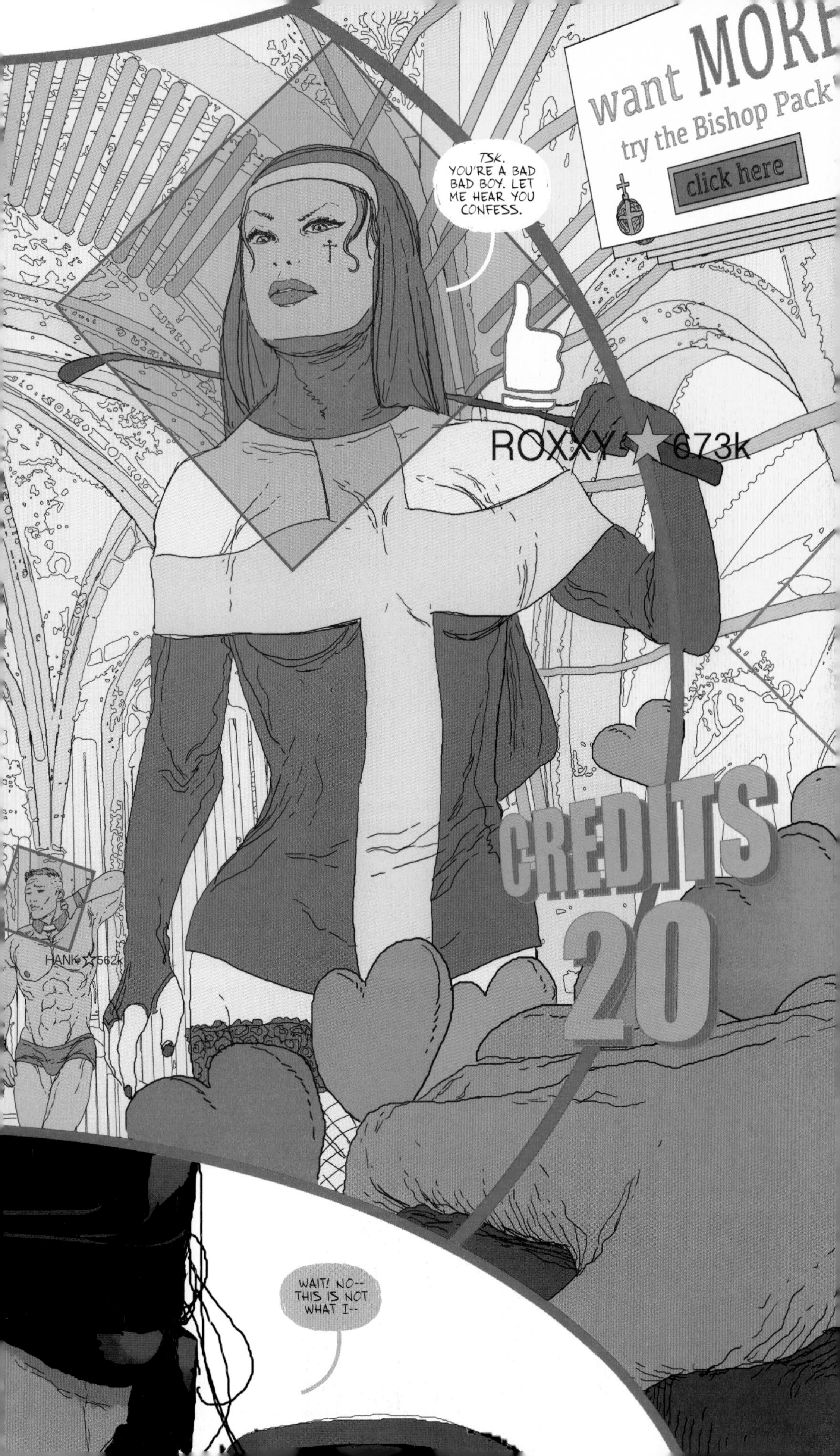
want MORE
try the Bishop Pack
click here
TSK. YOU'RE A BAD BAD BOY. LET ME HEAR YOU CONFESS.
ROXXY 673k
HANK 562k
CREDITS 20
WAIT! NO-- THIS IS NOT WHAT I--

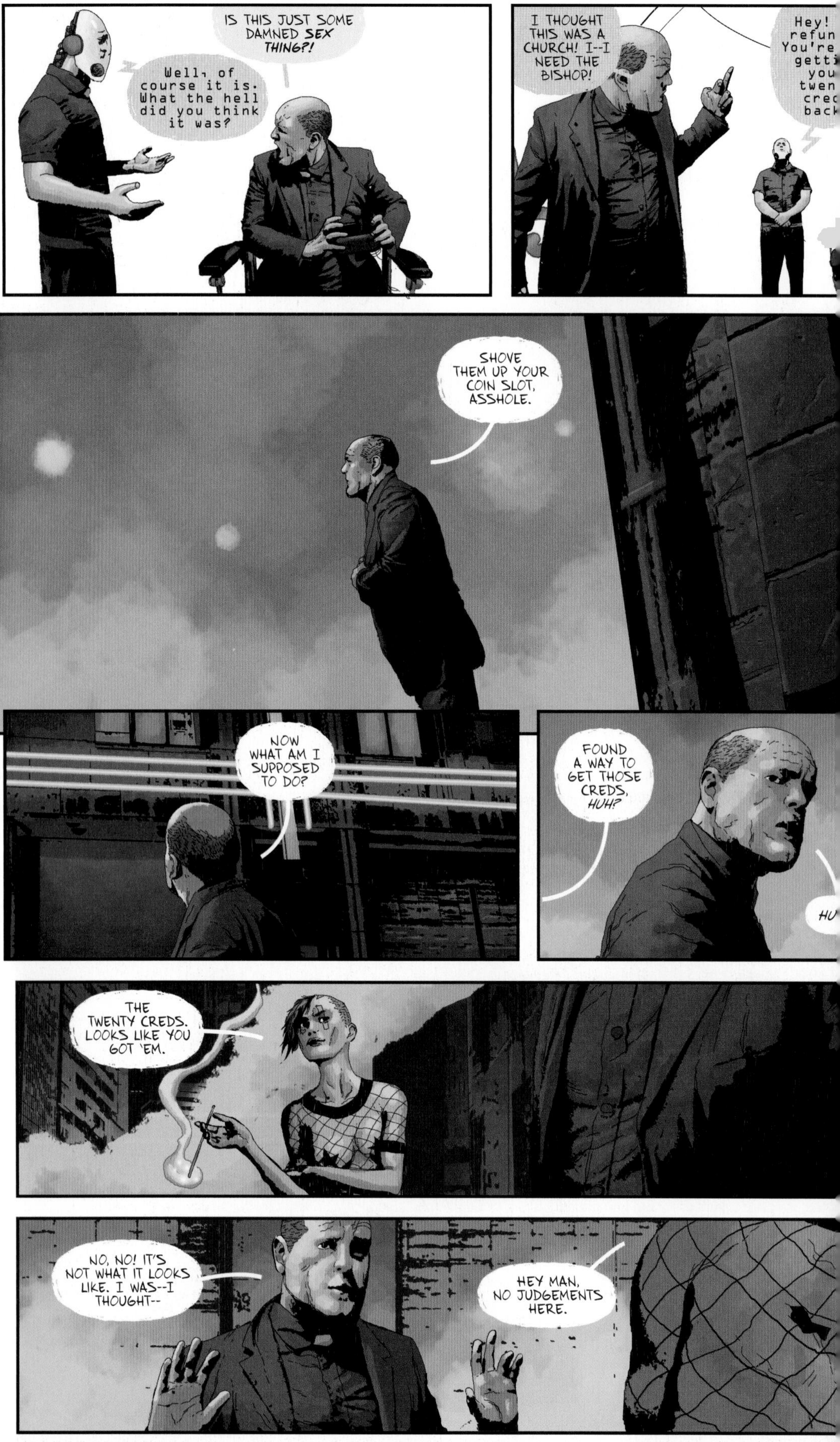
IS THIS JUST SOME DAMNED SEX THING?!
Well, of course it is. What the hell did you think it was?
I THOUGHT THIS WAS A CHURCH! I--I NEED THE BISHOP!
Hey!
SHOVE THEM UP YOUR COIN SLOT, ASSHOLE.
NOW WHAT AM I SUPPOSED TO DO?
FOUND A WAY TO GET THOSE CREDS, HUH?
THE TWENTY CREDS. LOOKS LIKE YOU GOT 'EM.
NO, NO! IT'S NOT WHAT IT LOOKS LIKE. I WAS--I THOUGHT--
HEY MAN, NO JUDGEMENTS HERE.

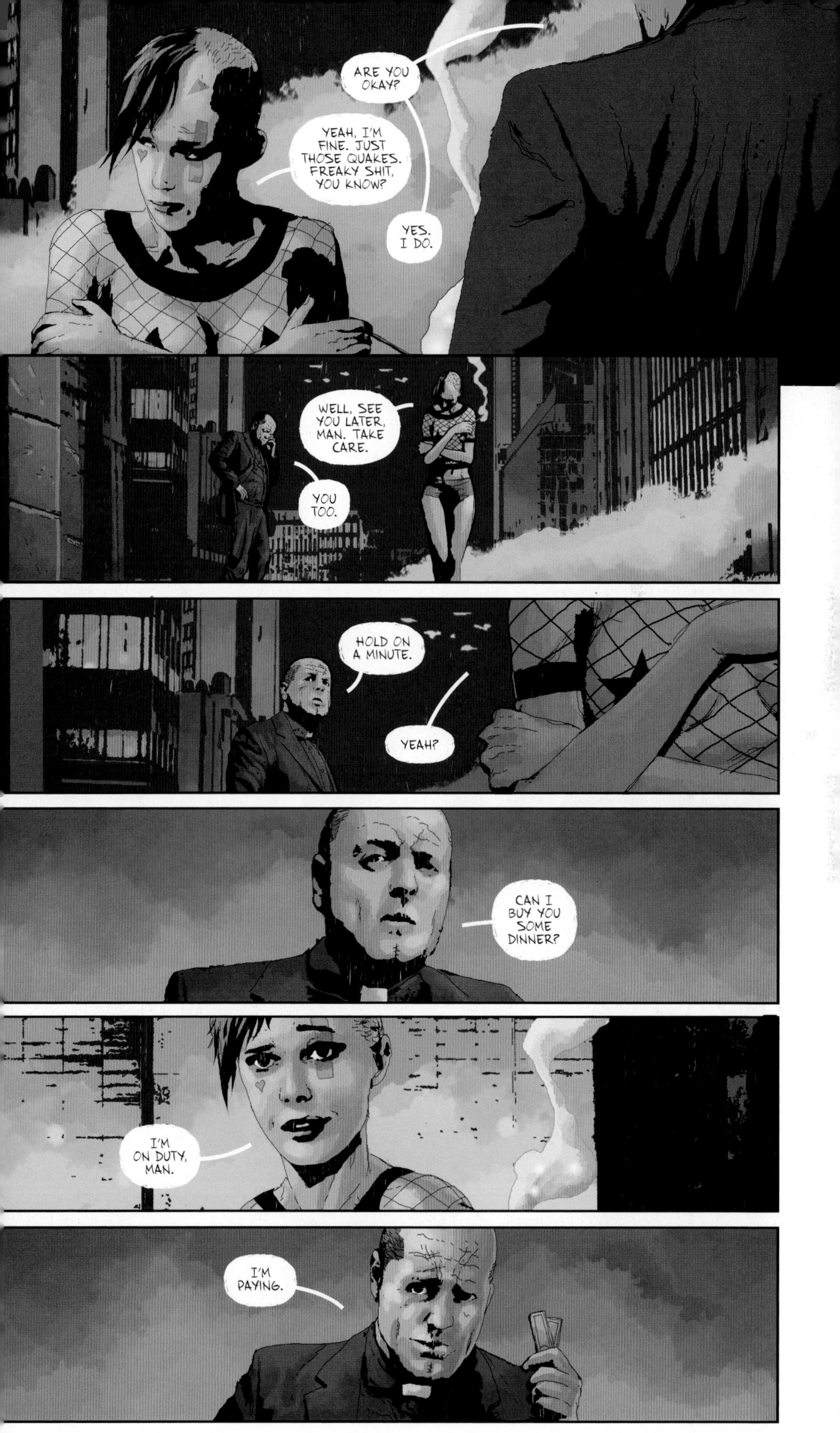
ARE YOU OKAY?
YEAH, I'M FINE. JUST THOSE QUAKES. FREAKY SHIT, YOU KNOW?
YES. I DO.
WELL, SEE YOU LATER, MAN. TAKE CARE.
YOU TOO.
HOLD ON A MINUTE.
YEAH?
CAN I BUY YOU SOME DINNER?
I'M ON DUTY, MAN.
I'M PAYING.

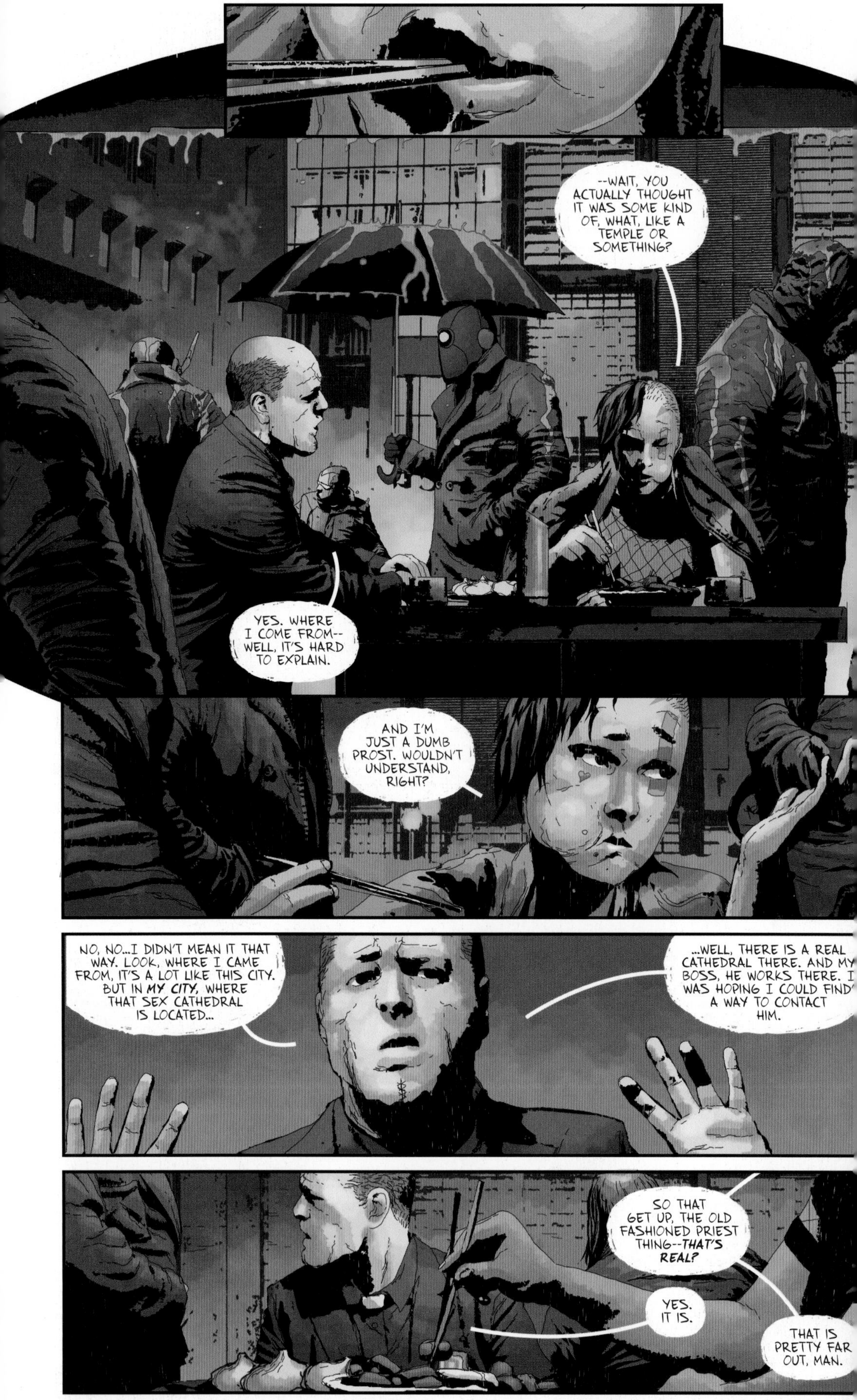
--WAIT, YOU ACTUALLY THOUGHT IT WAS SOME KIND OF, WHAT, LIKE A TEMPLE OR SOMETHING?
YES. WHERE I COME FROM--WELL, IT'S HARD TO EXPLAIN.
AND I'M JUST A DUMB PROST. WOULDN'T UNDERSTAND, RIGHT?
NO, NO...I DIDN'T MEAN IT THAT WAY. LOOK, WHERE I CAME FROM, IT'S A LOT LIKE THIS CITY. BUT IN MY CITY, WHERE THAT SEX CATHEDRAL IS LOCATED...
...WELL, THERE IS A REAL CATHEDRAL THERE. AND MY BOSS, HE WORKS THERE. I WAS HOPING I COULD FIND A WAY TO CONTACT HIM.
SO THAT GET UP, THE OLD FASHIONED PRIEST THING--THAT'S REAL?
YES. IT IS.
THAT IS PRETTY FAR OUT, MAN.

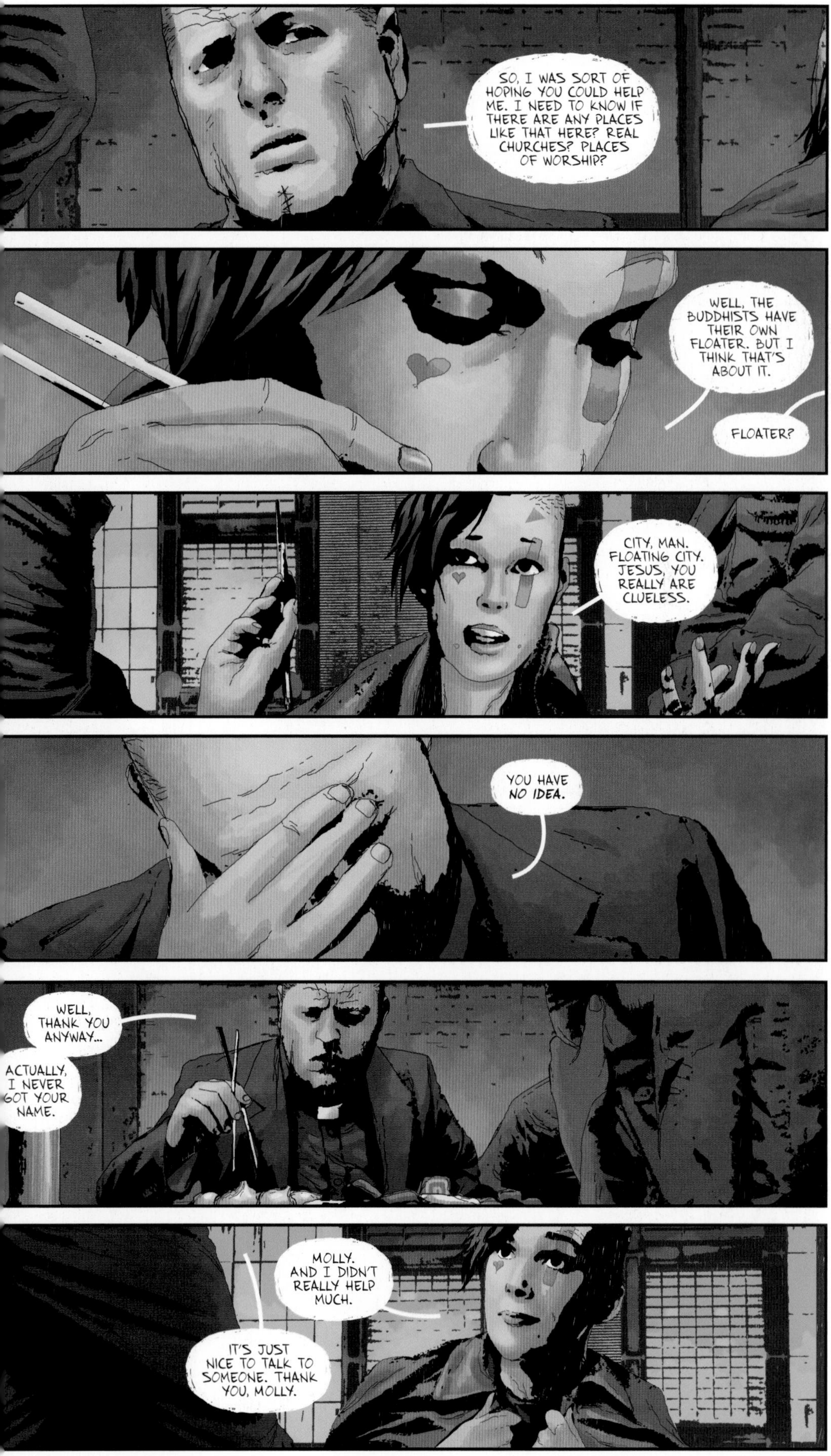
SO, I WAS SORT OF HOPING YOU COULD HELP ME. I NEED TO KNOW IF THERE ARE ANY PLACES LIKE THAT HERE? REAL CHURCHES? PLACES OF WORSHIP?
WELL, THE BUDDHISTS HAVE THEIR OWN FLOATER. BUT I THINK THAT'S ABOUT IT.
FLOATER?
CITY, MAN. FLOATING CITY. JESUS, YOU REALLY ARE CLUELESS.
YOU HAVE *NO IDEA.*
WELL, THANK YOU ANYWAY...
ACTUALLY, I NEVER GOT YOUR NAME.
MOLLY. AND I DIDN'T REALLY HELP MUCH.
IT'S JUST NICE TO TALK TO SOMEONE. THANK YOU, MOLLY.

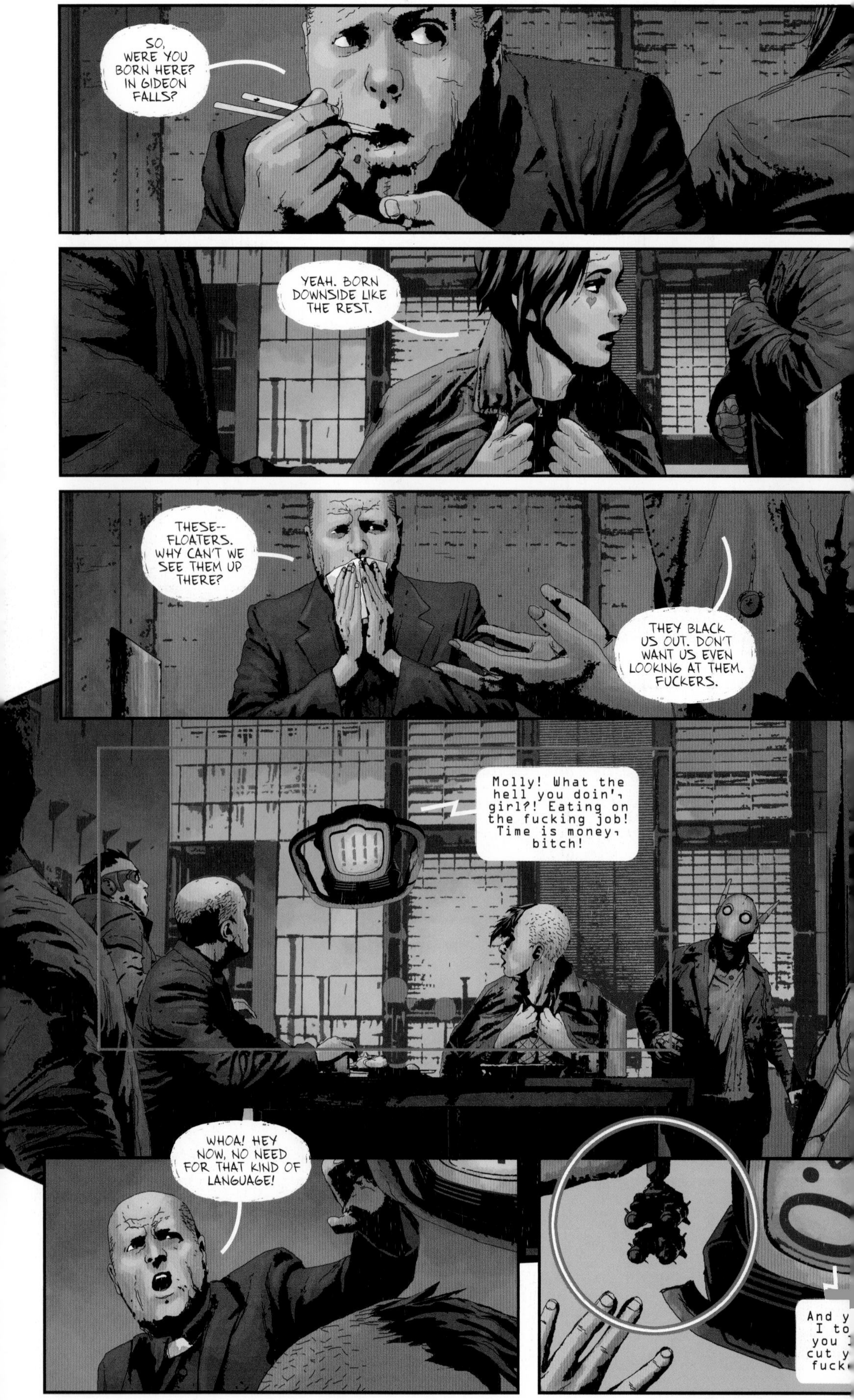
SO, WERE YOU BORN HERE? IN GIDEON FALLS?
YEAH. BORN DOWNSIDE LIKE THE REST.
THESE-- FLOATERS. WHY CAN'T WE SEE THEM UP THERE?
THEY BLACK US OUT. DON'T WANT US EVEN LOOKING AT THEM. FUCKERS.
Molly! What the hell you doin', girl?! Eating on the fucking job! Time is money, bitch!
WHOA! HEY NOW, NO NEED FOR THAT KIND OF LANGUAGE!
And y
I to
you
cut y
fuck

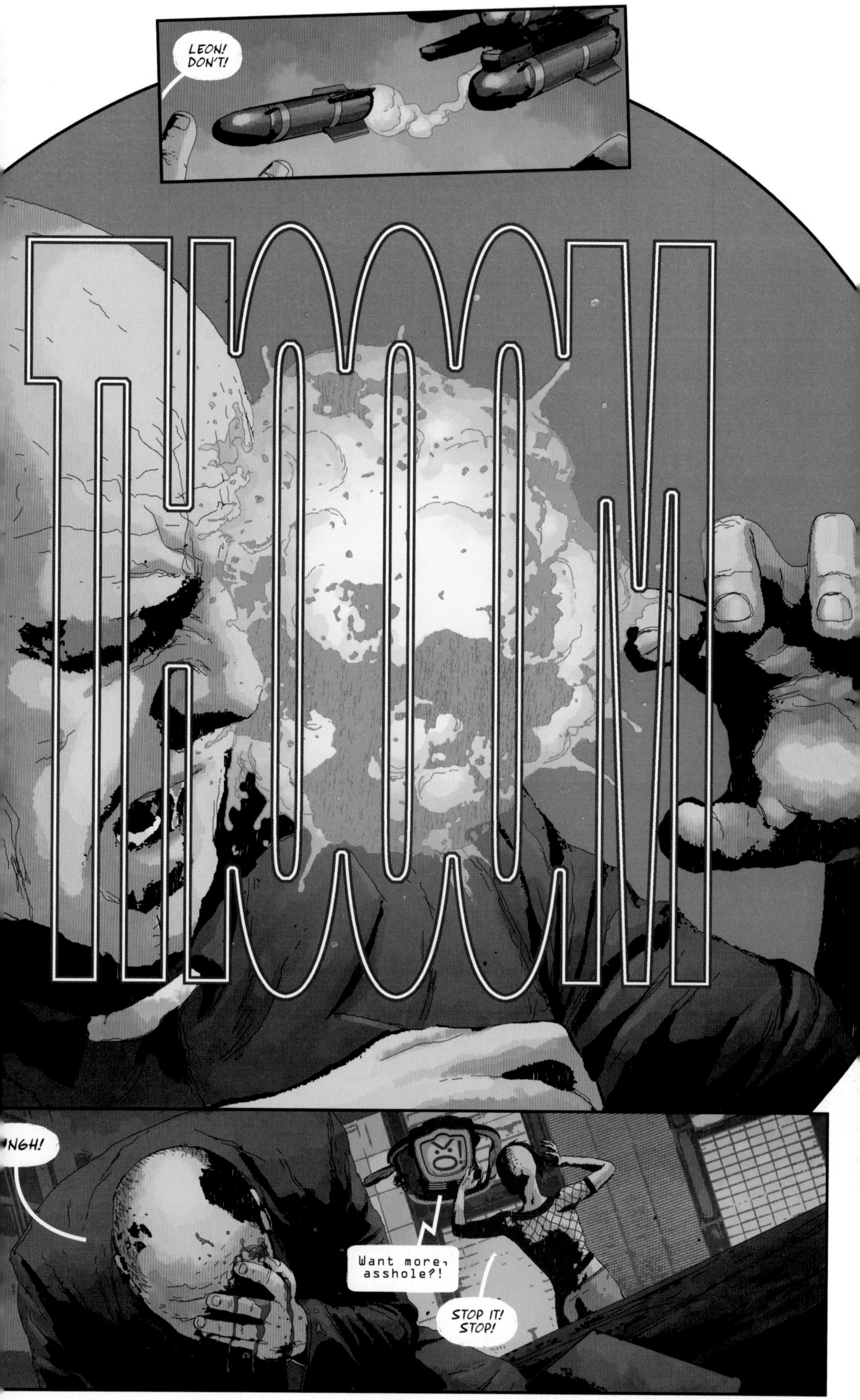
LEON! DON'T!
THOOOM
NGH!
Want more, asshole?!
STOP IT! STOP!

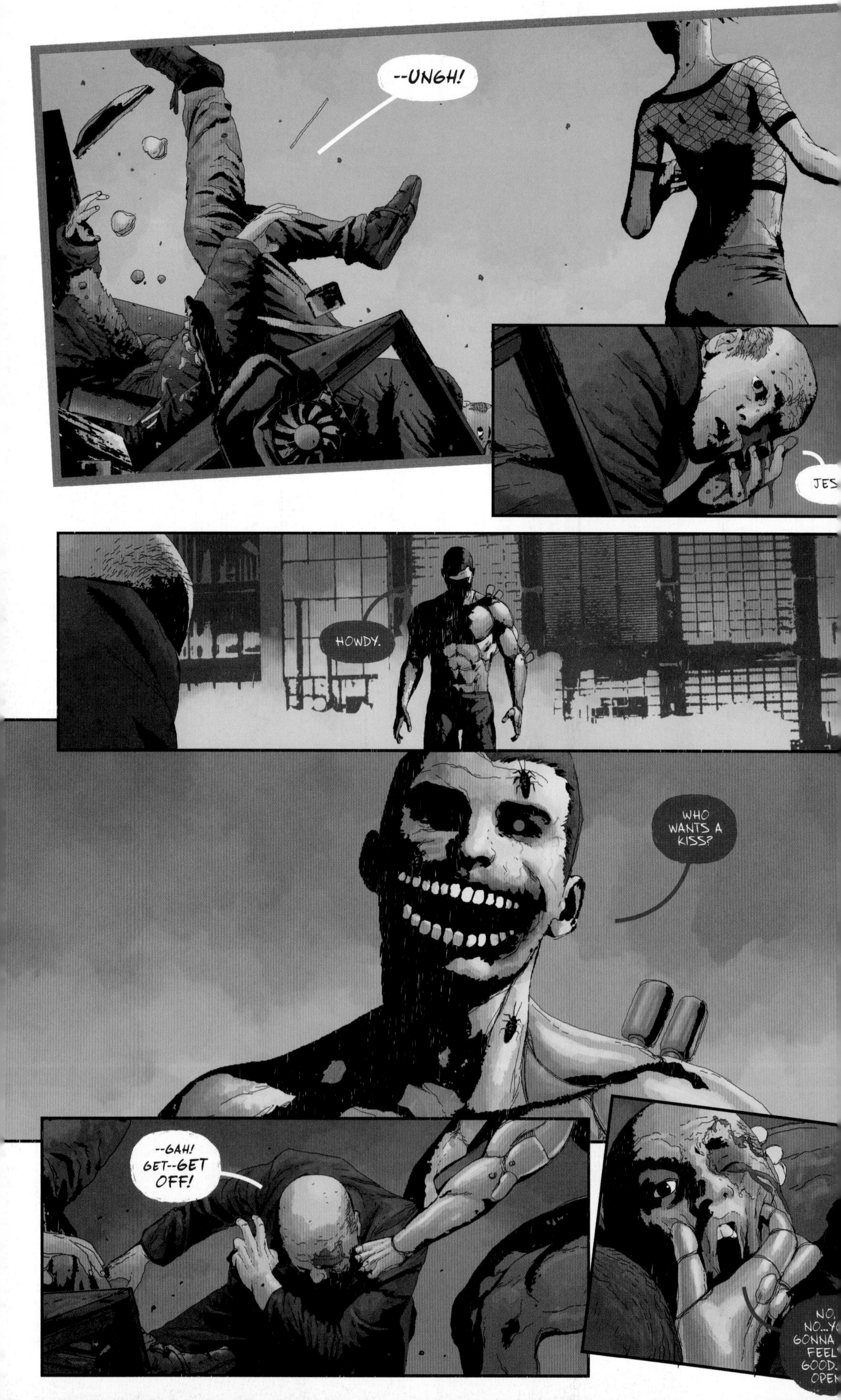
--UNGH!
JES
HOWDY.
WHO WANTS A KISS?
--GAH! GET--GET OFF!
NO, NO...YO GONNA FEEL GOOD. OPEN

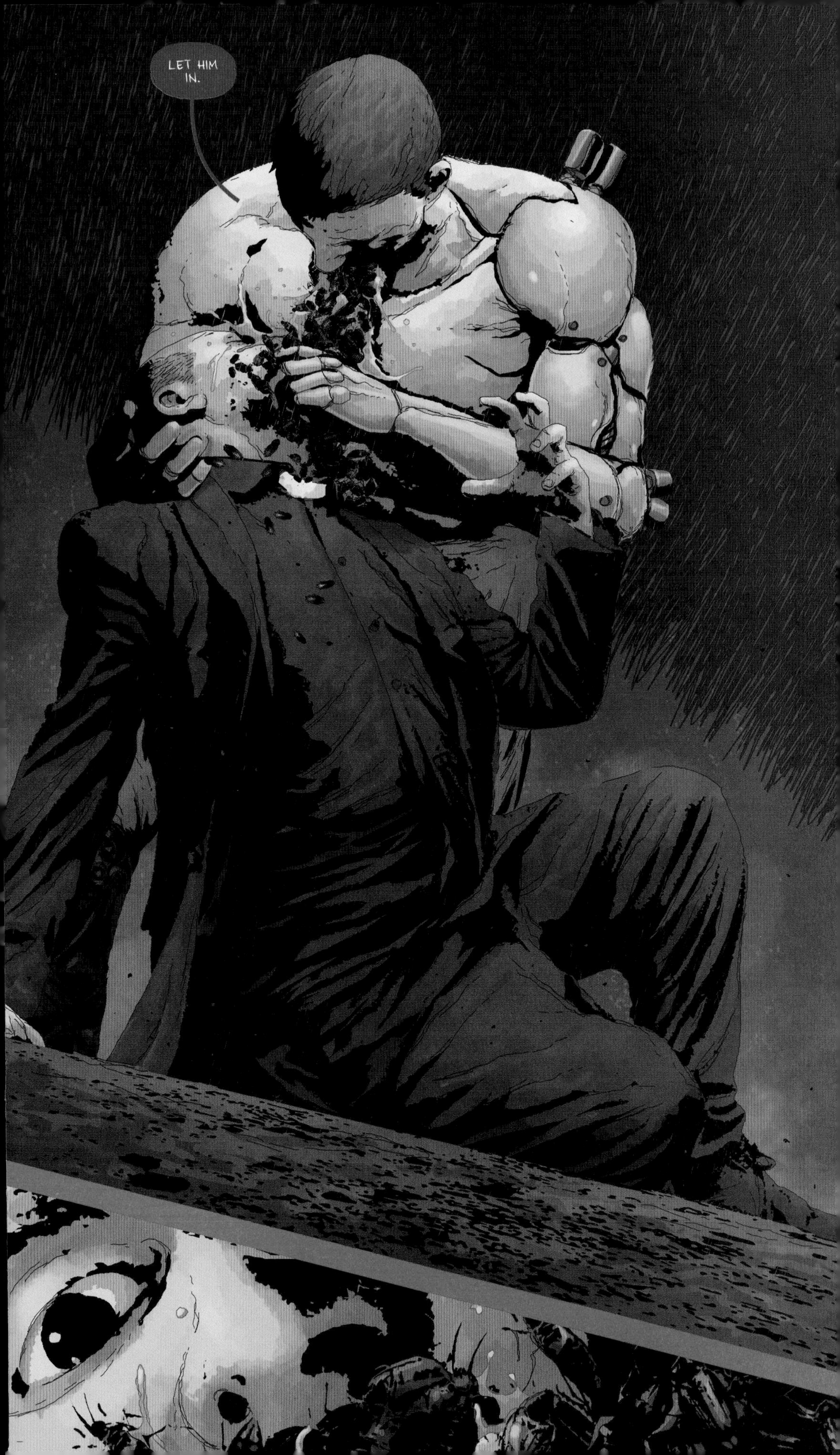
LET HIM IN.

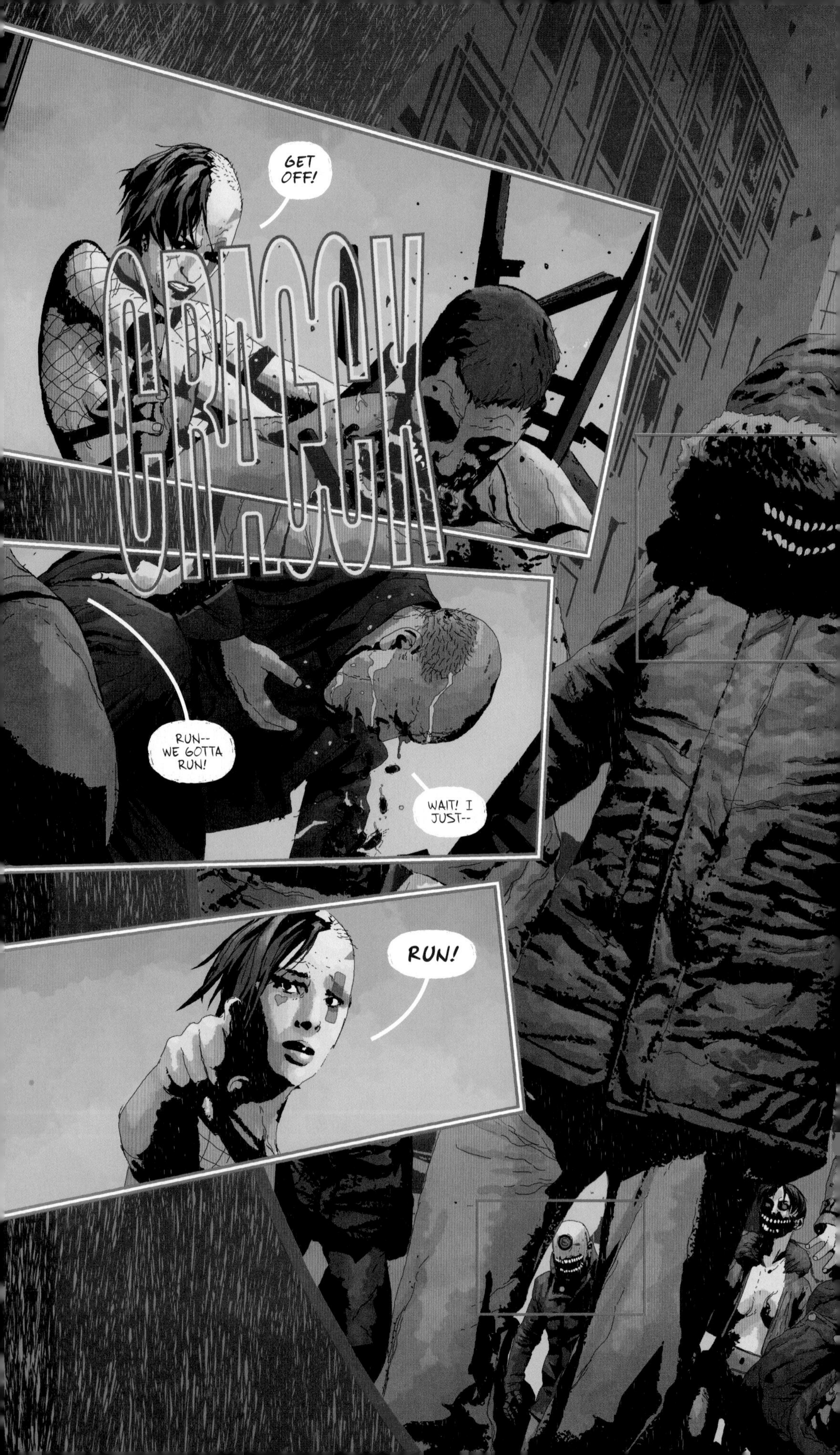
GET OFF!
CRACCK
RUN-- WE GOTTA RUN!
WAIT! I JUST--
RUN!

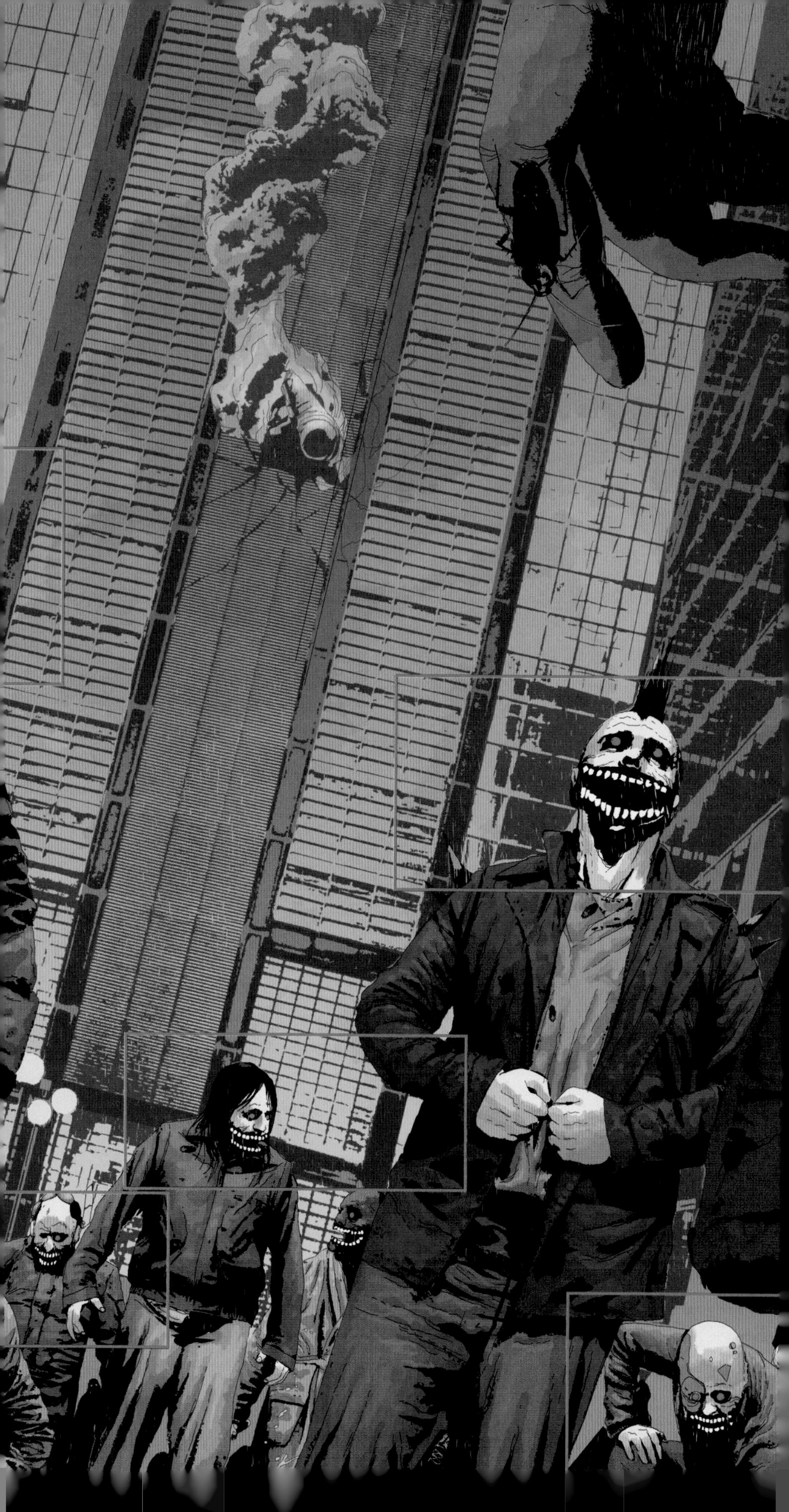

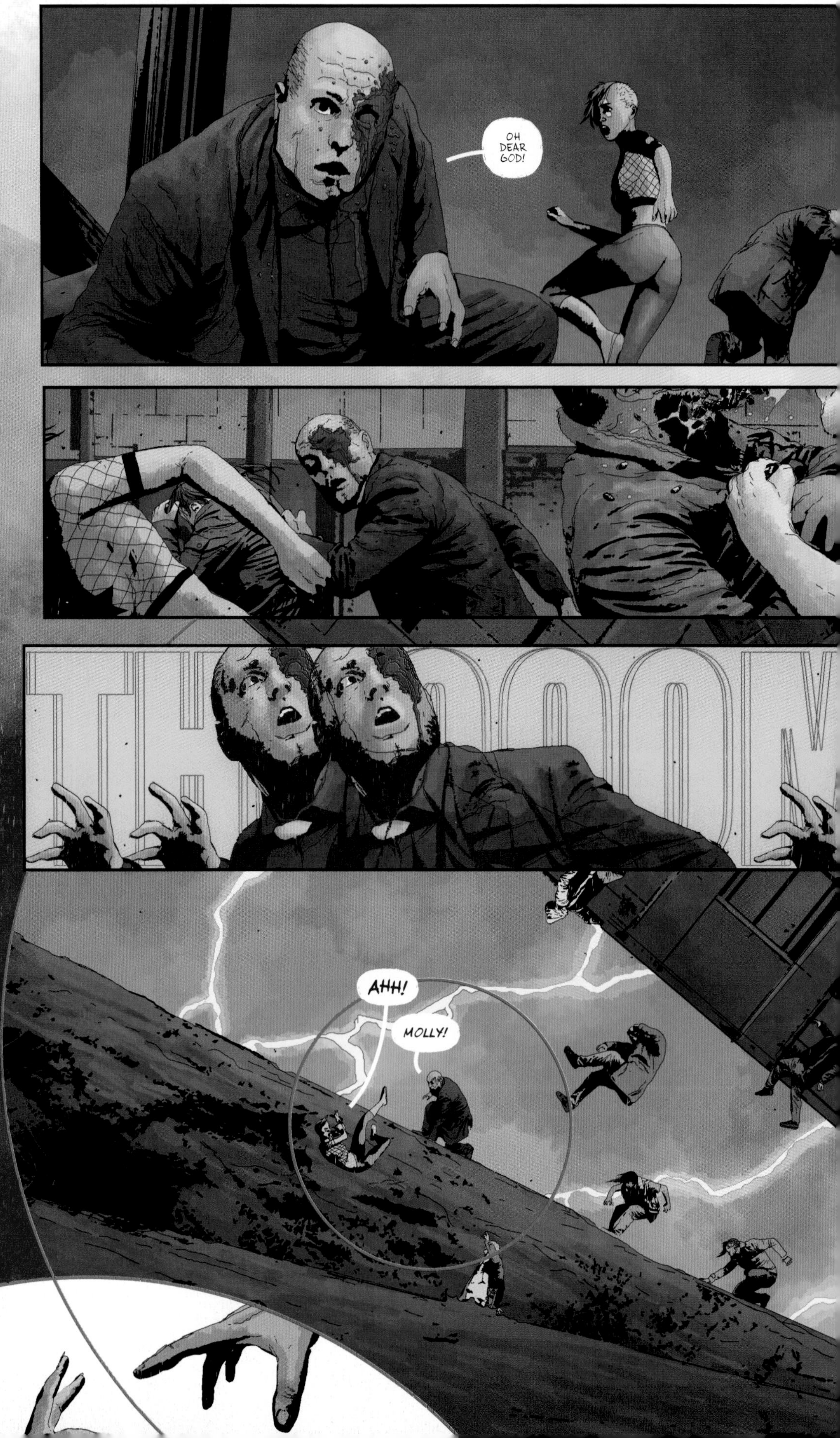
OH DEAR GOD!
AHH!
MOLLY!

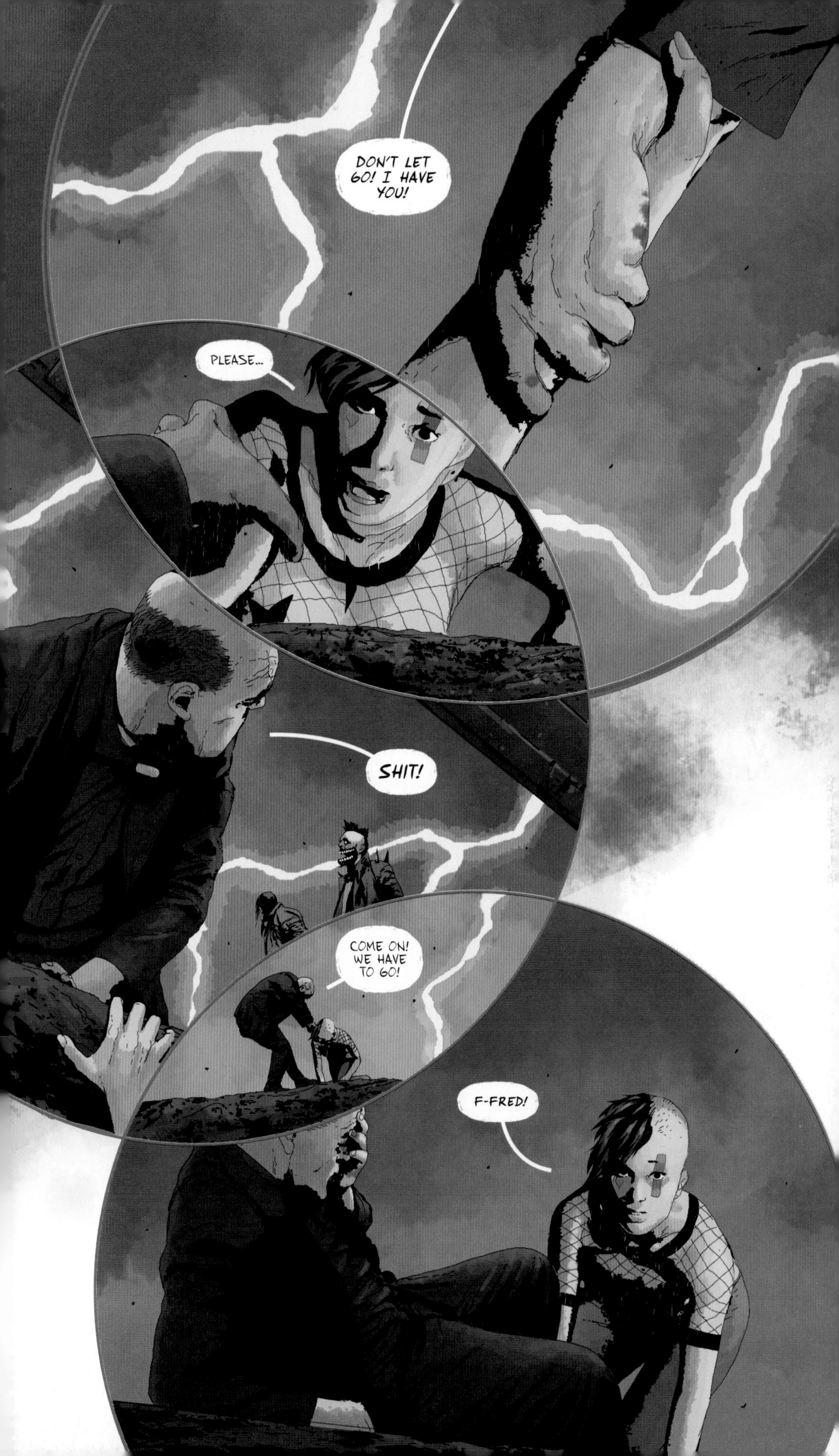
DON'T LET GO! I HAVE YOU!
PLEASE...
SHIT!
COME ON! WE HAVE TO GO!
F-FRED!

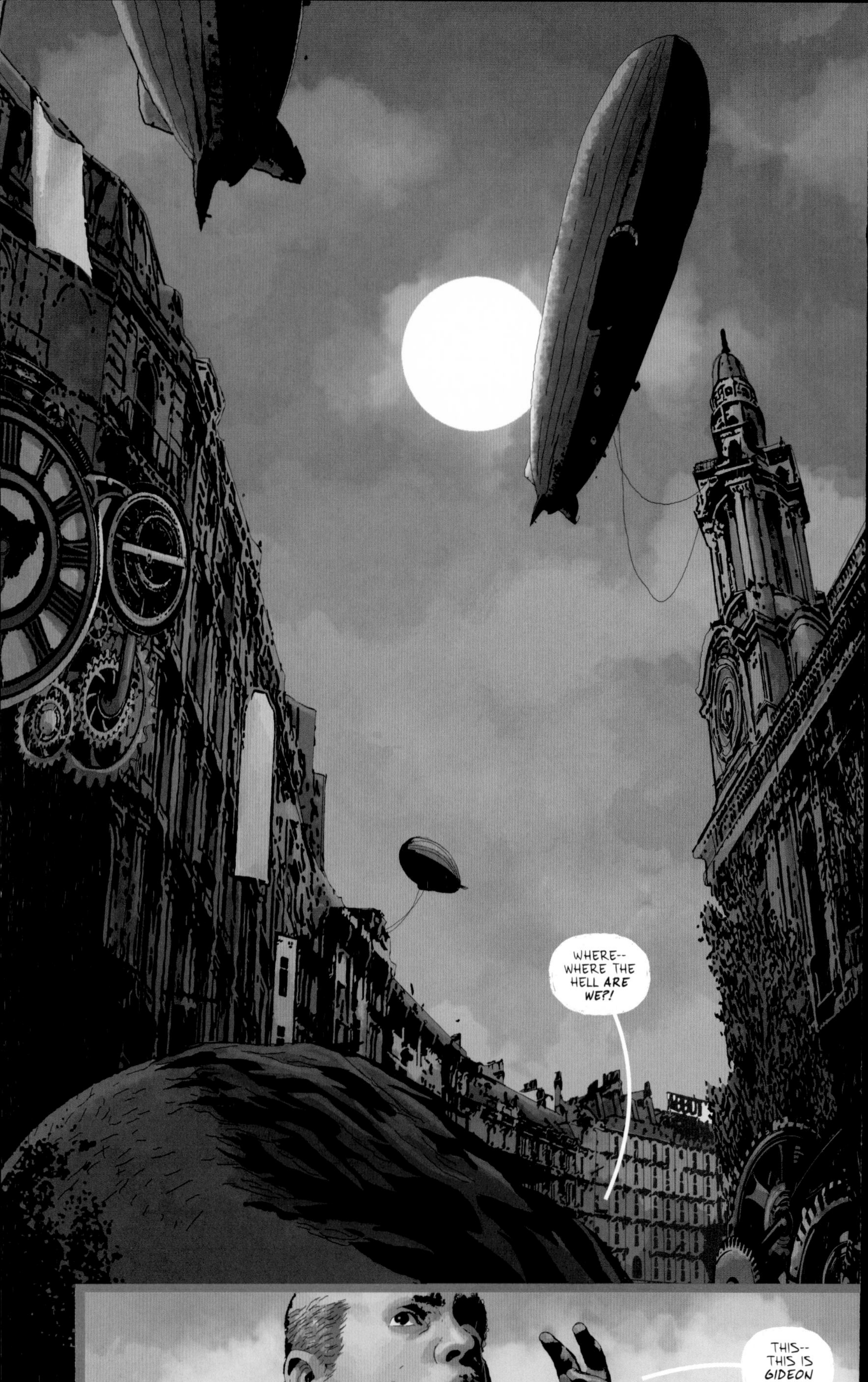
WHERE--
WHERE THE HELL ARE WE?!

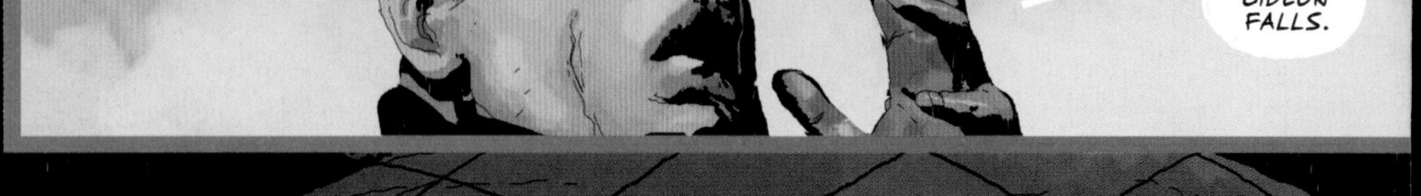
THIS--
THIS IS GIDEON FALLS.

GIDEON
FALLS

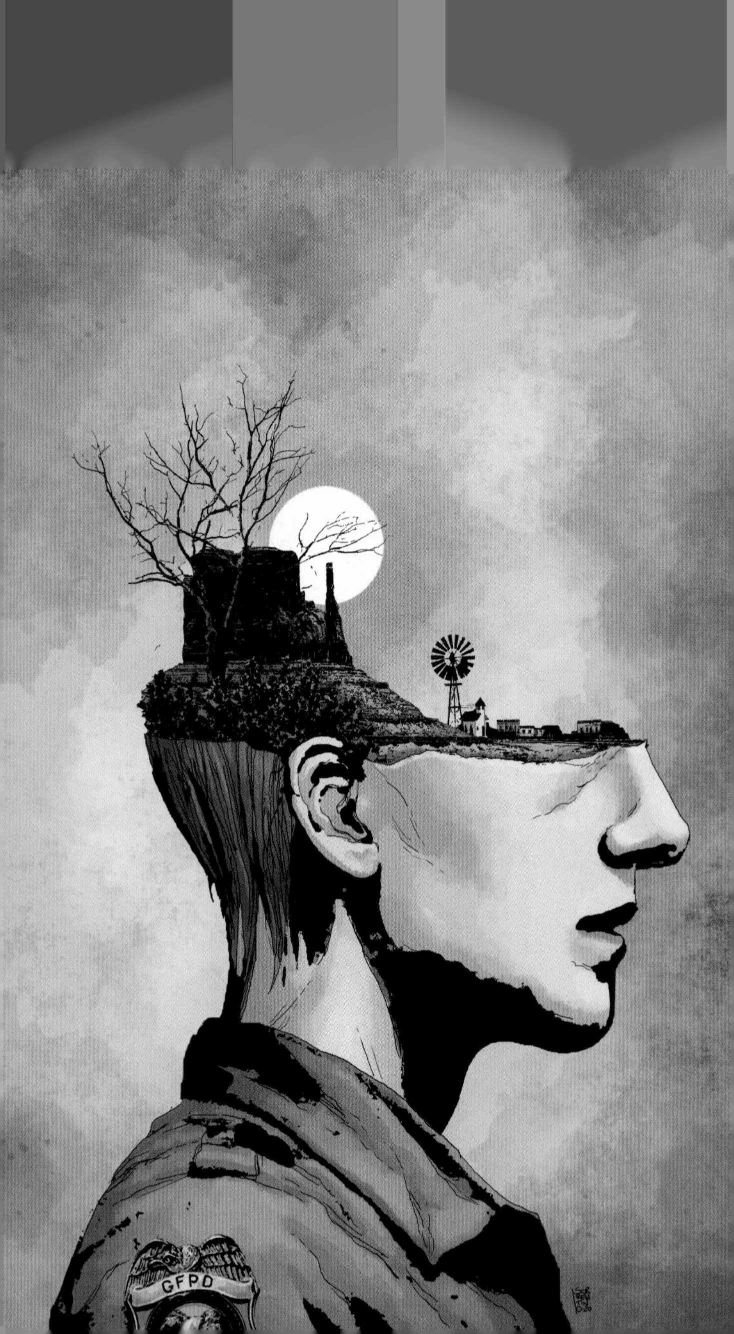
GFPD

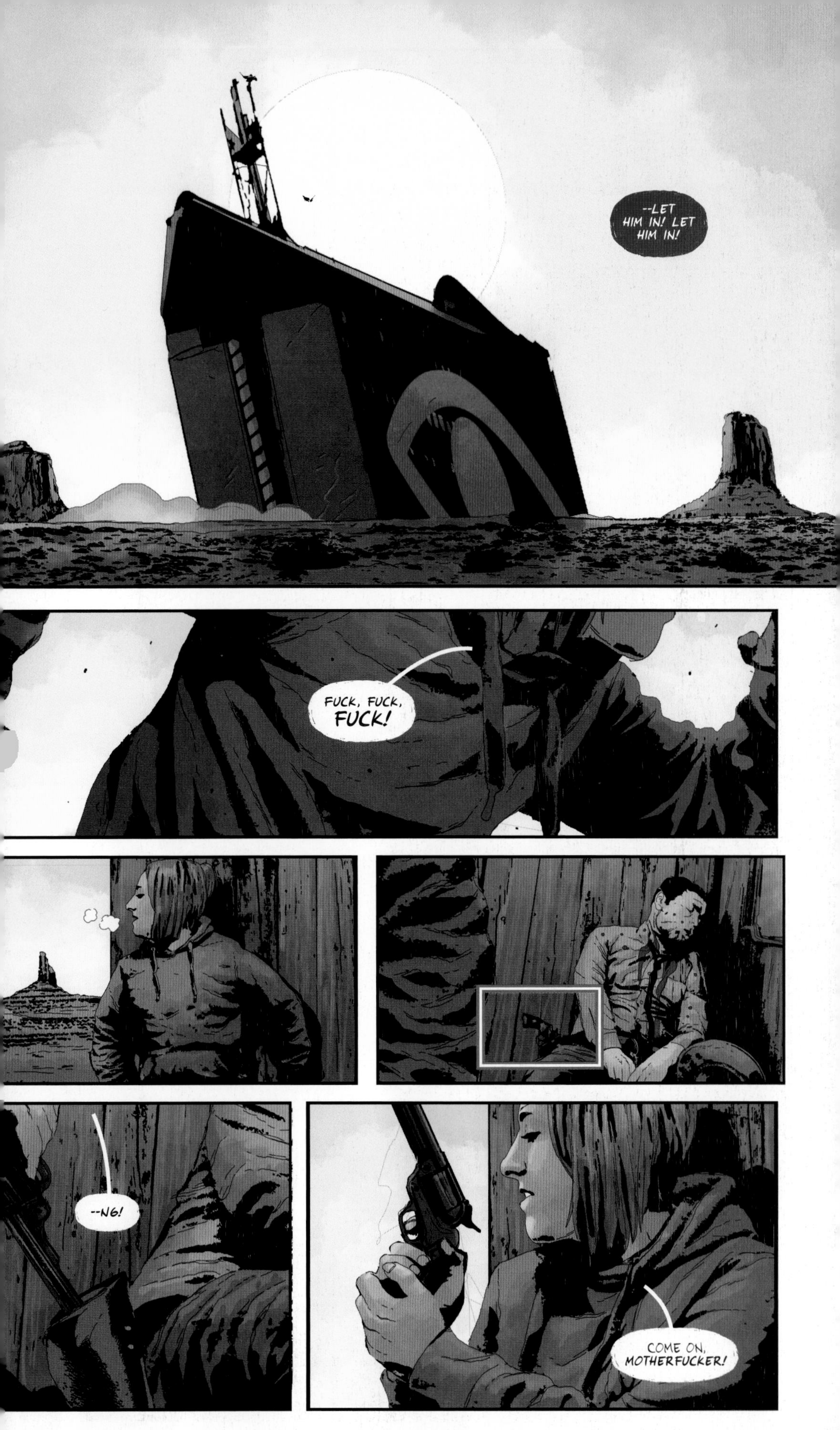
--LET HIM IN! LET HIM IN!
FUCK, FUCK, FUCK!
--NG!
COME ON, MOTHERFUCKER!

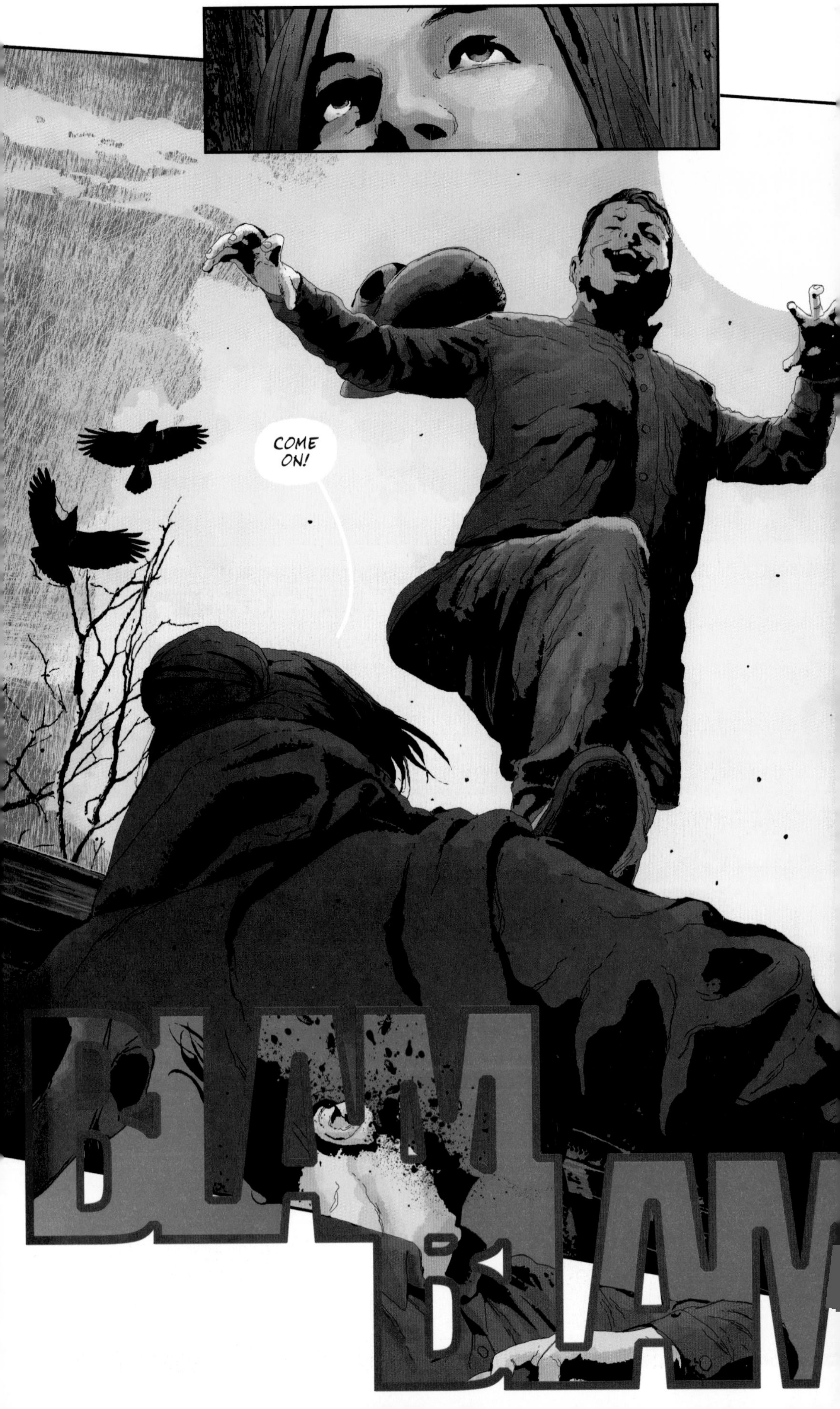
COME ON!
BLAM
BLAM

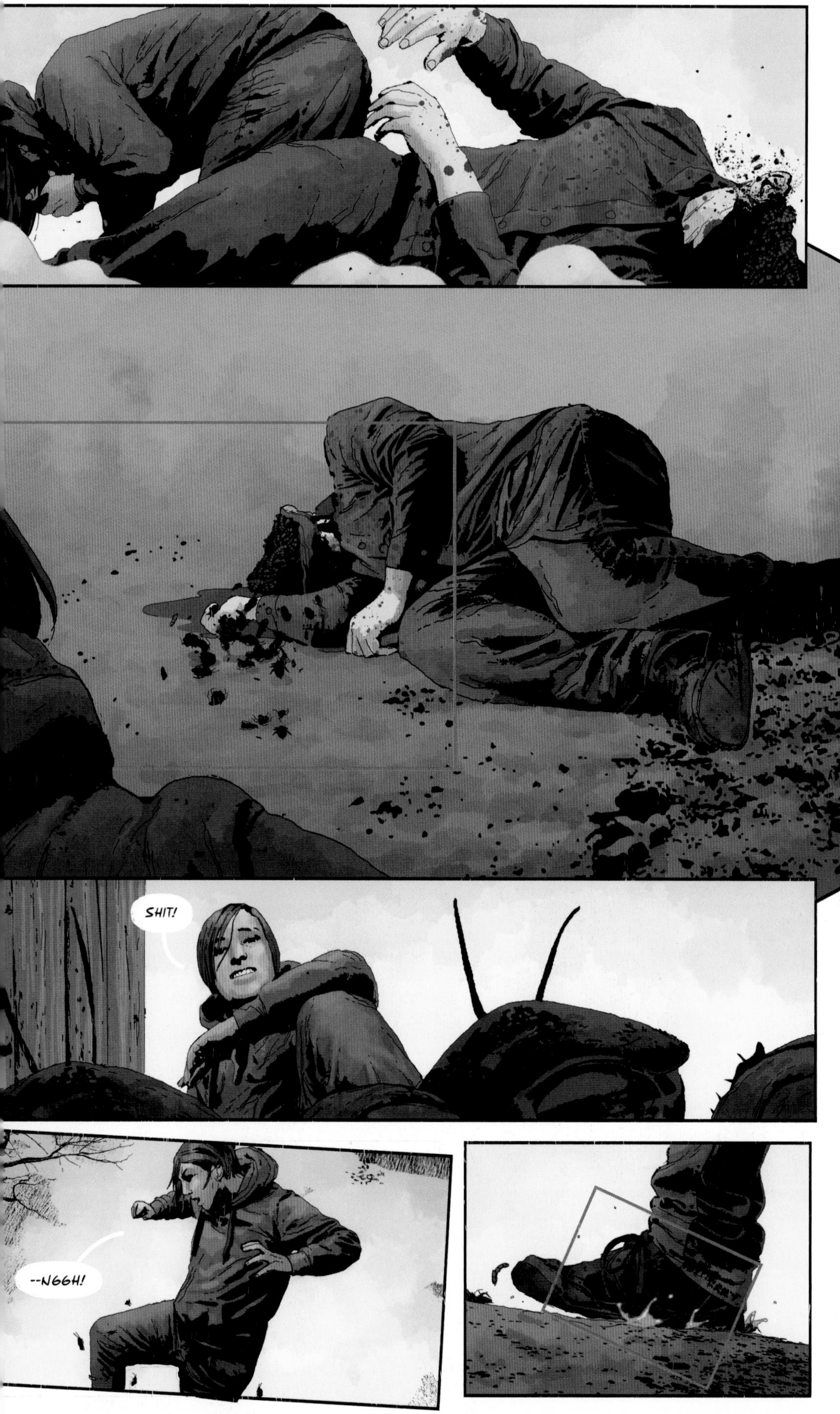
SHIT!
--NGGH!

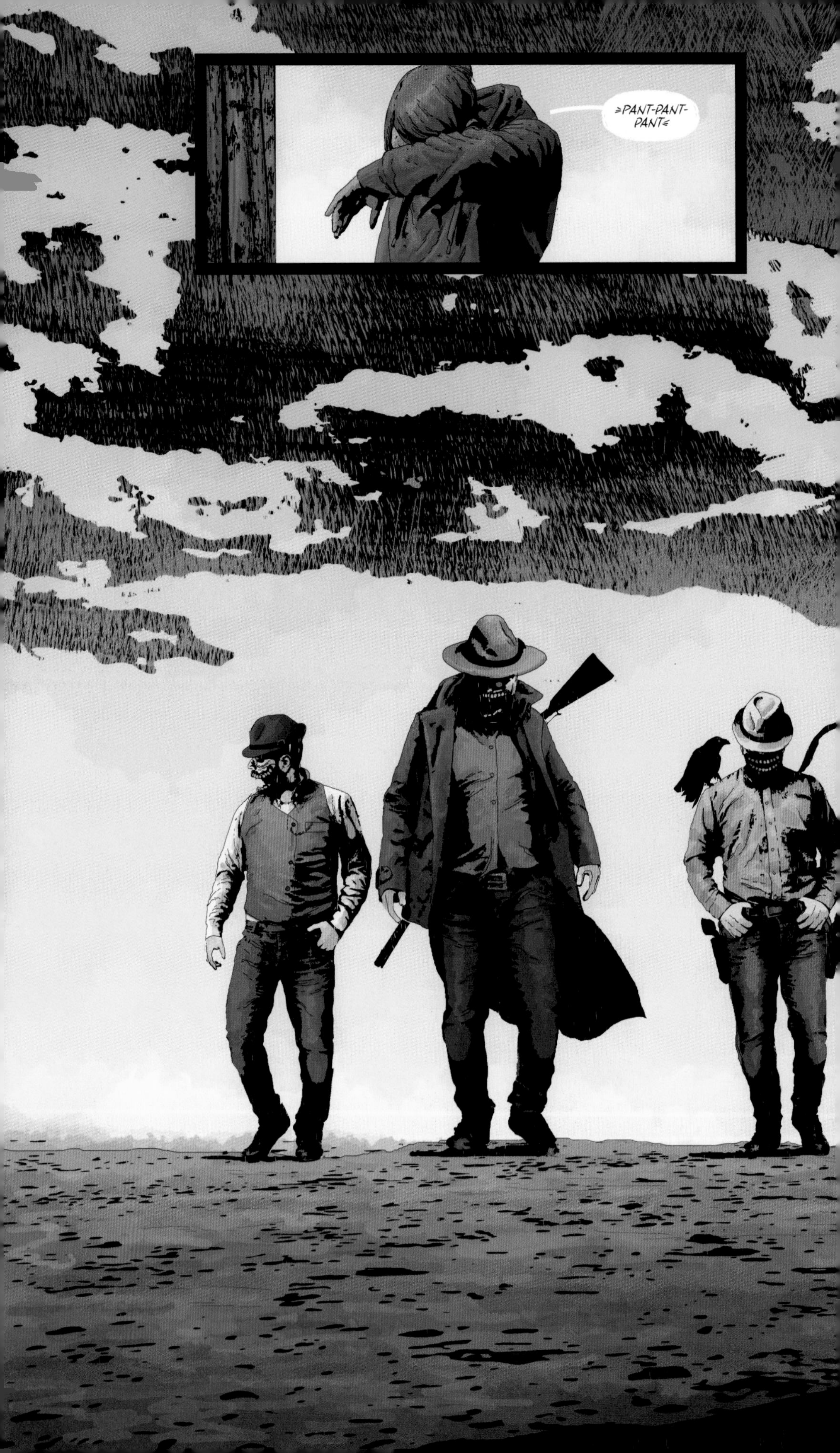
PANT-PANT-PANT

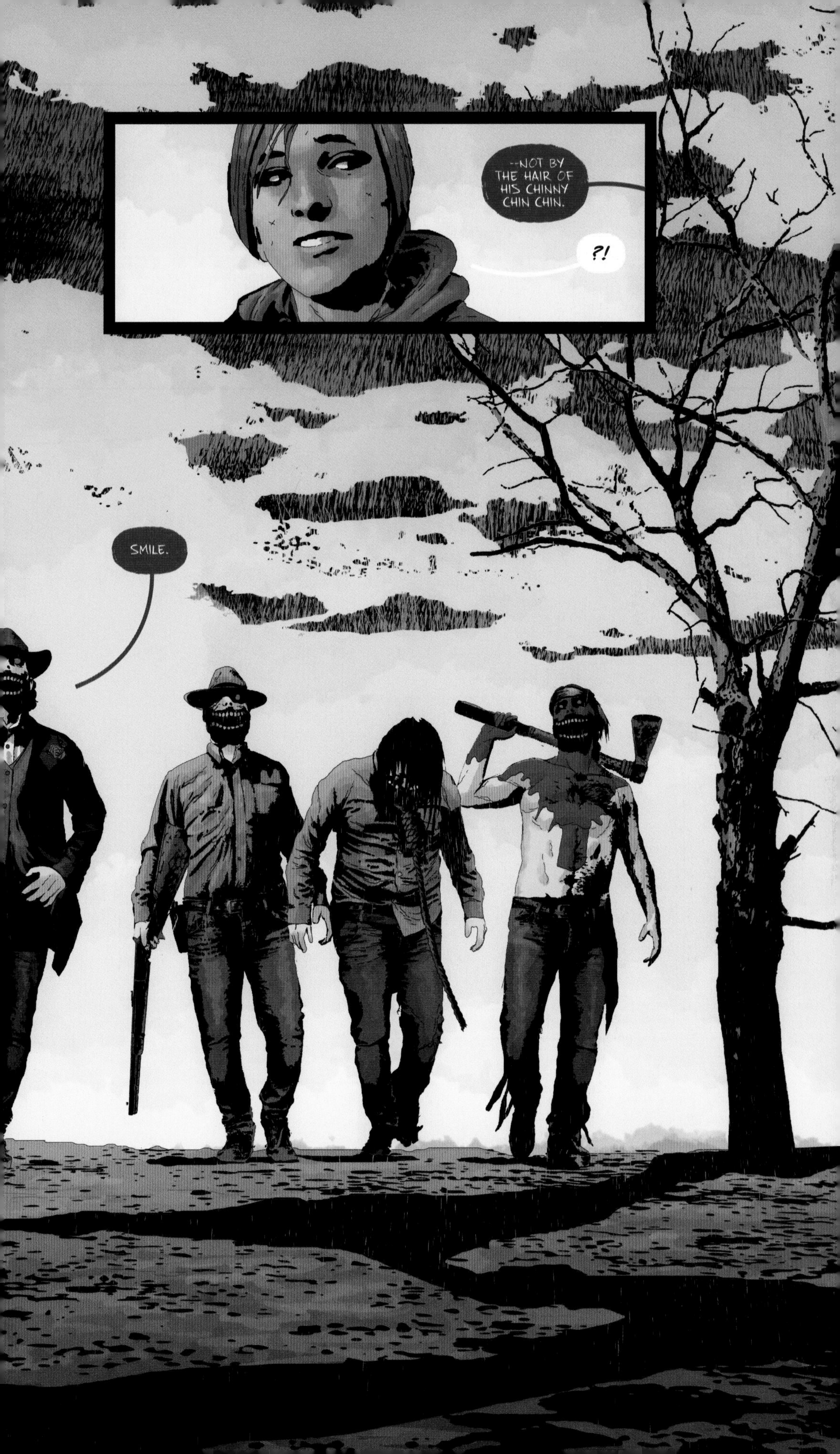
--NOT BY THE HAIR OF HIS CHINNY CHIN CHIN.
?!
SMILE.

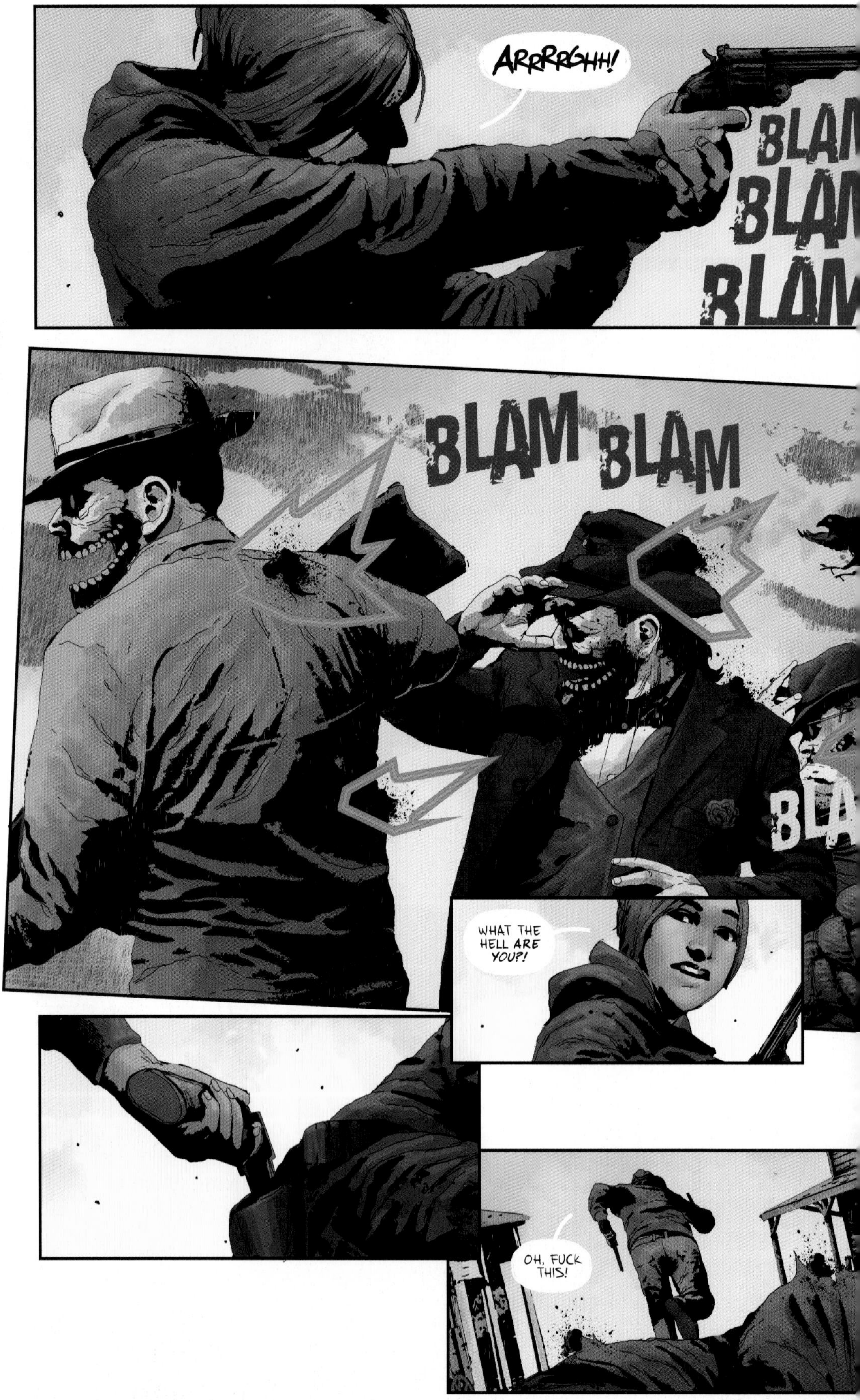
ARRRRGHH!
BLAM
BLAM
BLAM
BLAM BLAM
BLA
WHAT THE HELL ARE YOU?!
OH, FUCK THIS!

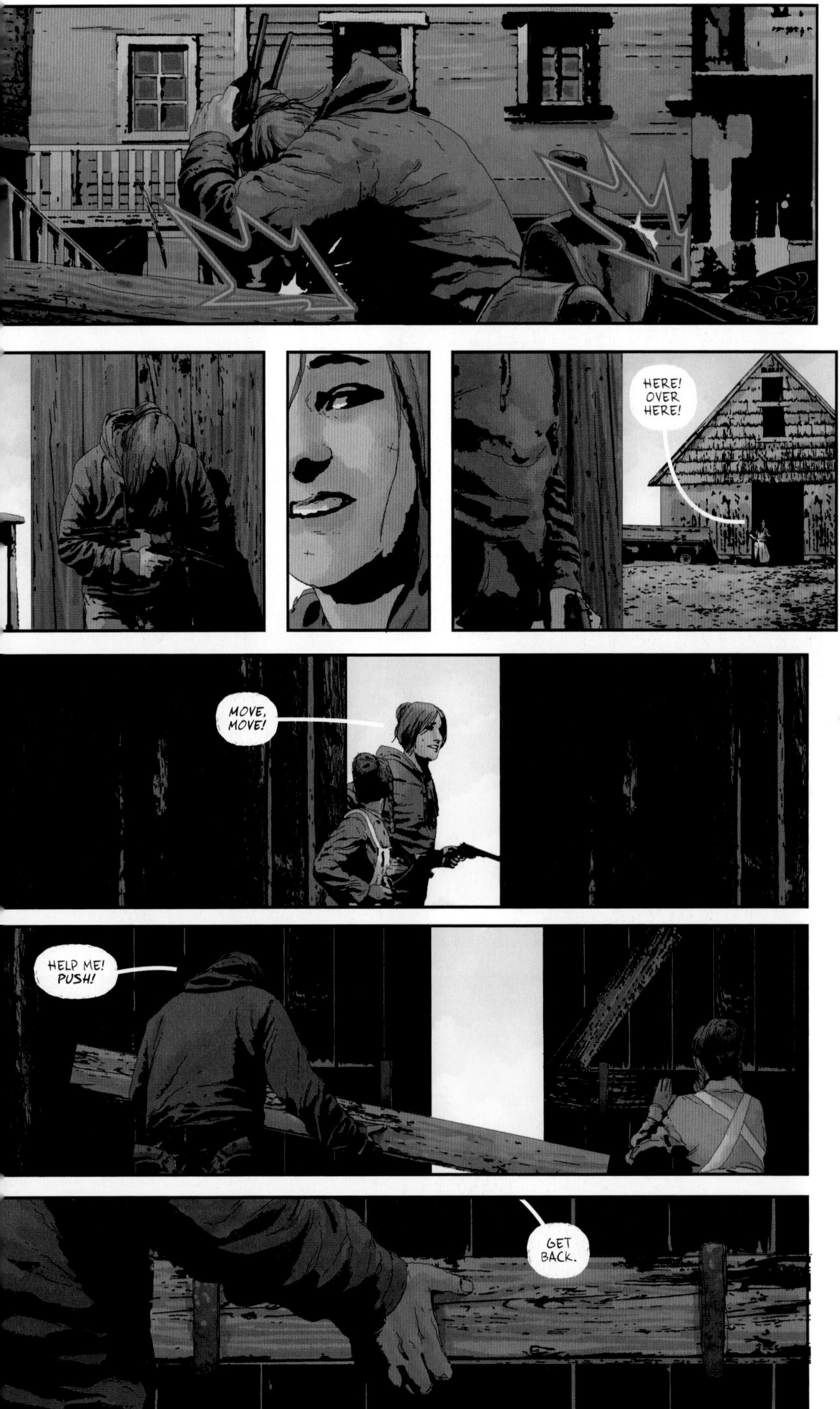
HERE! OVER HERE!
MOVE, MOVE!
HELP ME! PUSH!
GET BACK.

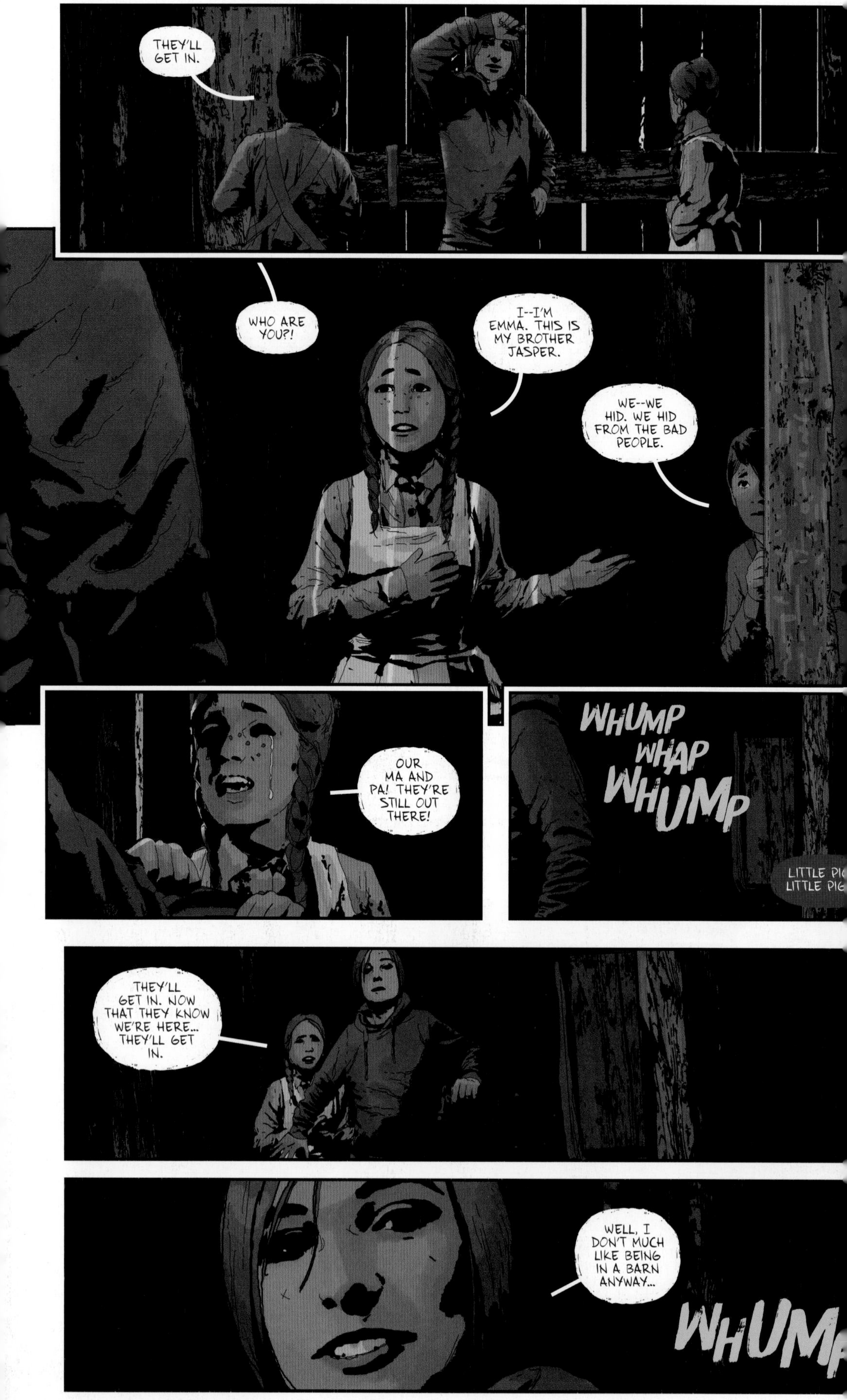

THEY'LL GET IN.
WHO ARE YOU?!
I--I'M EMMA. THIS IS MY BROTHER JASPER.
WE--WE HID. WE HID FROM THE BAD PEOPLE.
OUR MA AND PA! THEY'RE STILL OUT THERE!
WHUMP
WHAP
WHUMP
THEY'LL GET IN. NOW THAT THEY KNOW WE'RE HERE... THEY'LL GET IN.
WELL, I DON'T MUCH LIKE BEING IN A BARN ANYWAY...

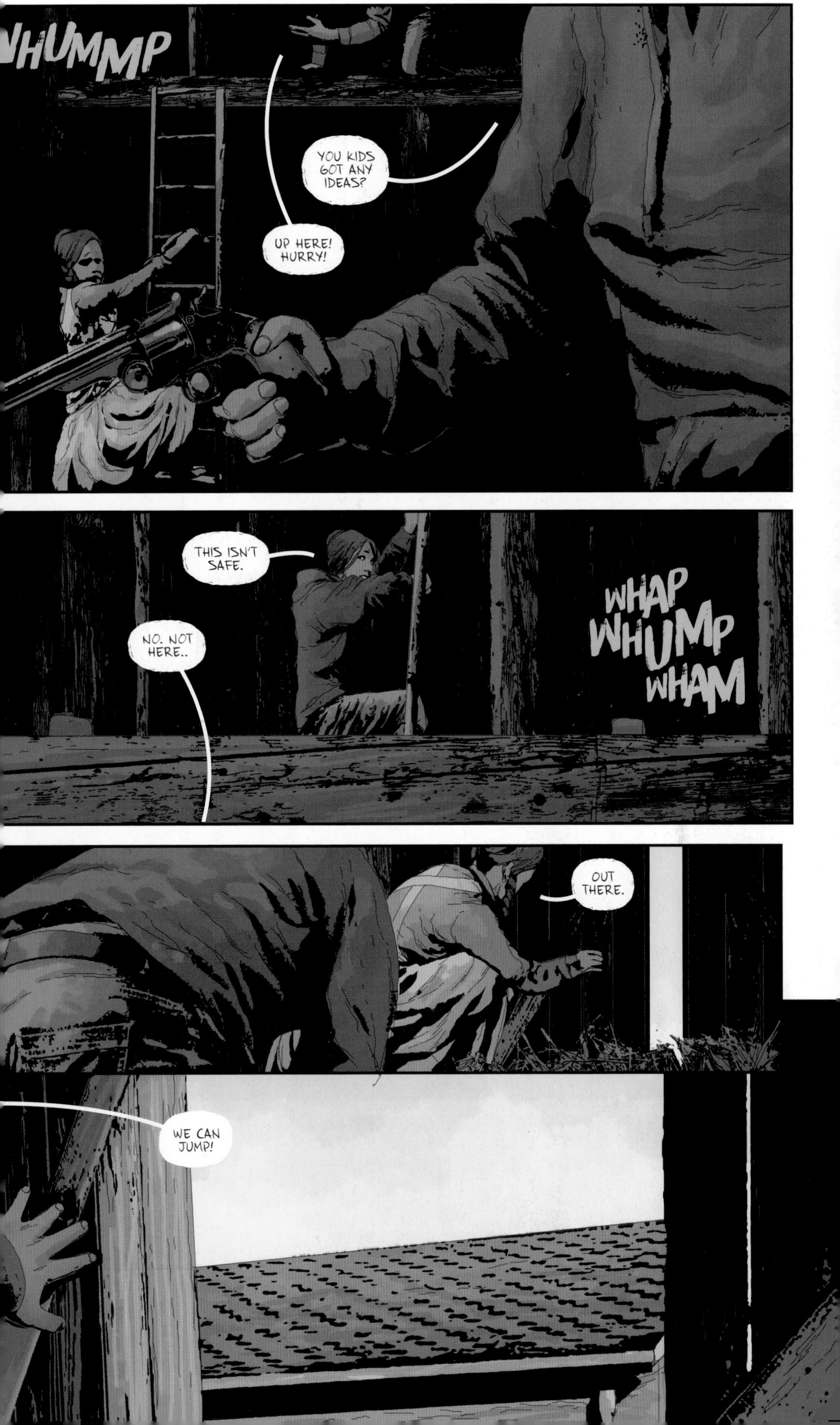
WHUMMP
YOU KIDS GOT ANY IDEAS?
UP HERE! HURRY!
THIS ISN'T SAFE.
NO. NOT HERE..
WHAP WHUMP WHAM
OUT THERE.
WE CAN JUMP!

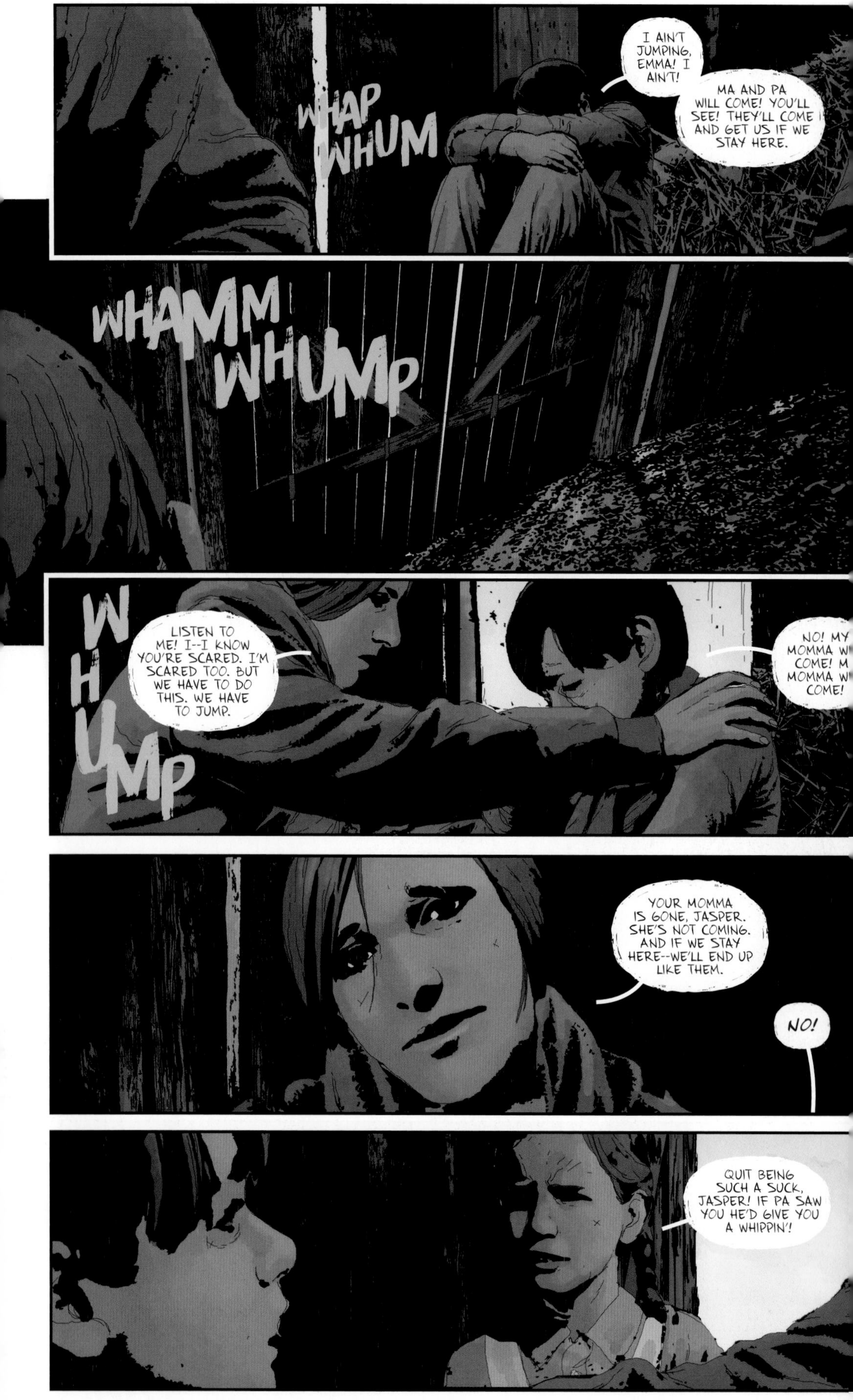
WHAP WHUM
I AIN'T JUMPING, EMMA! I AIN'T!
MA AND PA WILL COME! YOU'LL SEE! THEY'LL COME AND GET US IF WE STAY HERE.
WHAMM WHUMP
WHUMP
LISTEN TO ME! I--I KNOW YOU'RE SCARED. I'M SCARED TOO. BUT WE HAVE TO DO THIS. WE HAVE TO JUMP.
NO! MY MOMMA W COME! M MOMMA W COME!
YOUR MOMMA IS GONE, JASPER. SHE'S NOT COMING. AND IF WE STAY HERE--WE'LL END UP LIKE THEM.
NO!
QUIT BEING SUCH A SUCK, JASPER! IF PA SAW YOU HE'D GIVE YOU A WHIPPIN'!

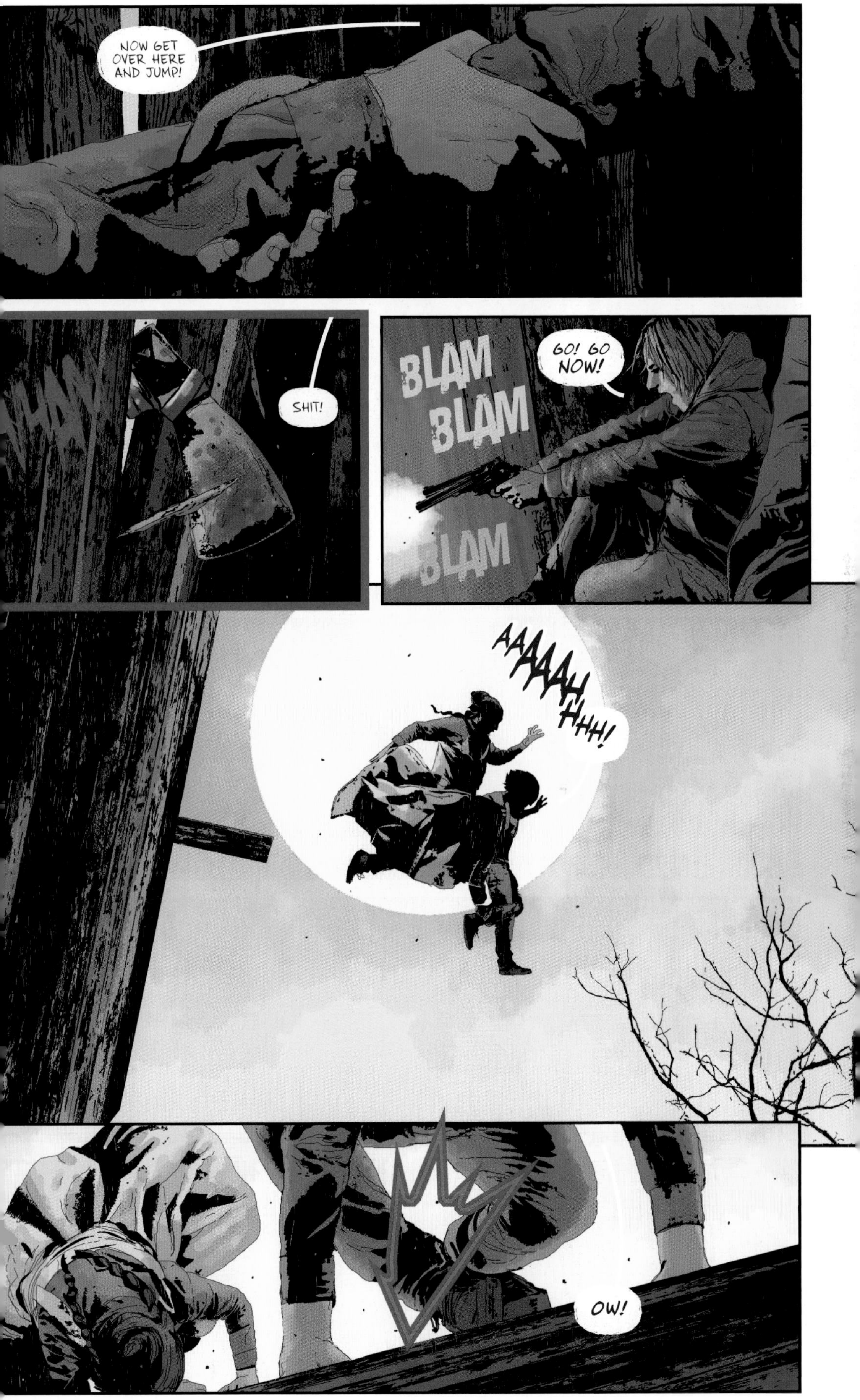
NOW GET OVER HERE AND JUMP!
SHIT!
BLAM
BLAM
BLAM
GO! GO NOW!
AAAAAHHHH!
OW!

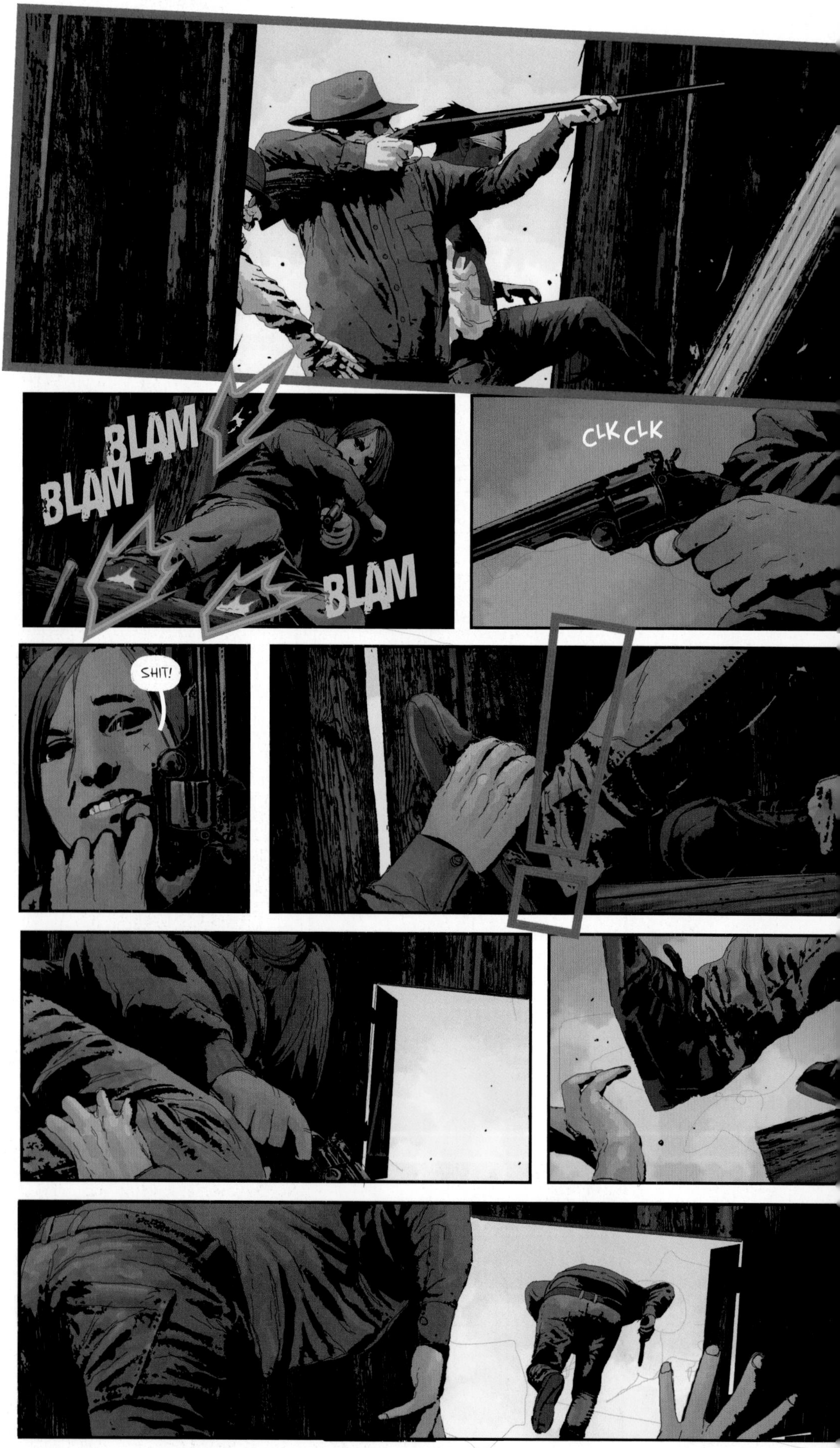
BLAM
BLAM
BLAM
CLK CLK
SHIT!

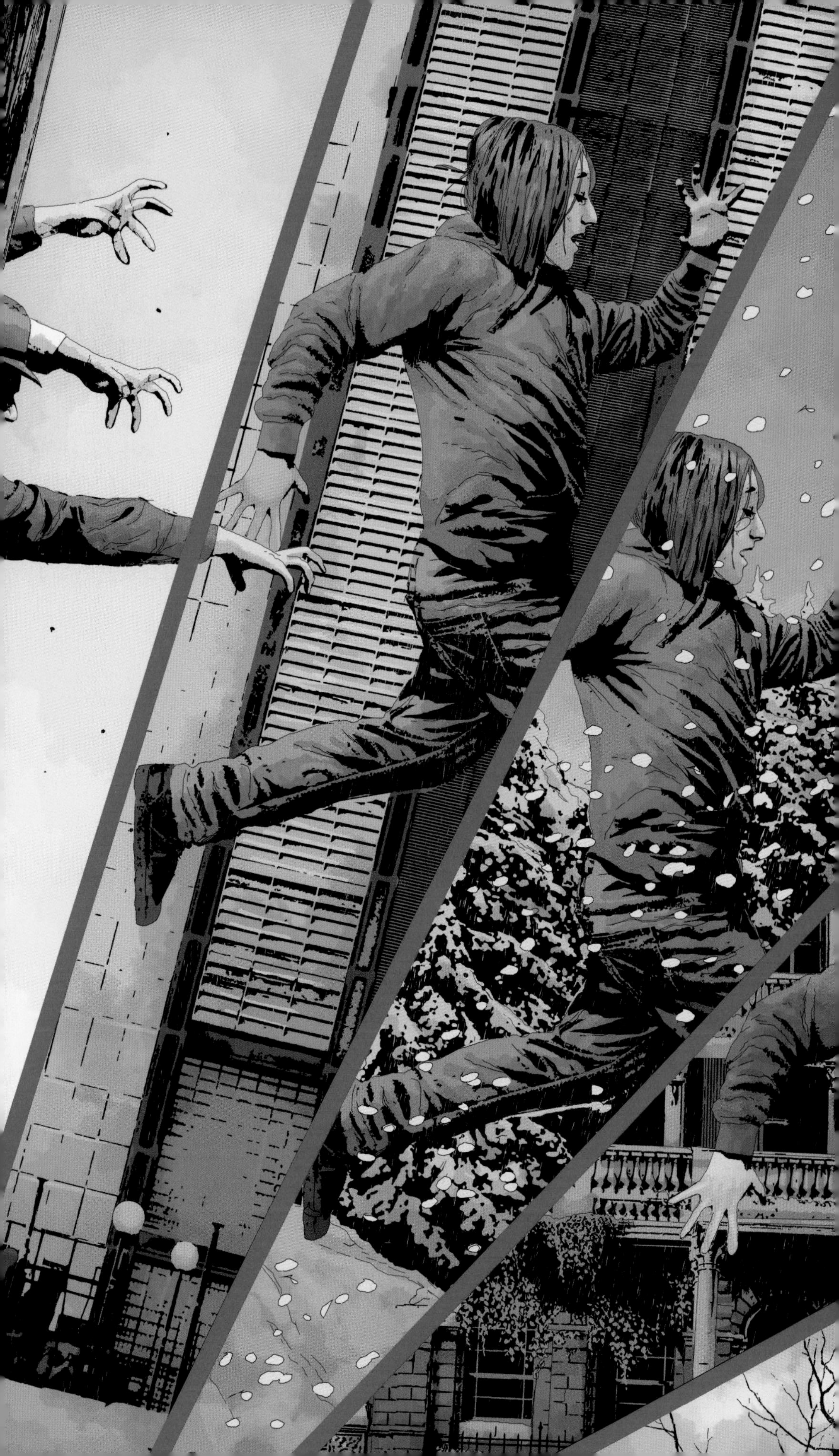

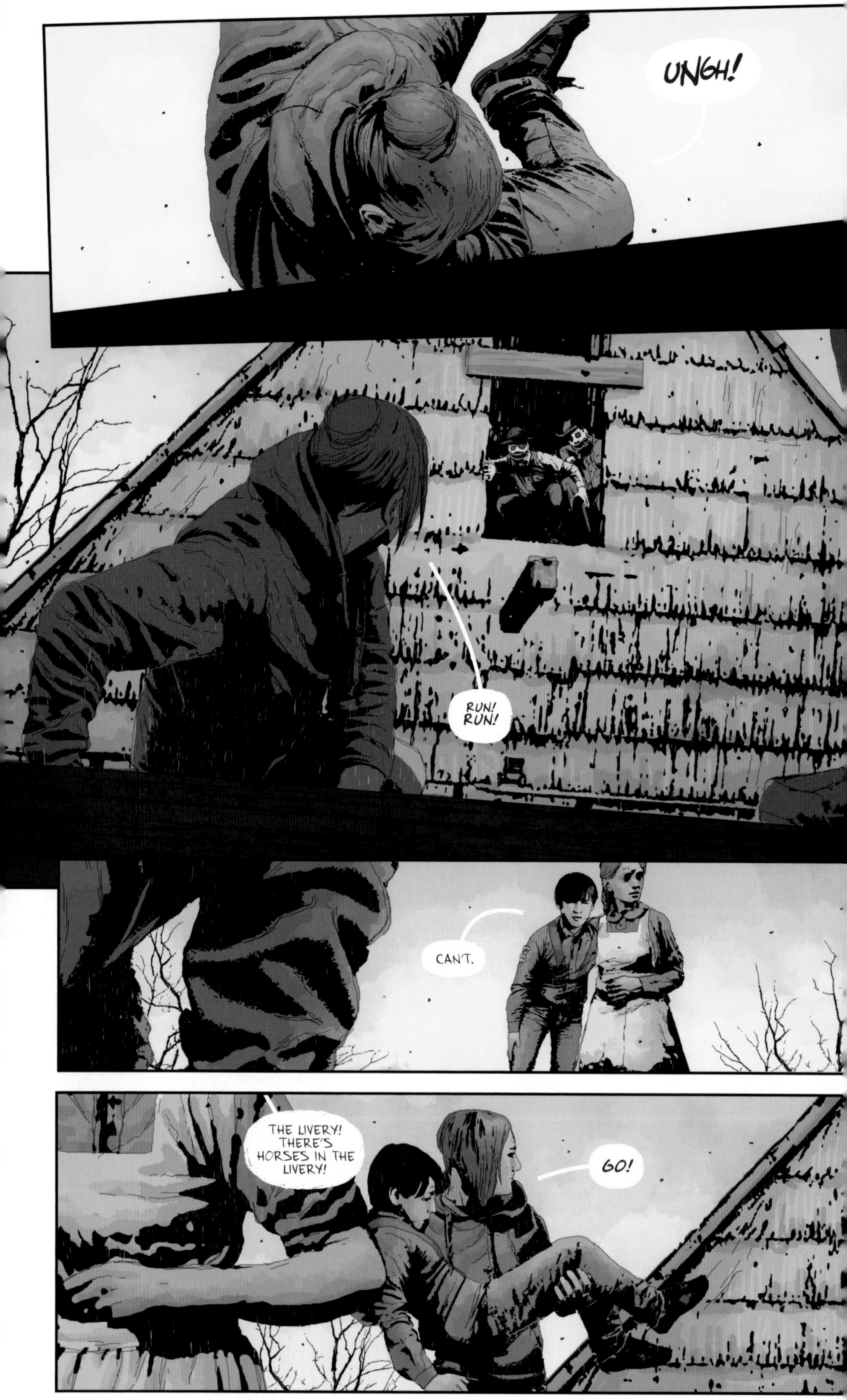
UNGH!
RUN! RUN!
CAN'T.
THE LIVERY! THERE'S HORSES IN THE LIVERY!
GO!

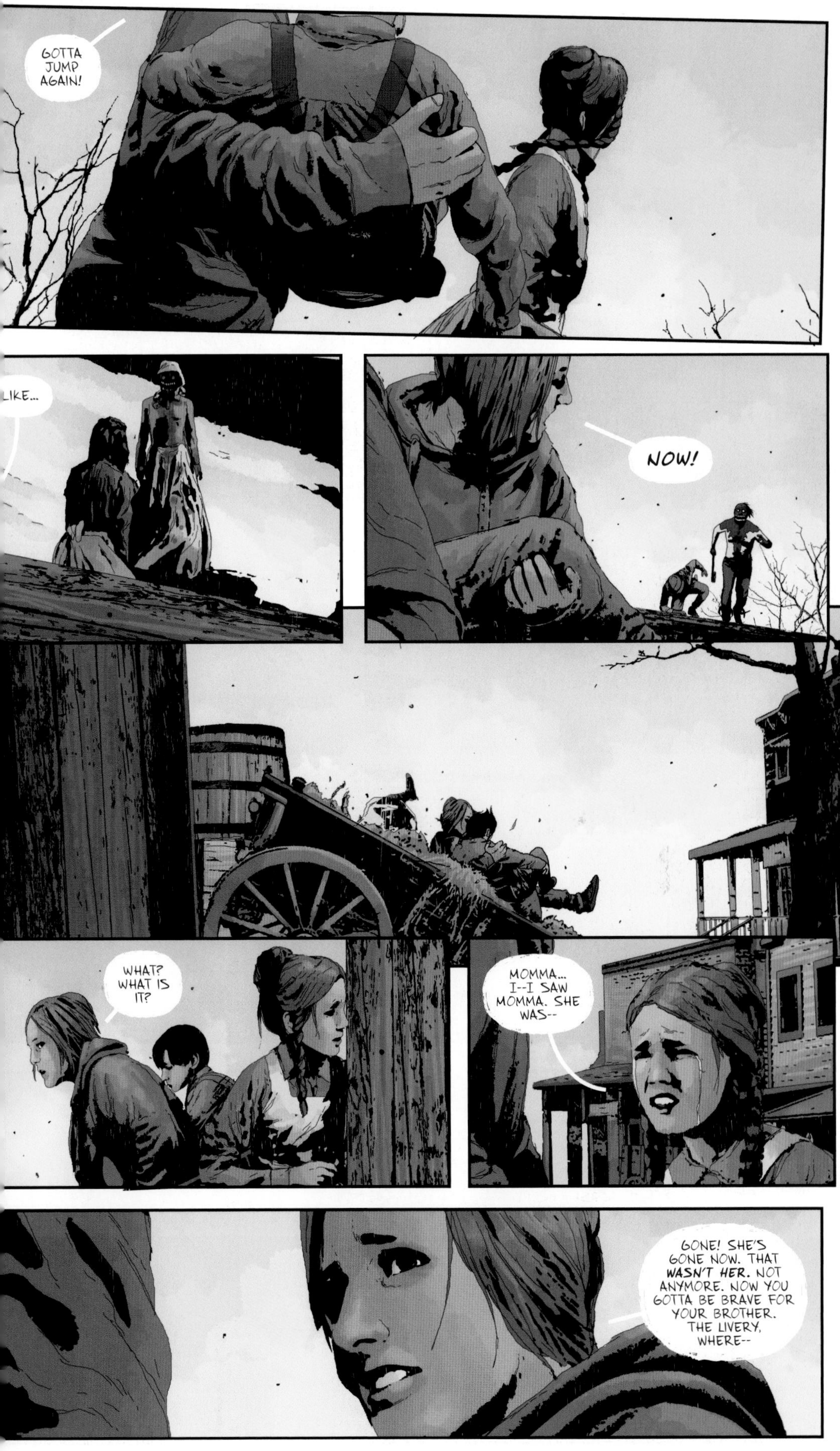
GOTTA JUMP AGAIN!
LIKE...
NOW!
WHAT? WHAT IS IT?
MOMMA... I--I SAW MOMMA. SHE WAS--
GONE! SHE'S GONE NOW. THAT WASN'T HER. NOT ANYMORE. NOW YOU GOTTA BE BRAVE FOR YOUR BROTHER. THE LIVERY, WHERE--

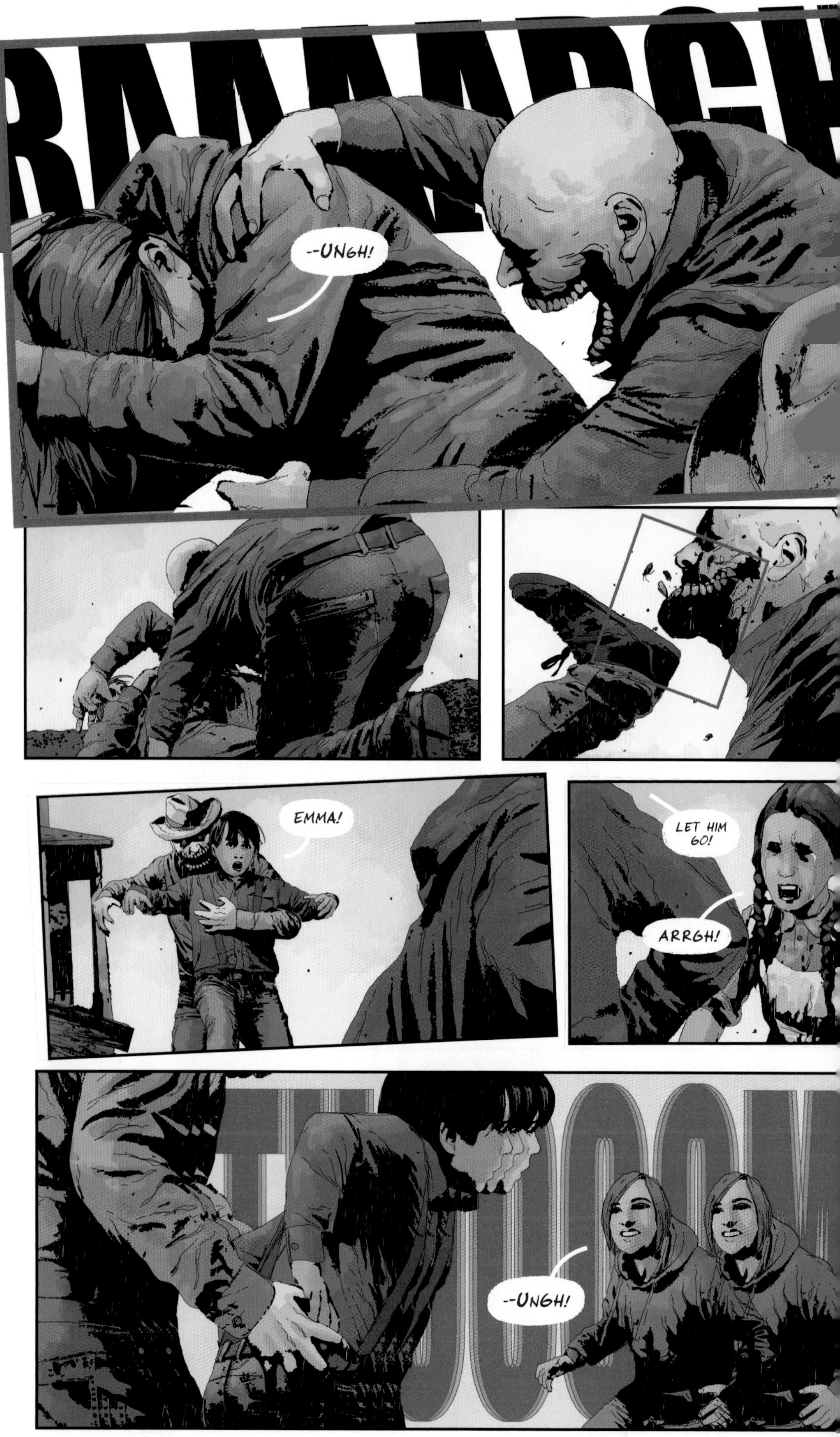
--UNGH!
EMMA!
LET HIM GO!
ARRGH!
--UNGH!

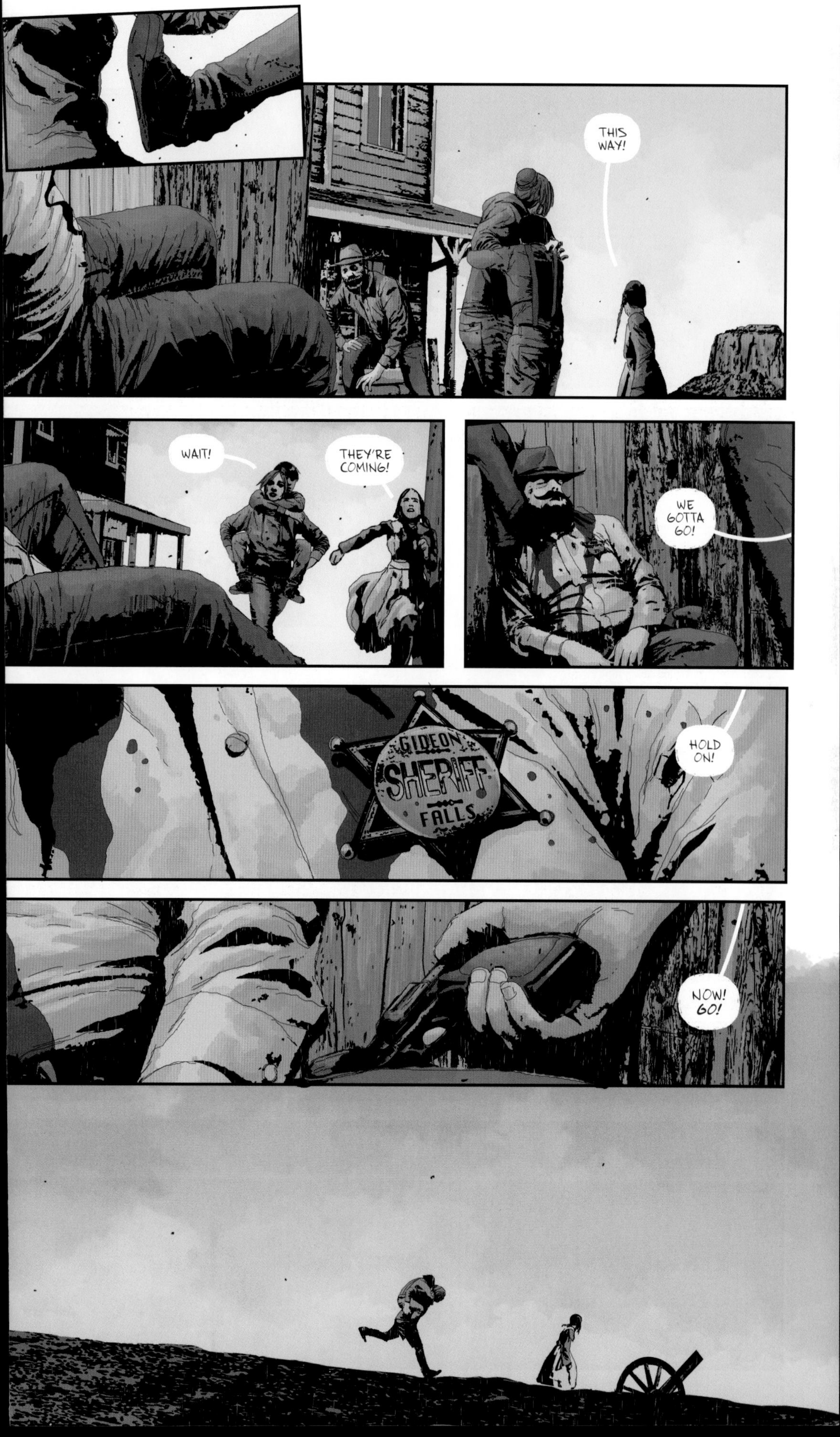
THIS WAY!
WAIT!
THEY'RE COMING!
WE GOTTA GO!
GIDEON SHERIFF FALLS
HOLD ON!
NOW! GO!

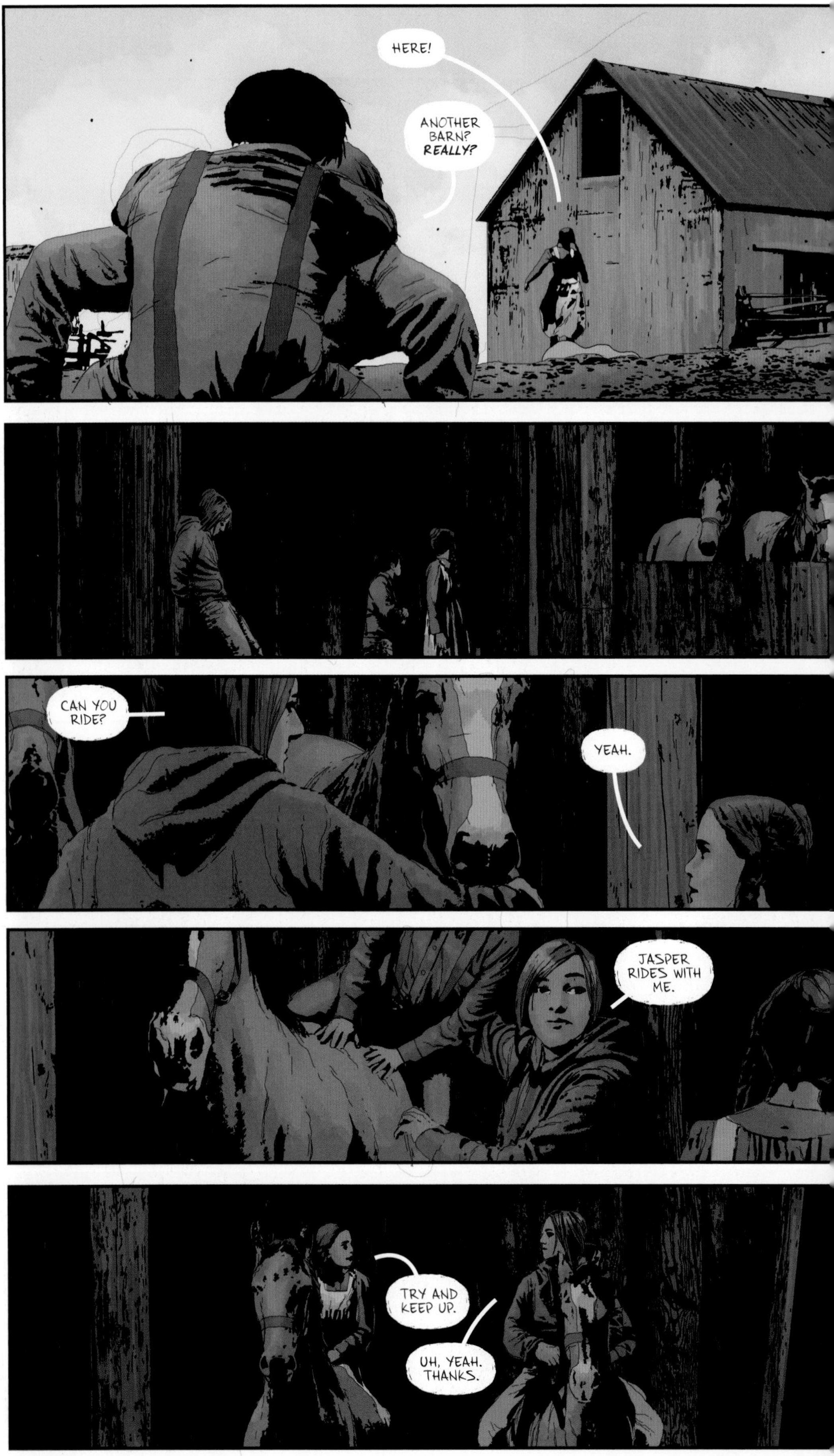
HERE!
ANOTHER BARN? REALLY?
CAN YOU RIDE?
YEAH.
JASPER RIDES WITH ME.
TRY AND KEEP UP.
UH, YEAH. THANKS.

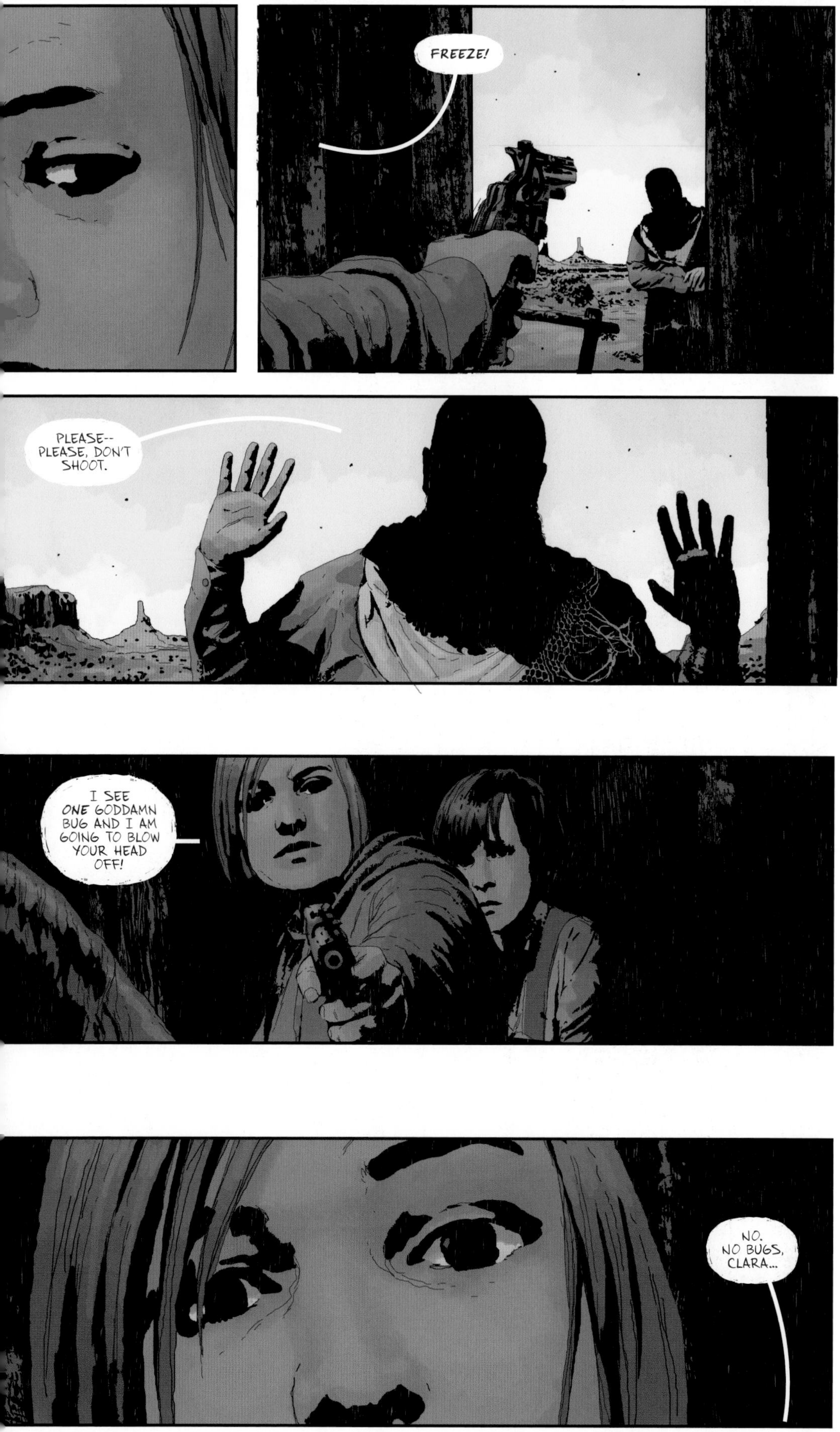
FREEZE!
PLEASE-- PLEASE, DON'T SHOOT.
I SEE ONE GODDAMN BUG AND I AM GOING TO BLOW YOUR HEAD OFF!
NO. NO BUGS, CLARA...

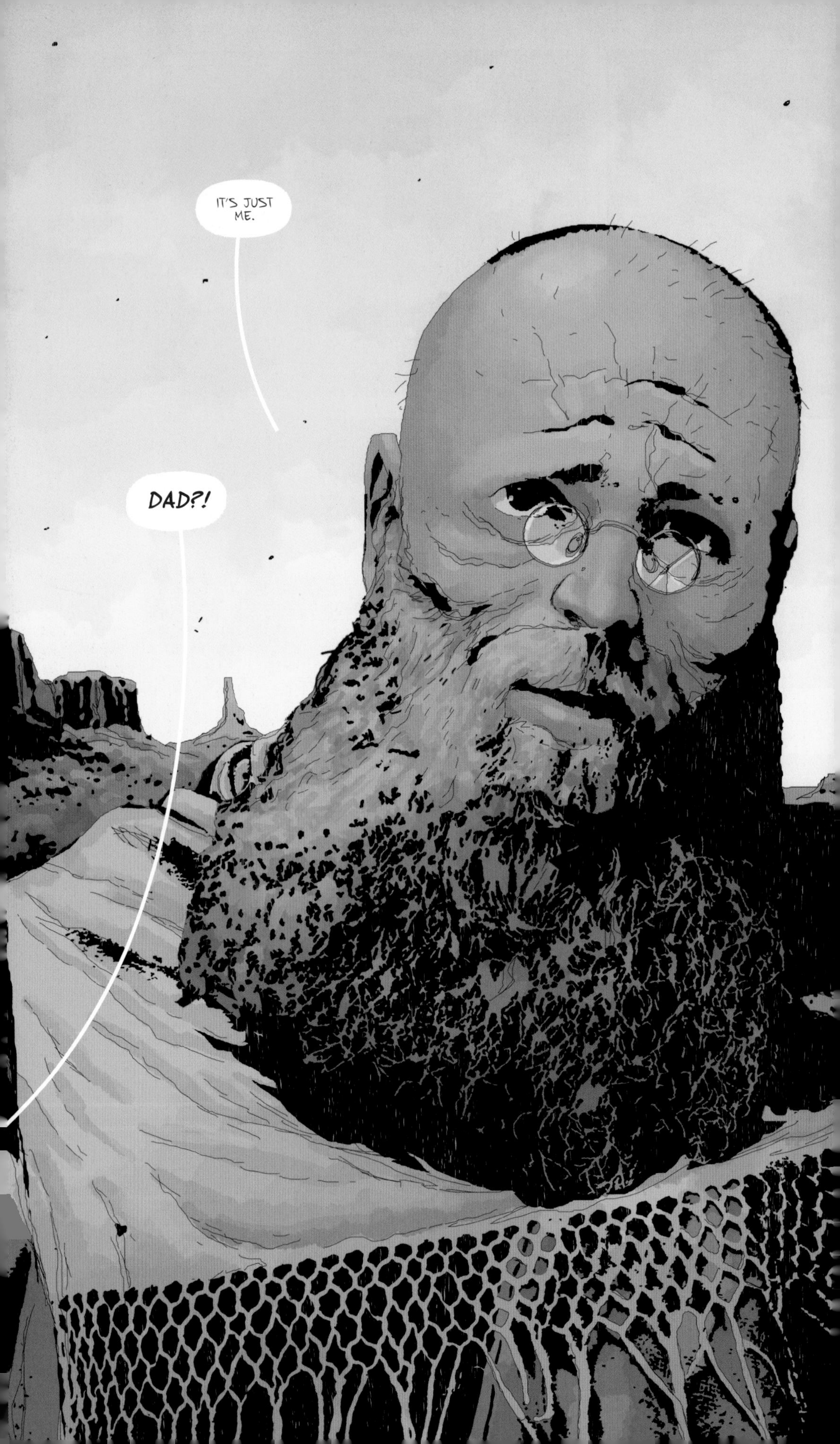
IT'S JUST ME.
DAD?!

GIDEON
FALLS

Twenty-Five

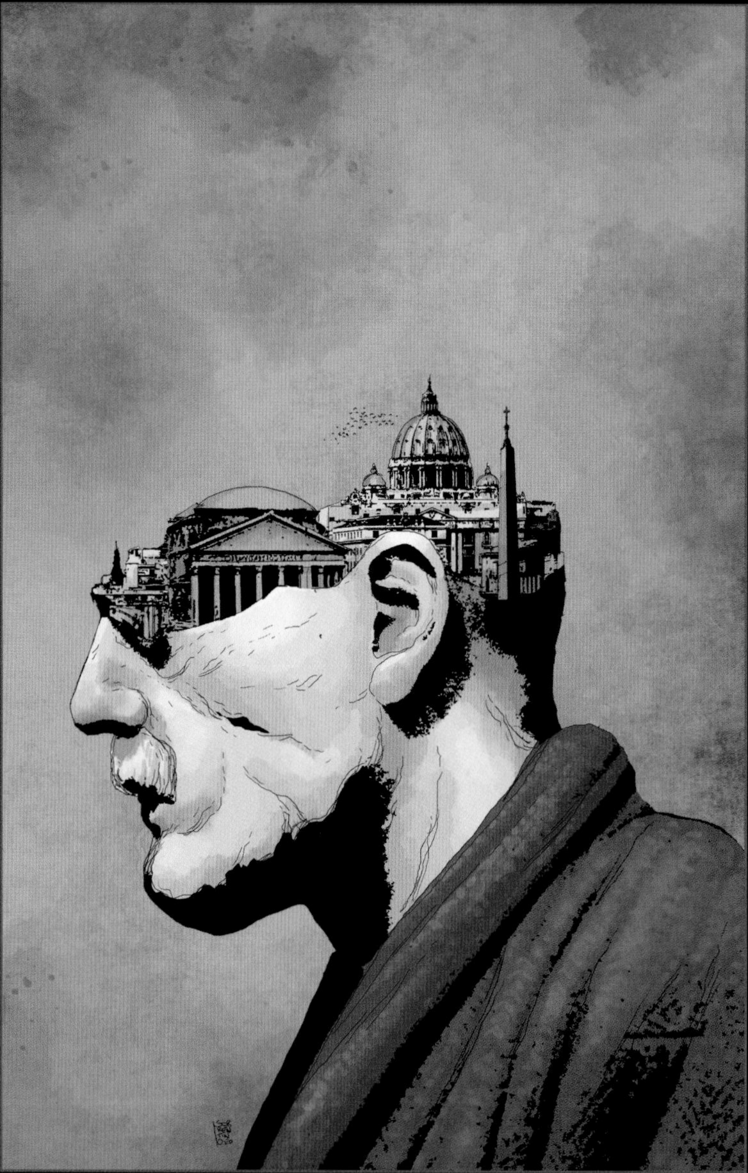

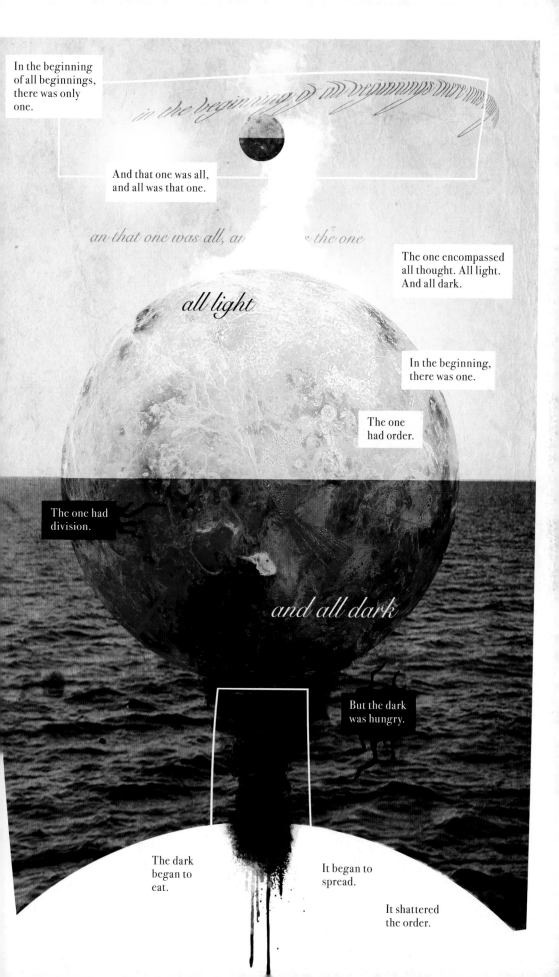

In the beginning of all beginnings, there was only one.

And that one was all, and all was that one.

an that one was all, a ~ the one

The one encompassed all thought. All light. And all dark.

all light

In the beginning, there was one.

The one had order.

The one had division.

and all dark

But the dark was hungry.

The dark began to eat.

It began to spread.

It shattered the order.

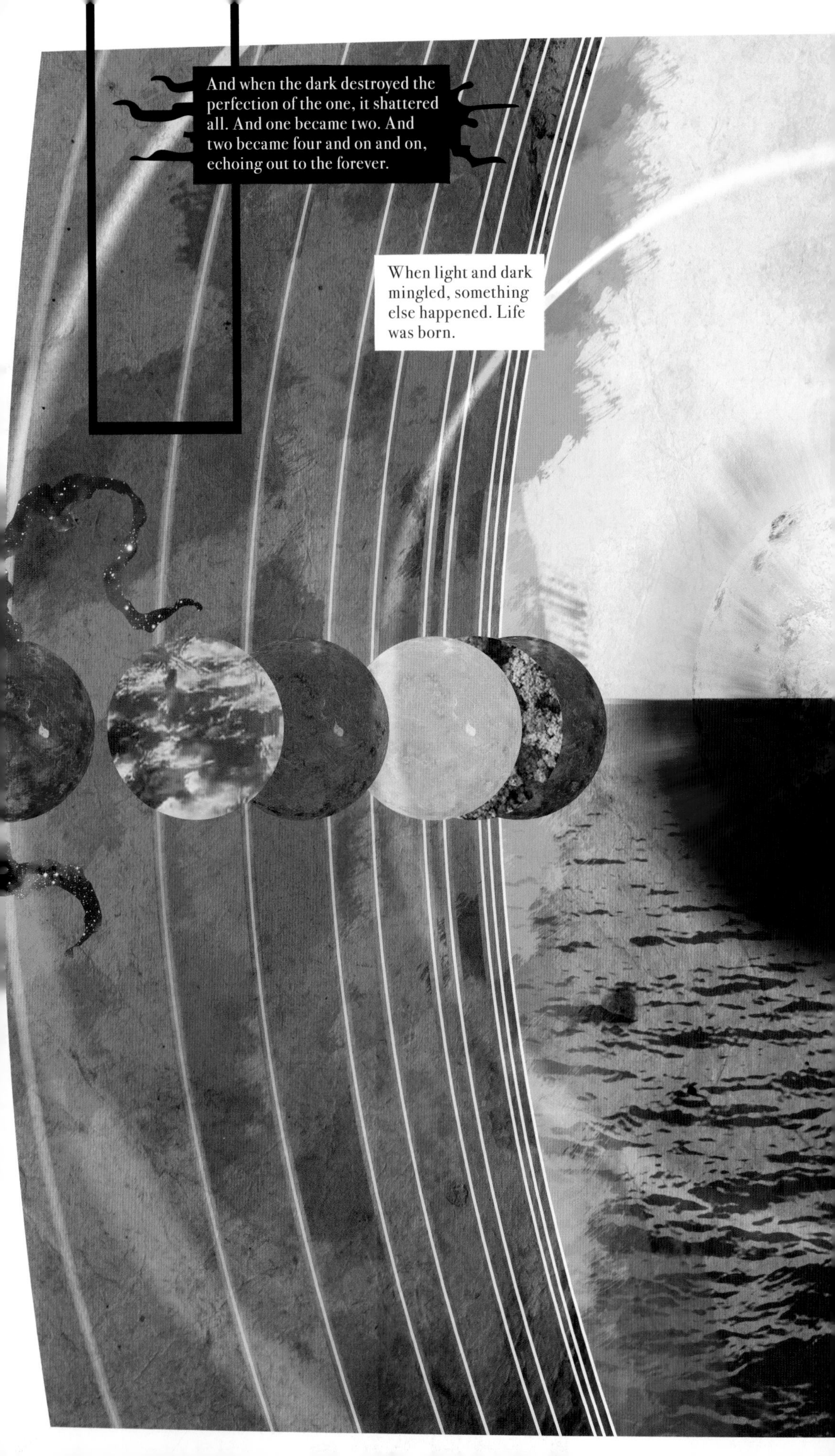
And when the dark destroyed the perfection of the one, it shattered all. And one became two. And two became four and on and on, echoing out to the forever.
When light and dark mingled, something else happened. Life was born.

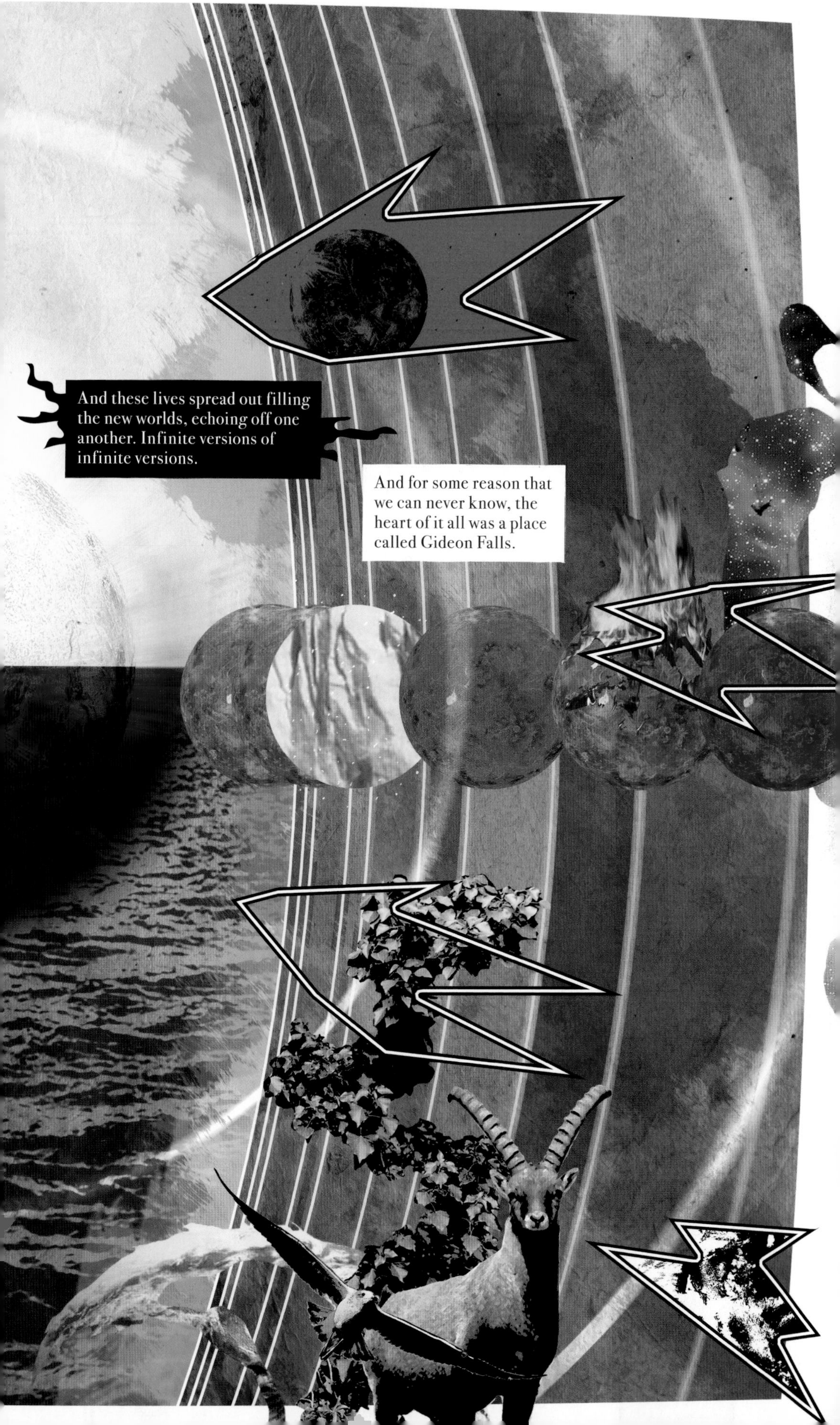
And these lives spread out filling the new worlds, echoing off one another. Infinite versions of infinite versions.
And for some reason that we can never know, the heart of it all was a place called Gideon Falls.

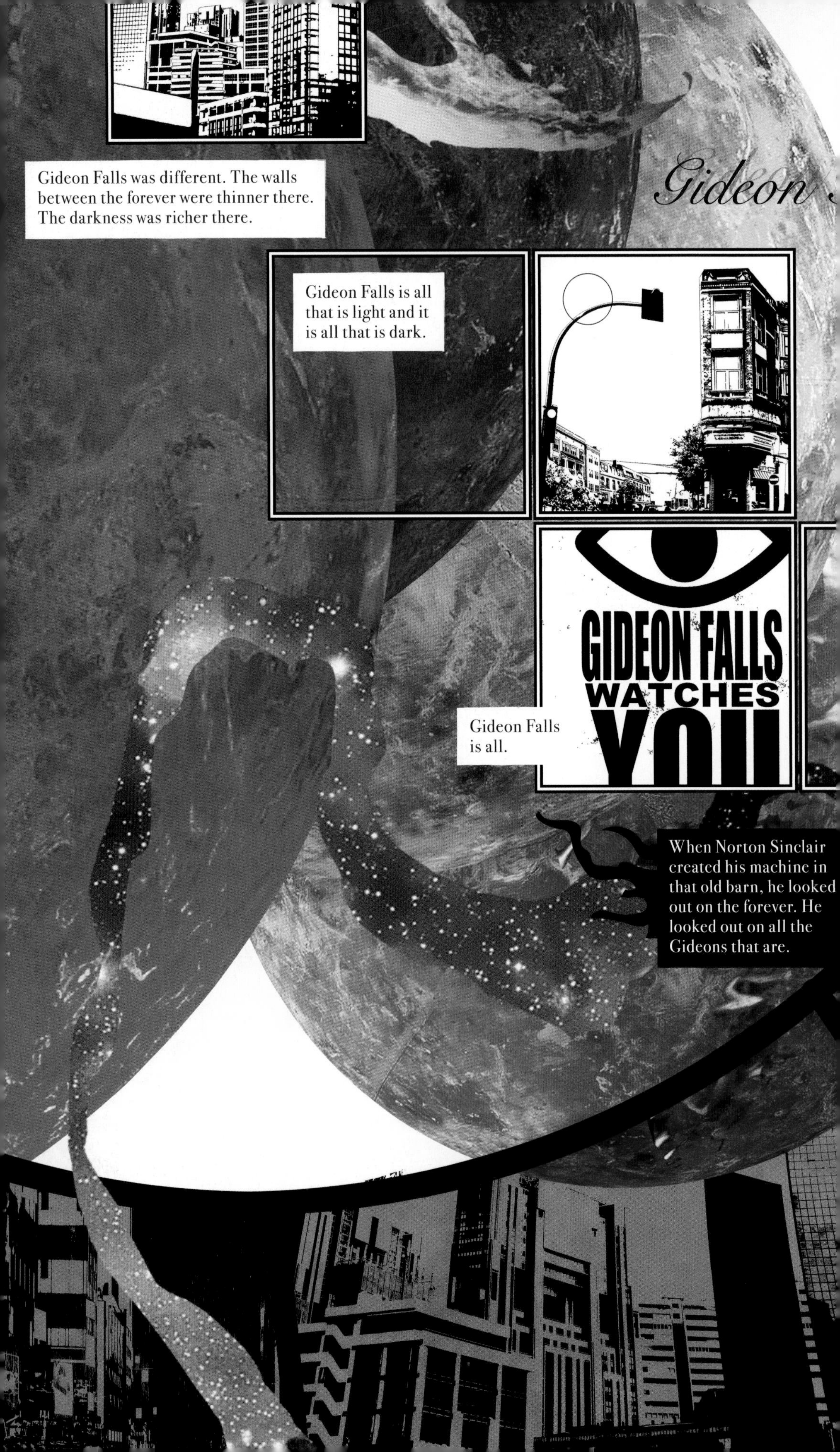

Gideon Falls was different. The walls between the forever were thinner there. The darkness was richer there.
Gideon
Gideon Falls is all that is light and it is all that is dark.
GIDEON FALLS WATCHES YOU
Gideon Falls is all.
When Norton Sinclair created his machine in that old barn, he looked out on the forever. He looked out on all the Gideons that are.

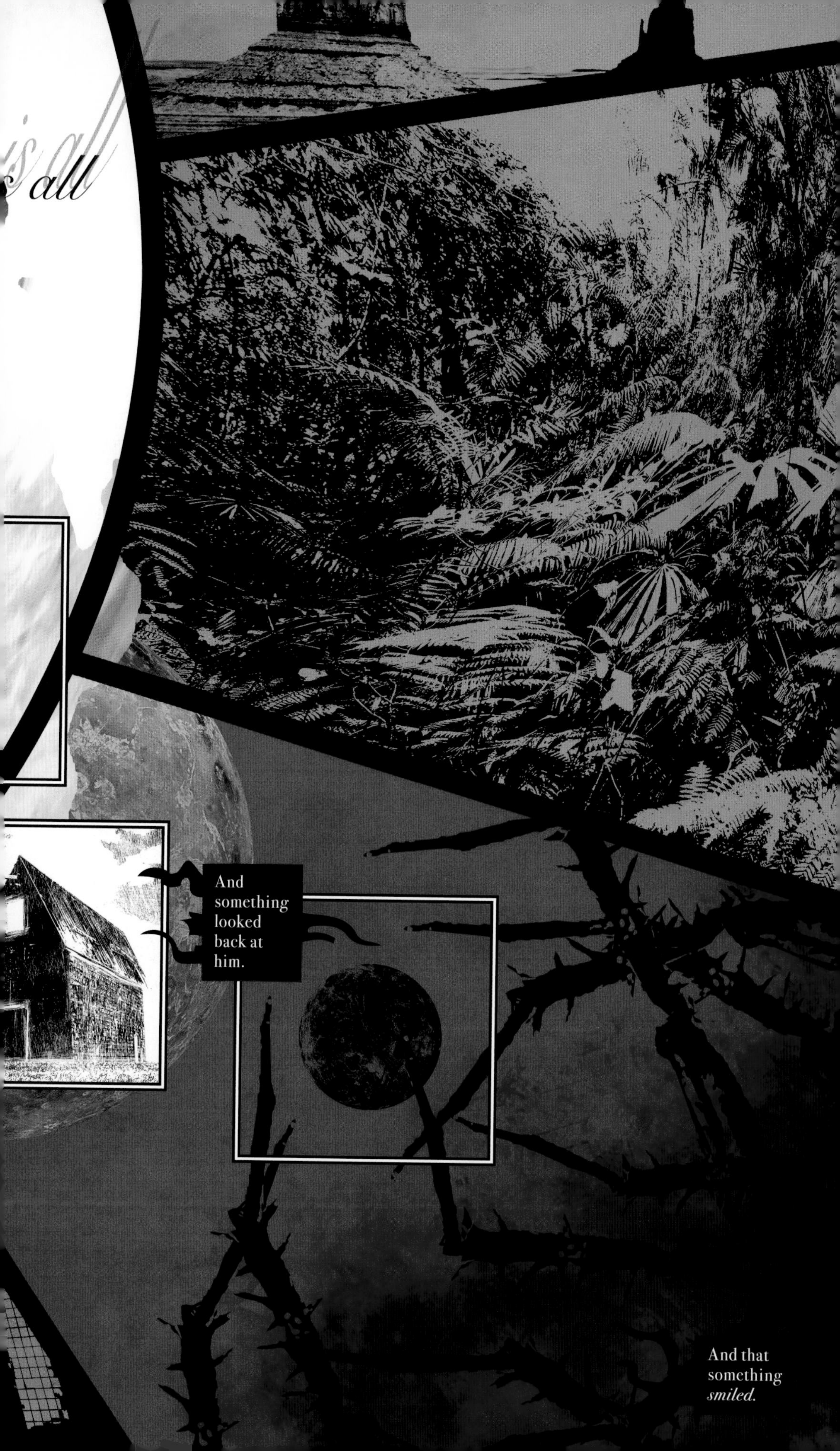

is all
And something looked back at him.
And that something *smiled.*

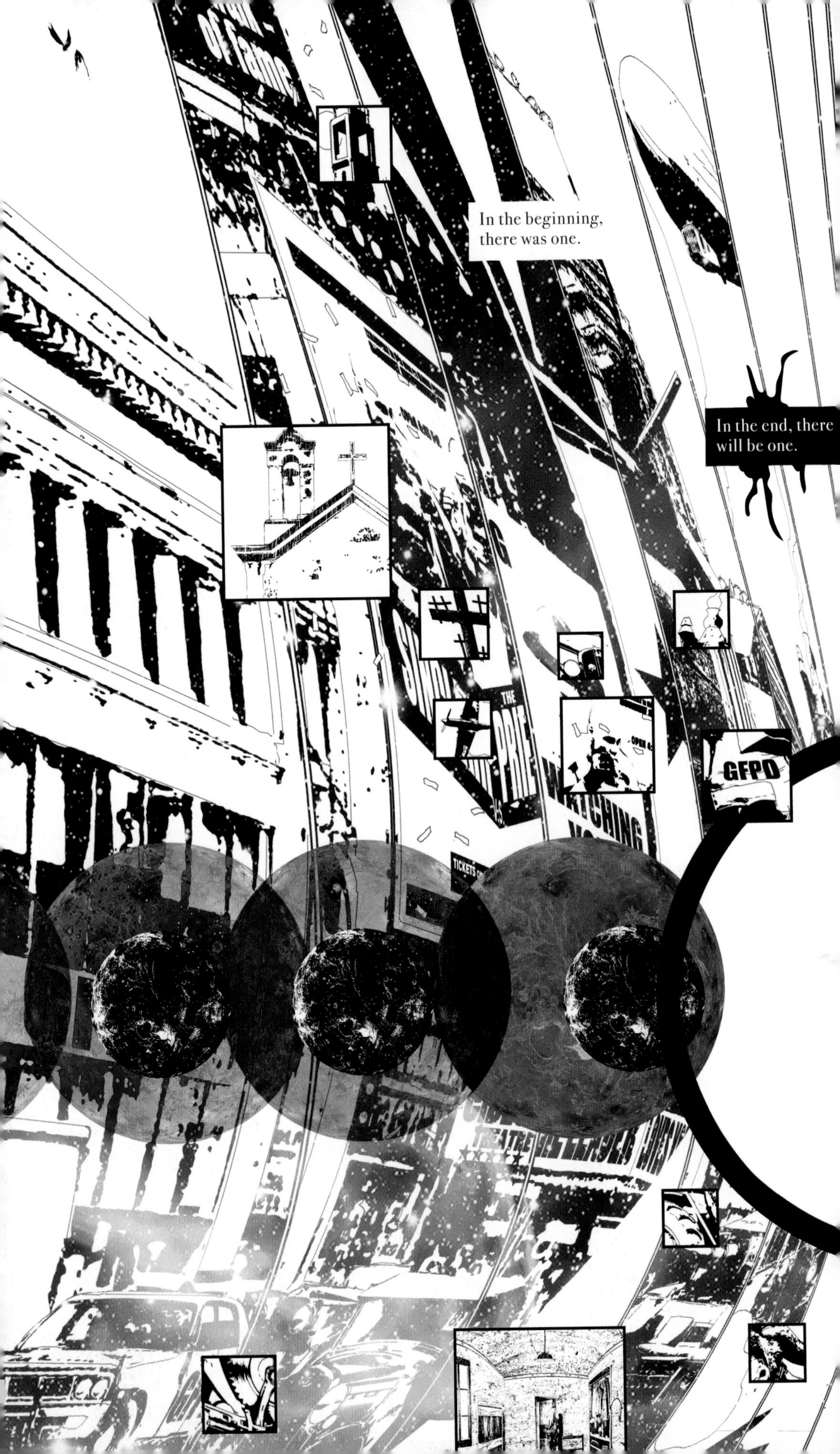
In the beginning, there was one.
In the end, there will be one.
GFPD

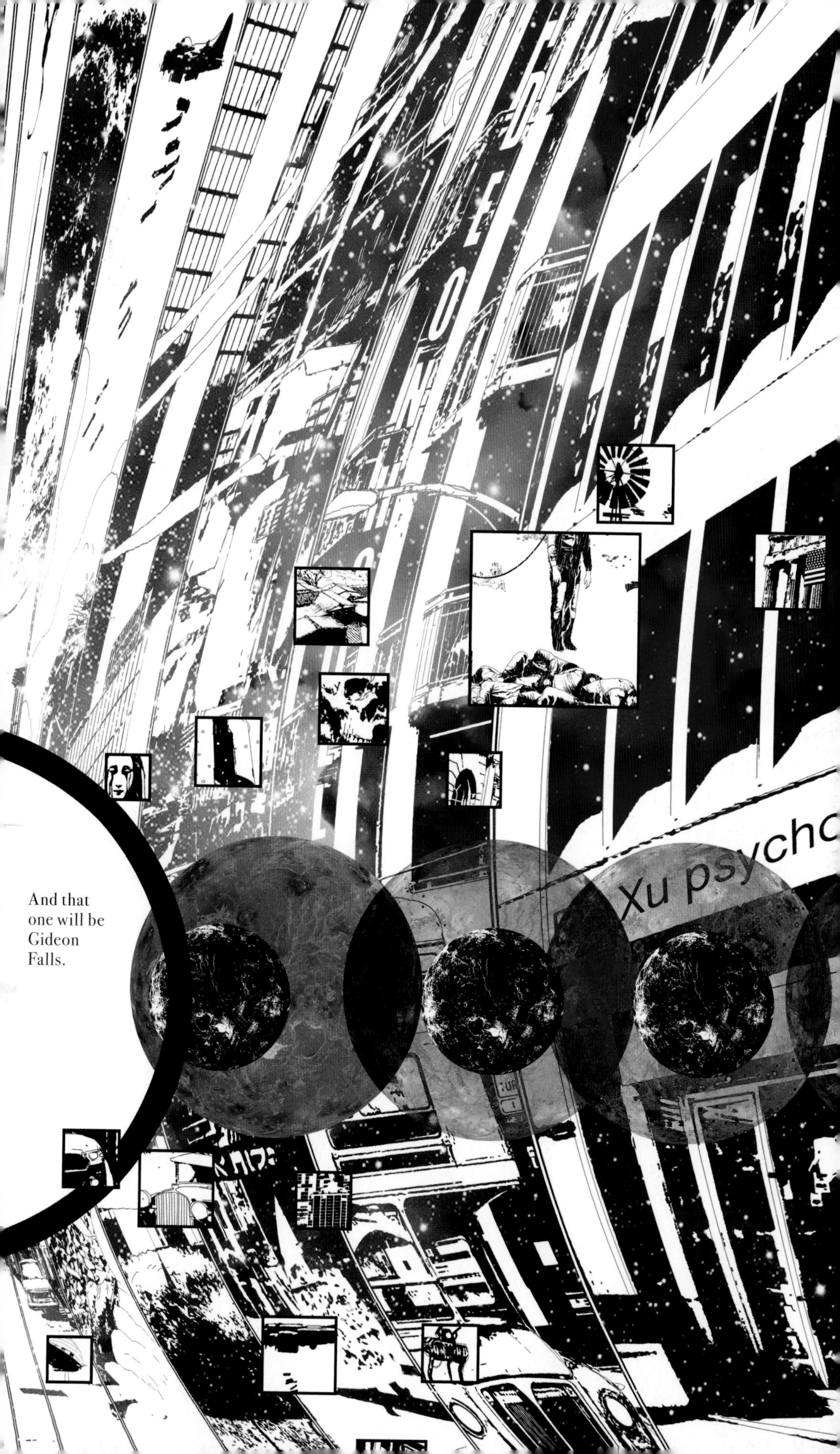
And that one will be Gideon Falls.
Xu psycho

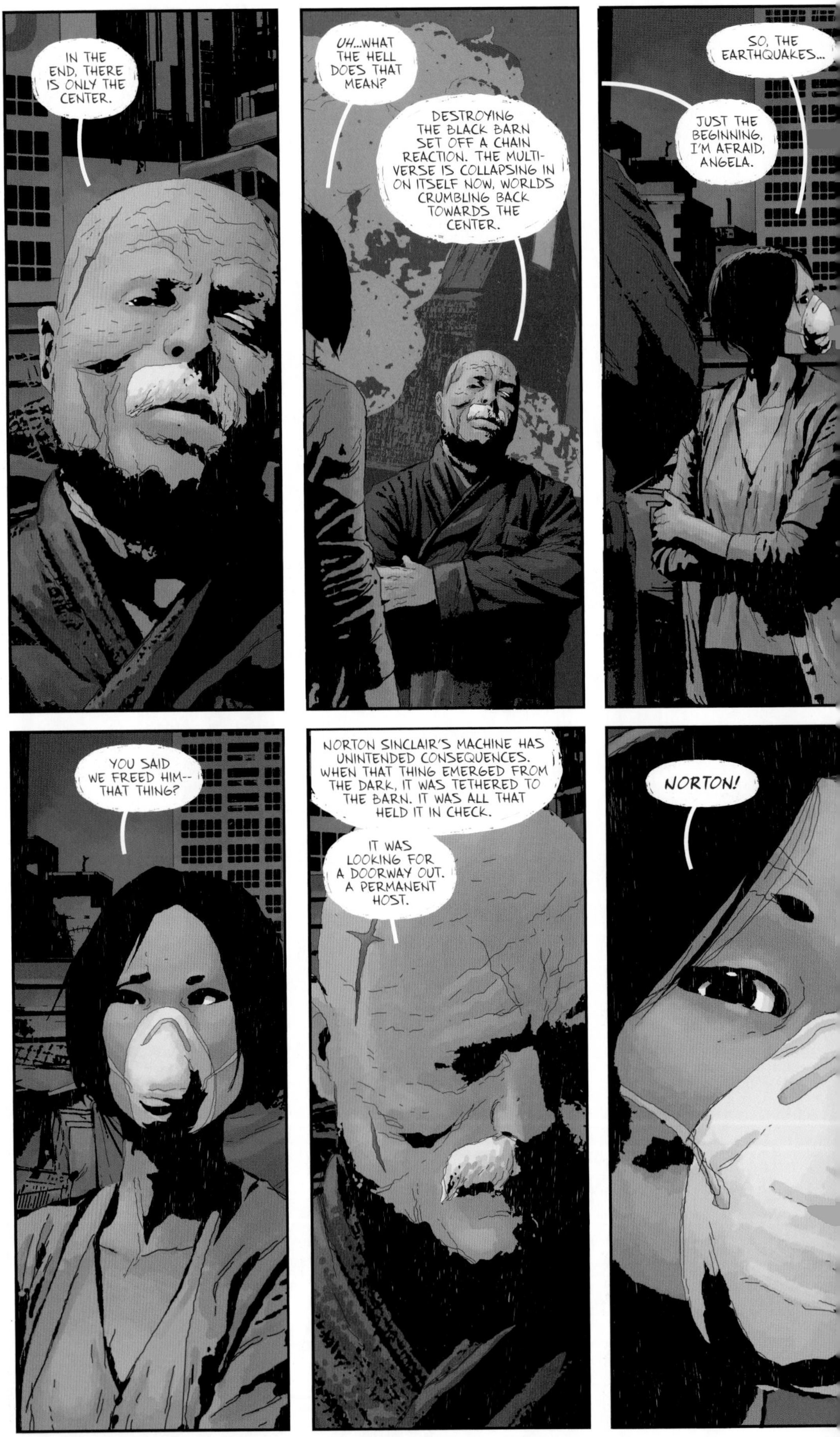
IN THE END, THERE IS ONLY THE CENTER.
UH...WHAT THE HELL DOES THAT MEAN?
DESTROYING THE BLACK BARN SET OFF A CHAIN REACTION. THE MULTIVERSE IS COLLAPSING IN ON ITSELF NOW, WORLDS CRUMBLING BACK TOWARDS THE CENTER.
SO, THE EARTHQUAKES...
JUST THE BEGINNING, I'M AFRAID, ANGELA.
YOU SAID WE FREED HIM--THAT THING?
NORTON SINCLAIR'S MACHINE HAS UNINTENDED CONSEQUENCES. WHEN THAT THING EMERGED FROM THE DARK, IT WAS TETHERED TO THE BARN. IT WAS ALL THAT HELD IT IN CHECK.
IT WAS LOOKING FOR A DOORWAY OUT. A PERMANENT HOST.
NORTON!

YES. THE MAN YOU KNEW AS NORTON. WHO, OF COURSE, WAS REALLY DANIEL SUTTON.

BUT THEN YOU DESTROYED THE BLACK BARN AND NOW THE DARKNESS IS FREE AND UNTETHERED. ALL IS LOST UNLESS WE ACT.

BUT WHERE IS HE?

WHERE IS DANIEL? AND THE OTHERS? HIS SISTER, HIS FATHER? FRED?

THAT IS WHY I AM HERE. IT IS TIME WE FOUND THEM. IT IS TIME WE GATHERED *THE FIVE TRAVELLERS.*

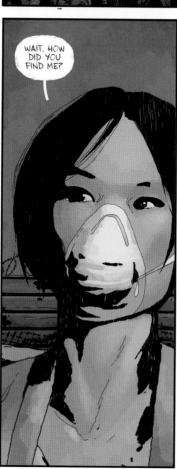

WAIT, HOW DID YOU FIND ME?

YOU TOLD ME YOU WOULD BE HERE, ANGELA.

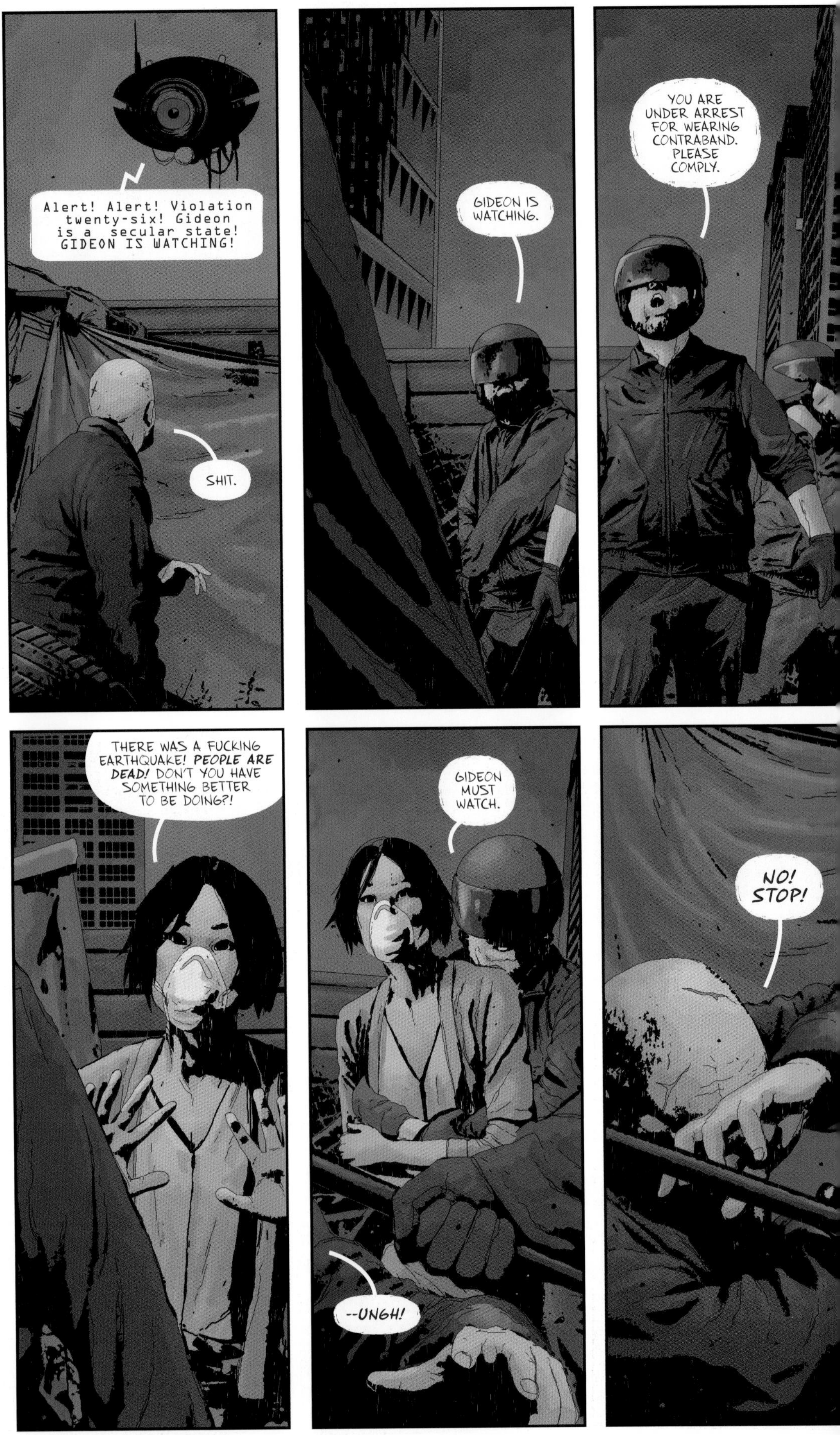
Alert! Alert! Violation twenty-six! Gideon is a secular state! GIDEON IS WATCHING!
SHIT.
GIDEON IS WATCHING.
YOU ARE UNDER ARREST FOR WEARING CONTRABAND. PLEASE COMPLY.
THERE WAS A FUCKING EARTHQUAKE! PEOPLE ARE DEAD! DON'T YOU HAVE SOMETHING BETTER TO BE DOING?!
GIDEON MUST WATCH.
--UNGH!
NO! STOP!

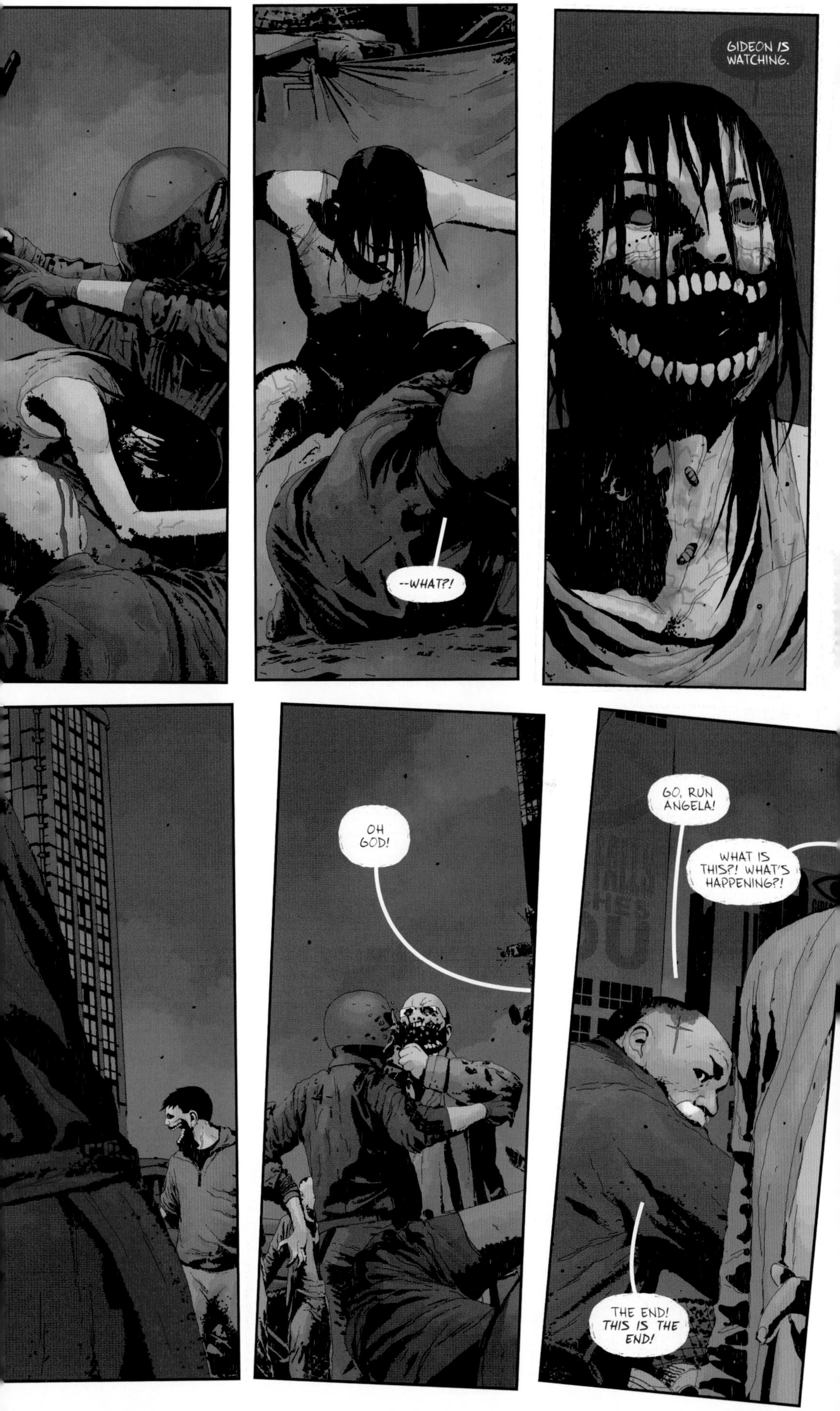
--WHAT?!
GIDEON IS WATCHING.
OH GOD!
GO, RUN ANGELA!
WHAT IS THIS?! WHAT'S HAPPENING?!
THE END! THIS IS THE END!

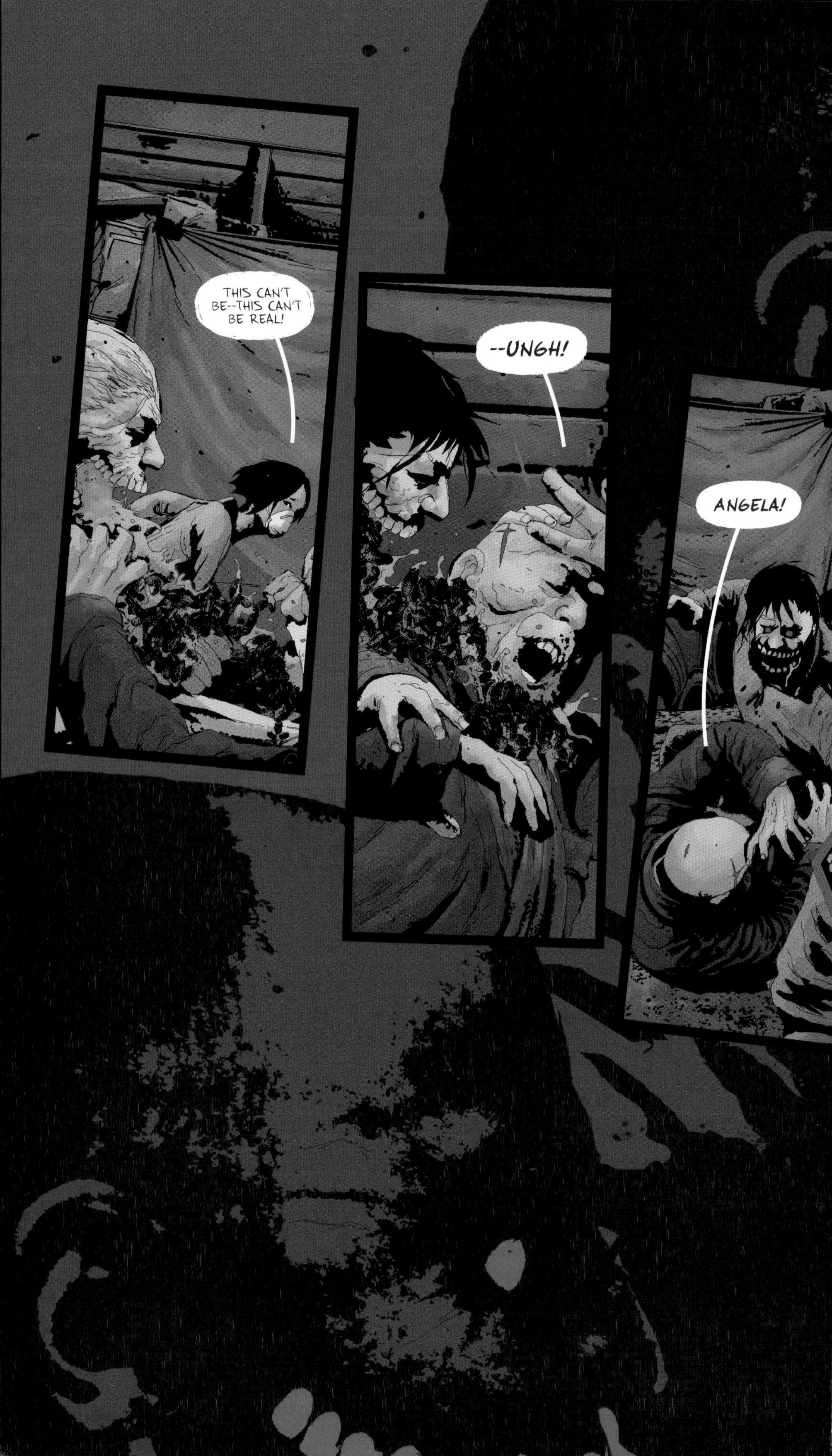
THIS CAN'T BE--THIS CAN'T BE REAL!
--UNGH!
ANGELA!

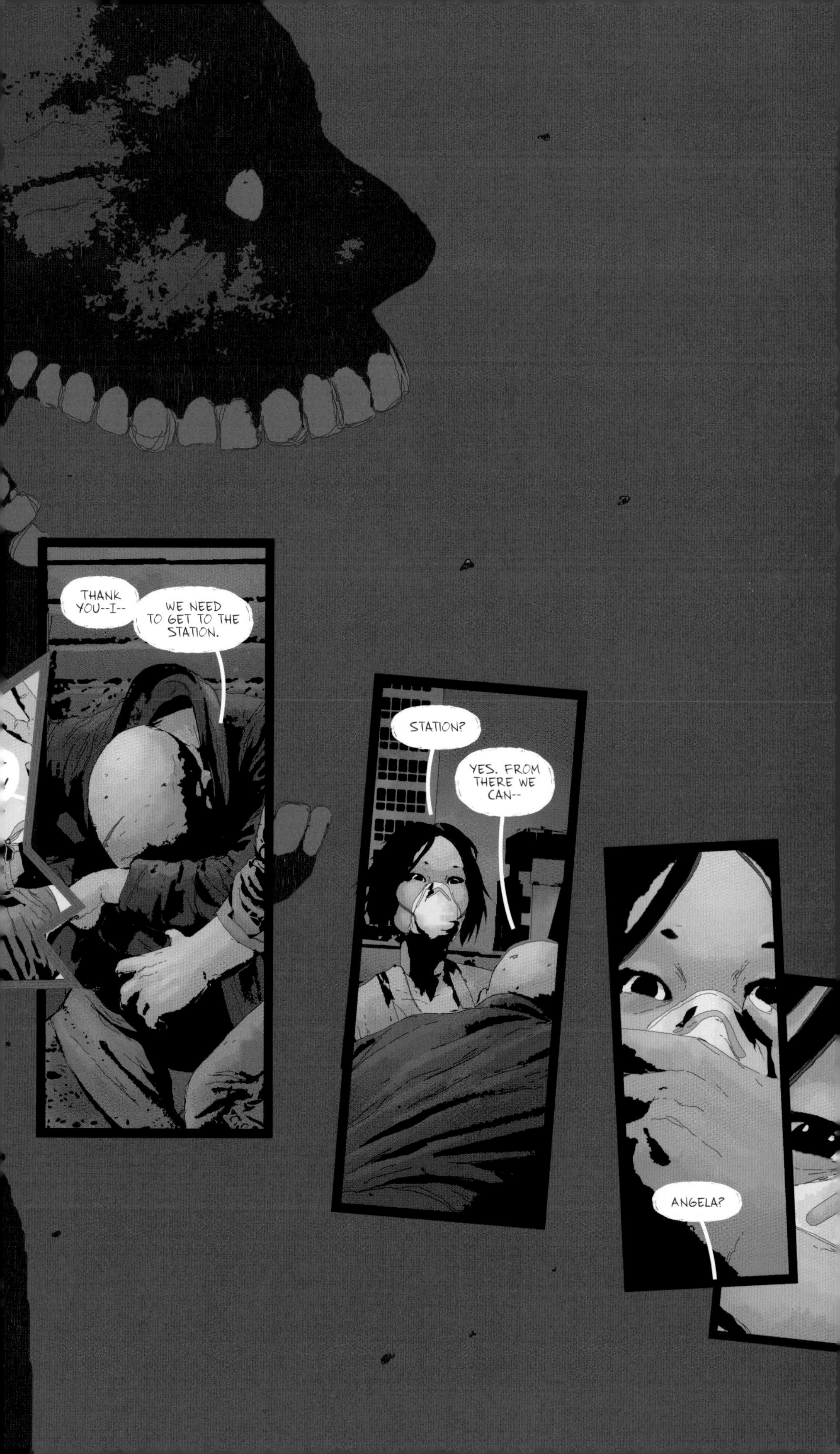
THANK YOU--I--
WE NEED TO GET TO THE STATION.
STATION?
YES. FROM THERE WE CAN--
ANGELA?

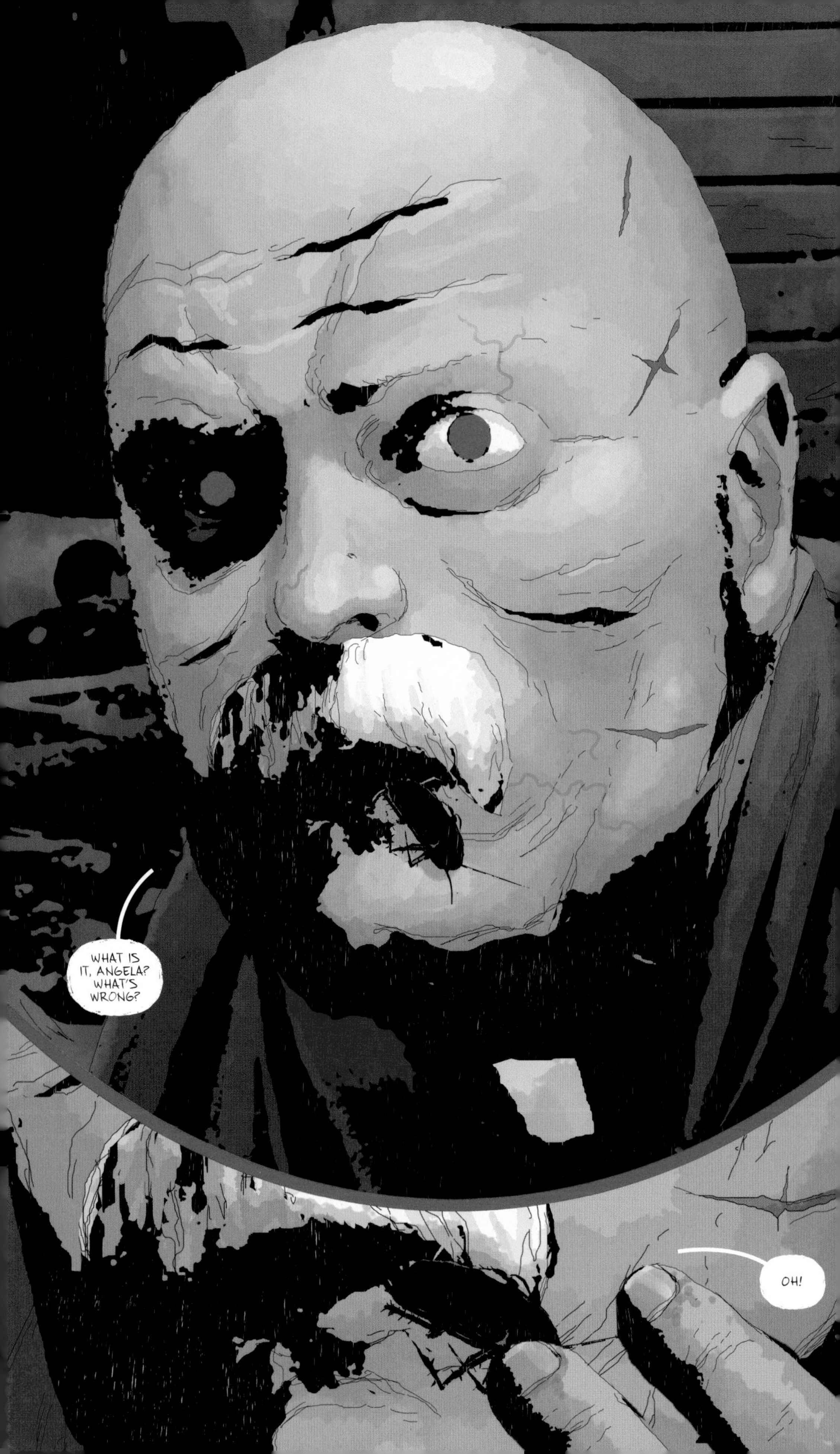
WHAT IS IT, ANGELA? WHAT'S WRONG?
OH!

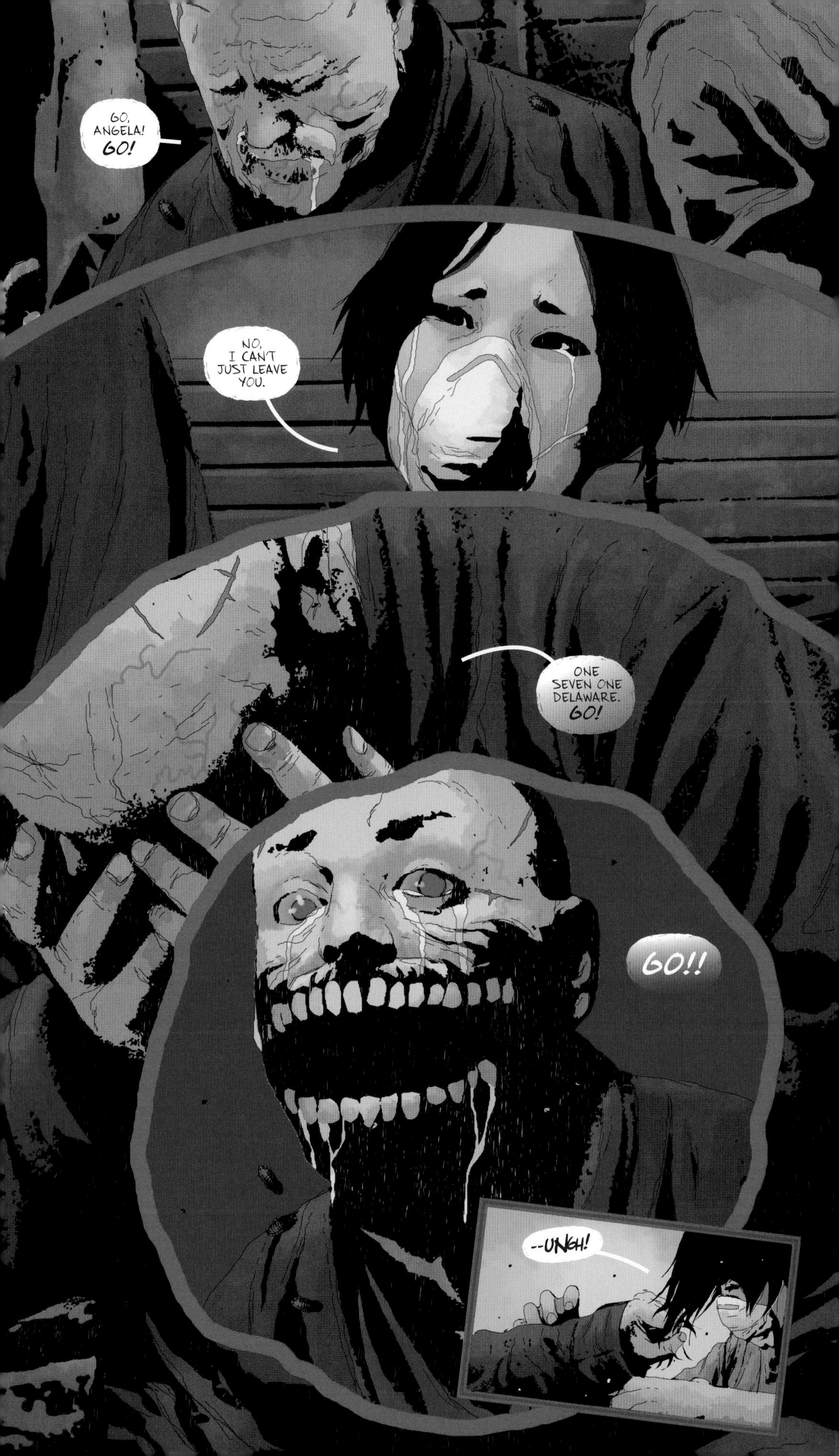
GO, ANGELA! GO!
NO, I CAN'T JUST LEAVE YOU.
ONE SEVEN ONE DELAWARE. GO!
GO!!
--UNGH!

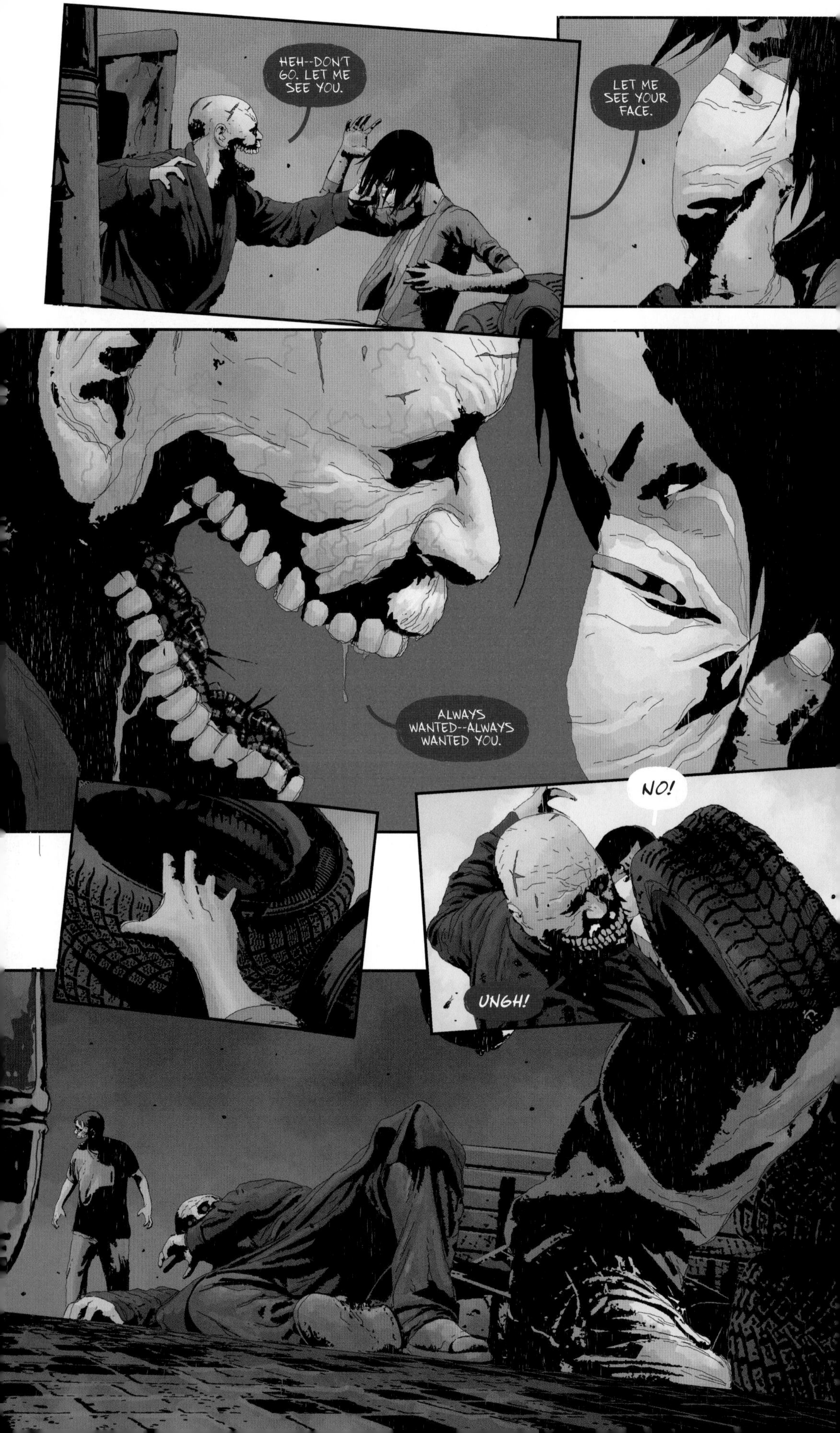
HEH--DON'T GO. LET ME SEE YOU.
LET ME SEE YOUR FACE.
ALWAYS WANTED--ALWAYS WANTED YOU.
NO!
UNGH!

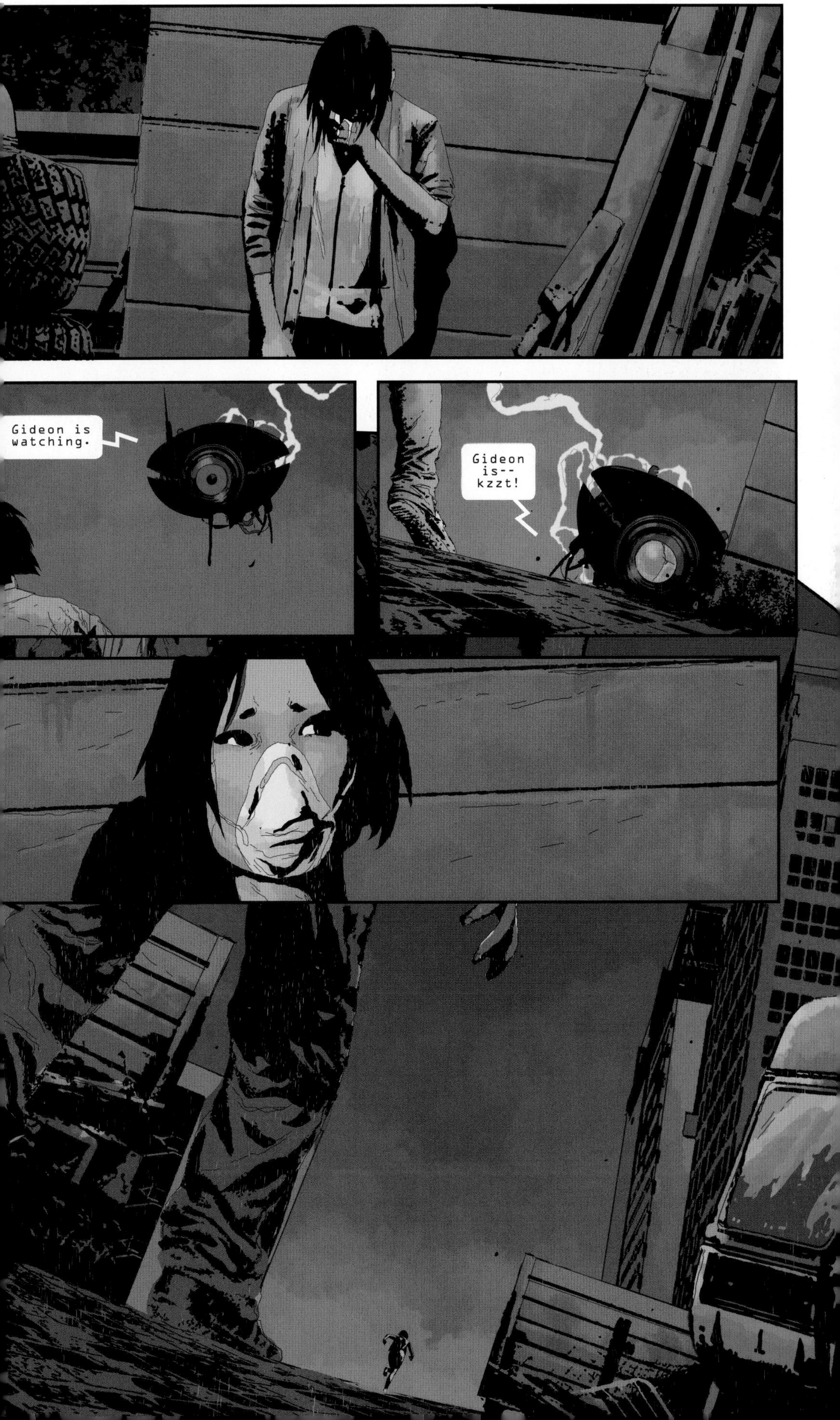
Gideon is watching.
Gideon is-- kzzt!

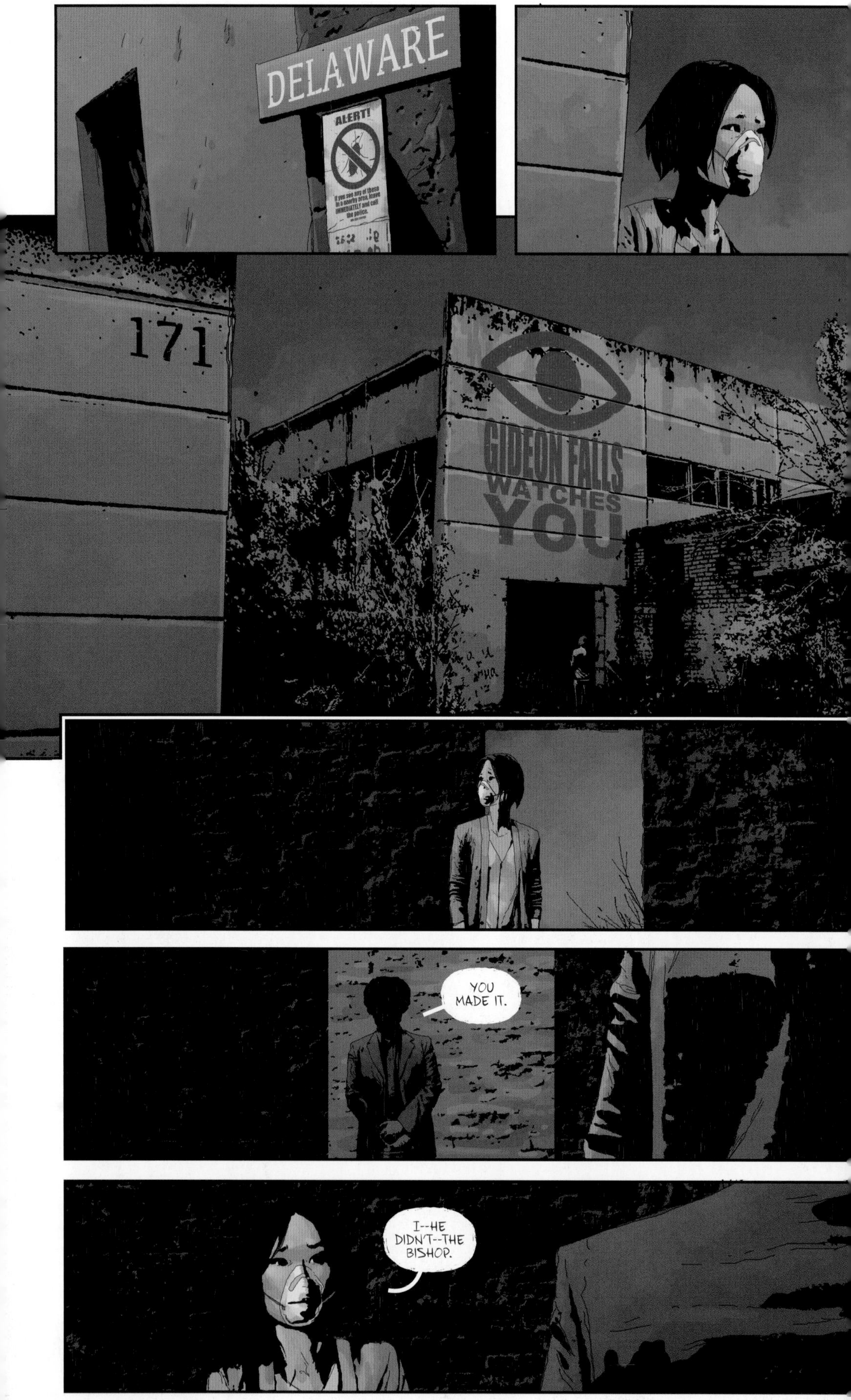
DELAWARE
ALERT!
If you see any of these in a nearby area, leave IMMEDIATELY and call the police.
171
GIDEON FALLS
WATCHES
YOU
YOU MADE IT.
I--HE DIDN'T--THE BISHOP.

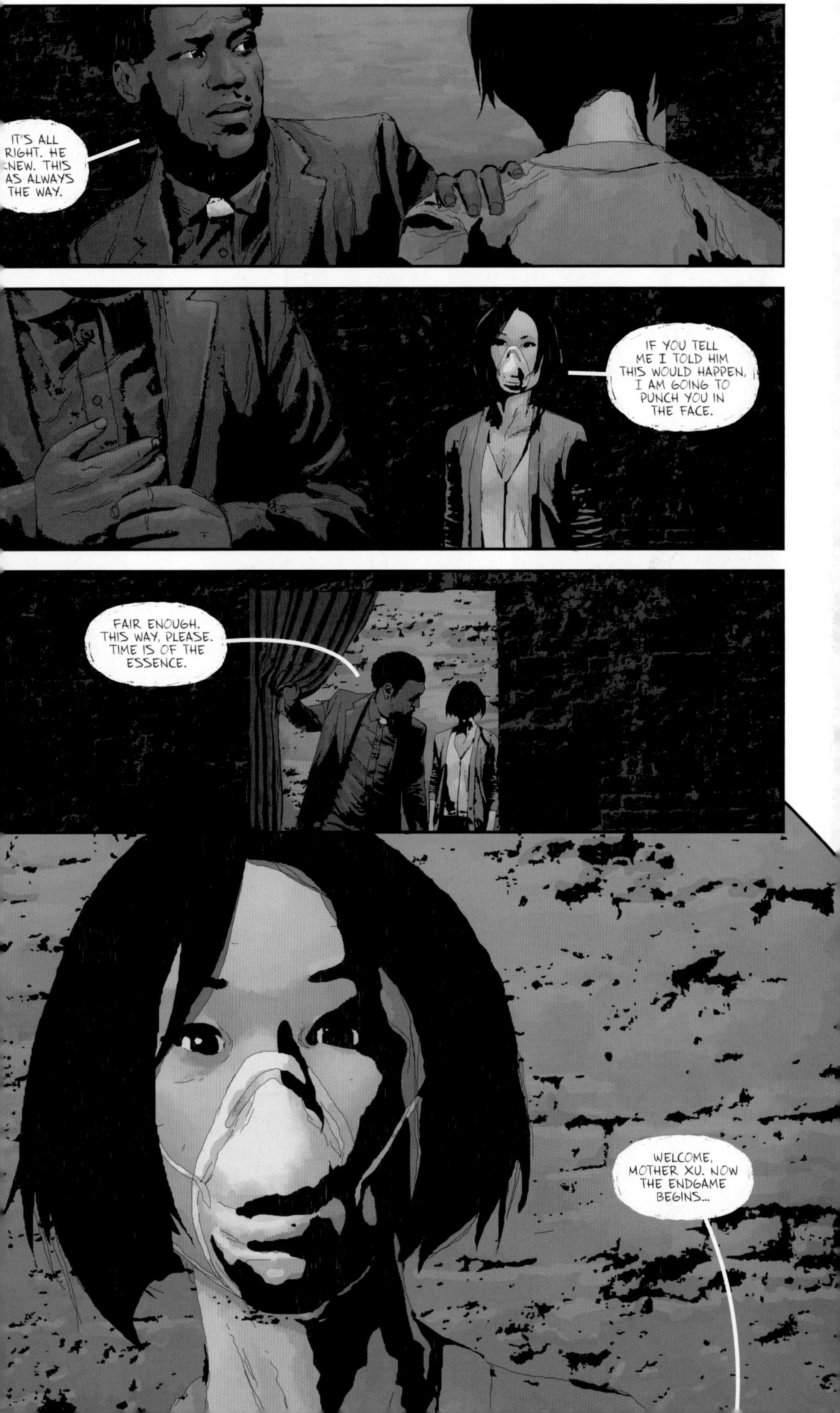
IT'S ALL RIGHT. HE KNEW. THIS WAS ALWAYS THE WAY.
IF YOU TELL ME I TOLD HIM THIS WOULD HAPPEN, I AM GOING TO PUNCH YOU IN THE FACE.
FAIR ENOUGH. THIS WAY, PLEASE. TIME IS OF THE ESSENCE.
WELCOME, MOTHER XU. NOW THE ENDGAME BEGINS...

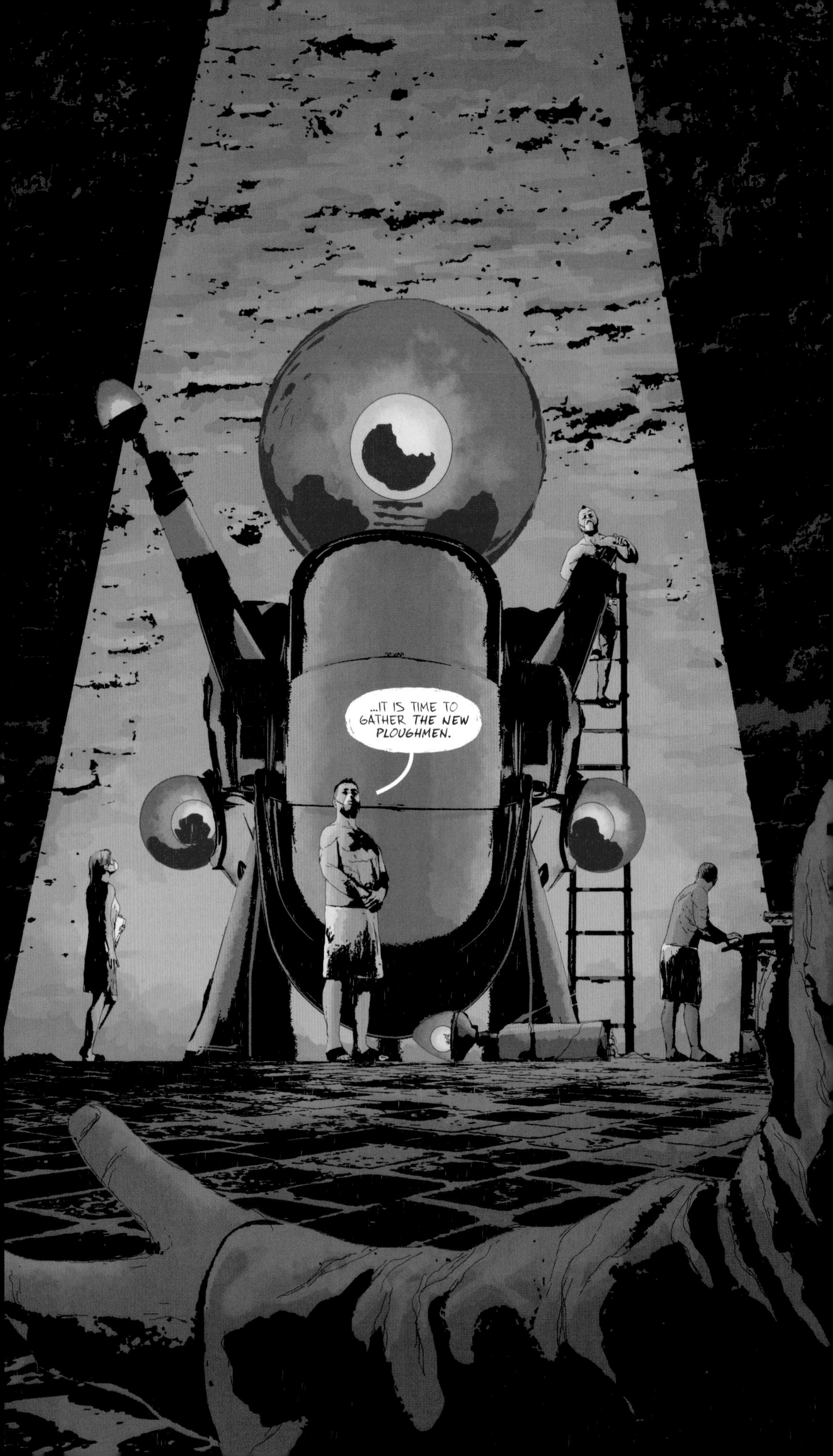
...IT IS TIME TO GATHER THE NEW PLOUGHMEN.

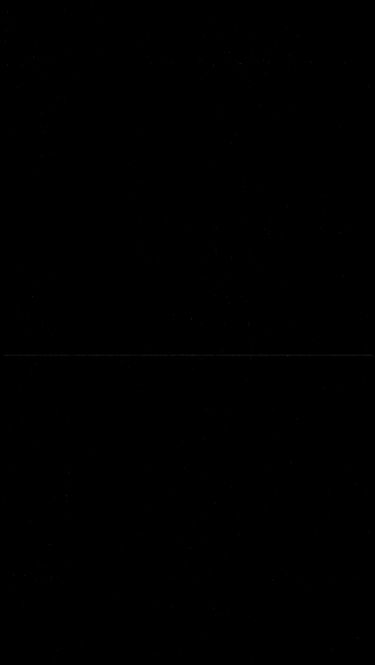

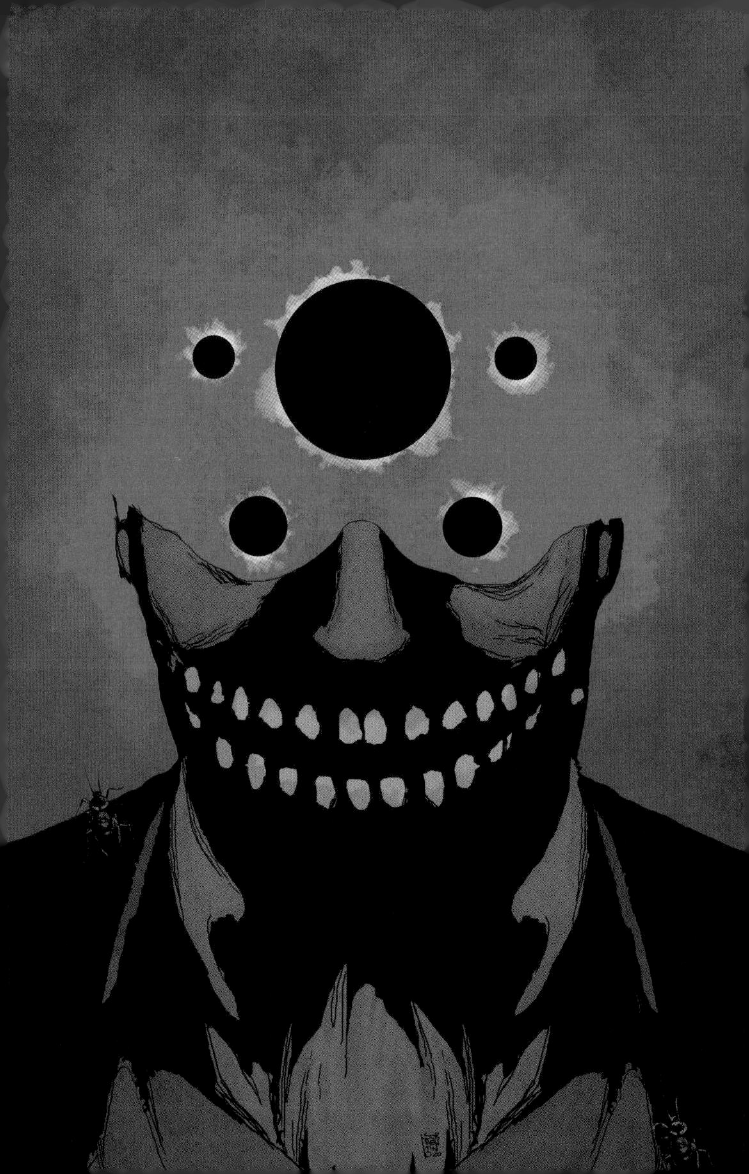

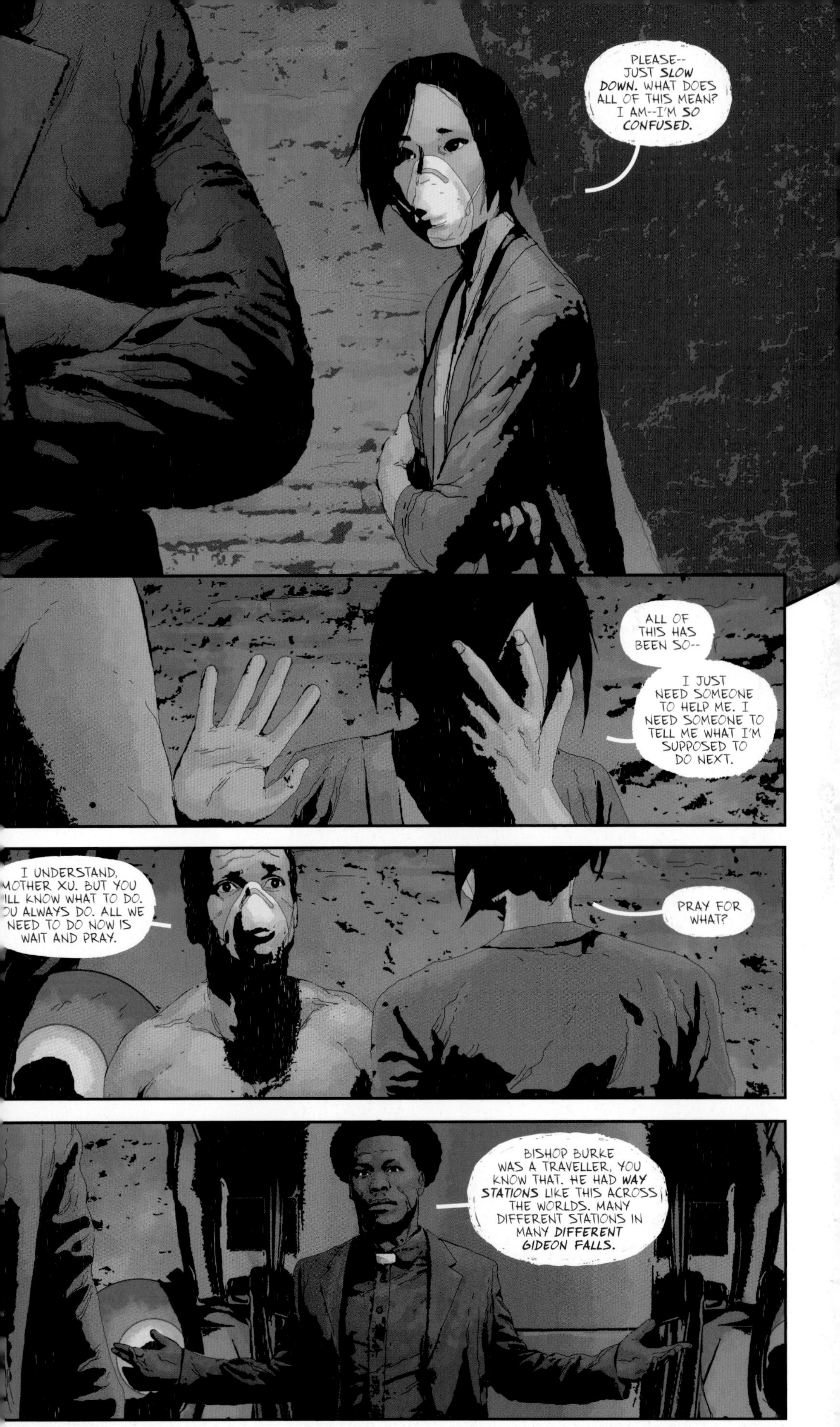
PLEASE-- JUST SLOW DOWN. WHAT DOES ALL OF THIS MEAN? I AM--I'M SO CONFUSED.
ALL OF THIS HAS BEEN SO--
I JUST NEED SOMEONE TO HELP ME. I NEED SOMEONE TO TELL ME WHAT I'M SUPPOSED TO DO NEXT.
I UNDERSTAND, MOTHER XU. BUT YOU ILL KNOW WHAT TO DO. OU ALWAYS DO. ALL WE NEED TO DO NOW IS WAIT AND PRAY.
PRAY FOR WHAT?
BISHOP BURKE WAS A TRAVELLER, YOU KNOW THAT. HE HAD WAY STATIONS LIKE THIS ACROSS THE WORLDS. MANY DIFFERENT STATIONS IN MANY DIFFERENT GIDEON FALLS.

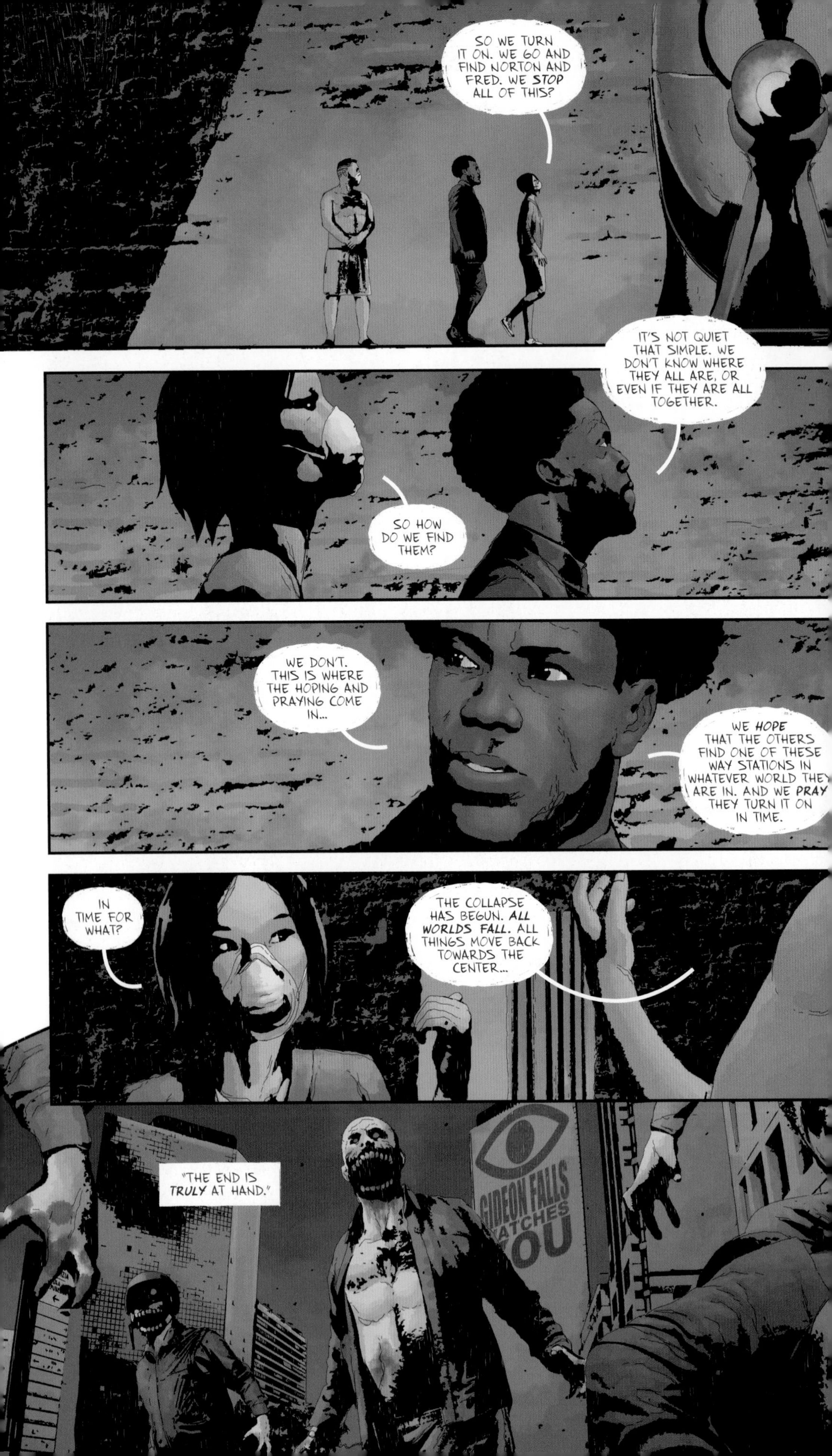
SO WE TURN IT ON. WE GO AND FIND NORTON AND FRED. WE STOP ALL OF THIS?
IT'S NOT QUIET THAT SIMPLE. WE DON'T KNOW WHERE THEY ALL ARE, OR EVEN IF THEY ARE ALL TOGETHER.
SO HOW DO WE FIND THEM?
WE DON'T. THIS IS WHERE THE HOPING AND PRAYING COME IN...
WE HOPE THAT THE OTHERS FIND ONE OF THESE WAY STATIONS IN WHATEVER WORLD THEY ARE IN. AND WE PRAY THEY TURN IT ON IN TIME.
IN TIME FOR WHAT?
THE COLLAPSE HAS BEGUN. ALL WORLDS FALL. ALL THINGS MOVE BACK TOWARDS THE CENTER...
"THE END IS TRULY AT HAND."
GIDEON FALLS WATCHES YOU

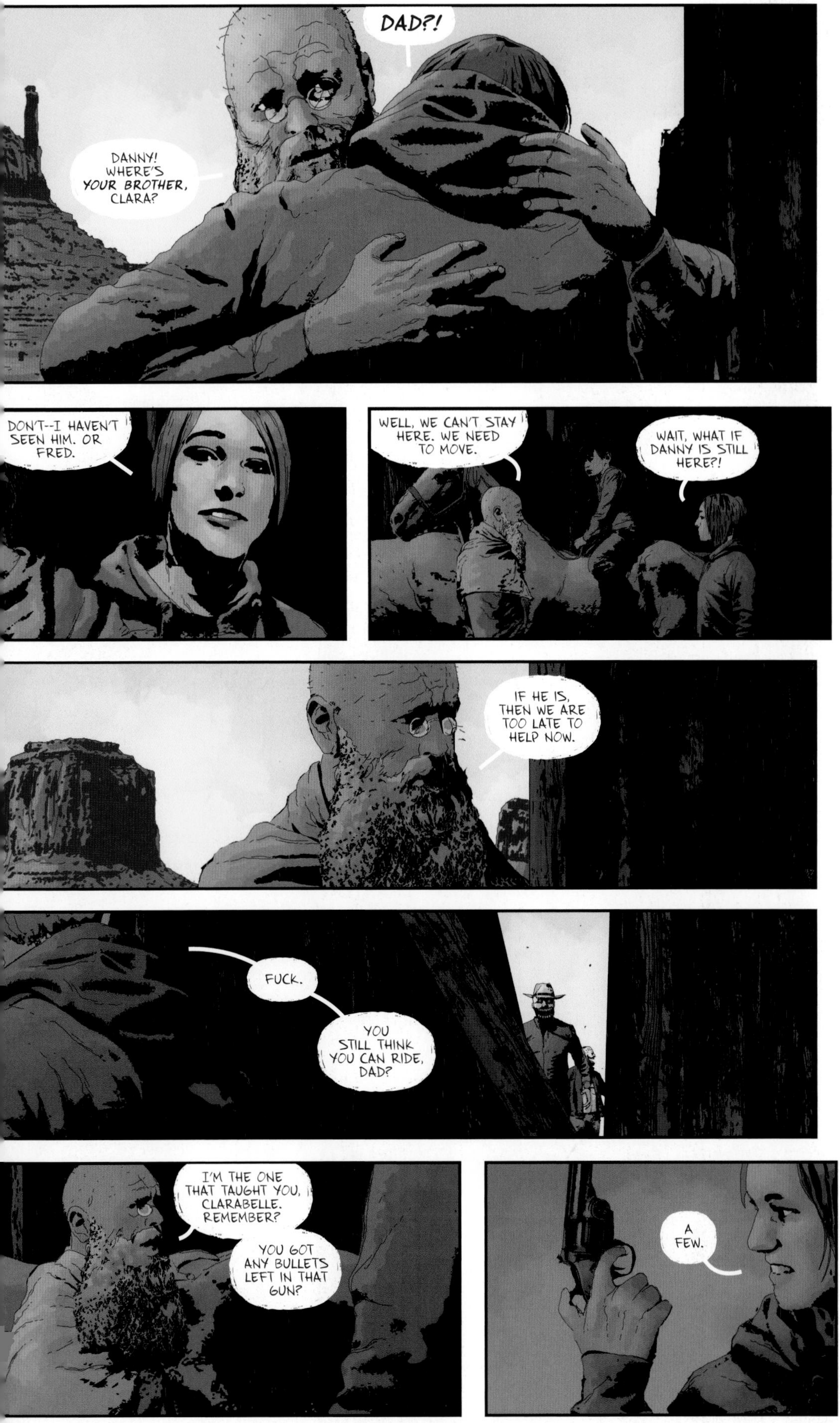
DAD?!
DANNY! WHERE'S YOUR BROTHER, CLARA?
DON'T--I HAVEN'T SEEN HIM. OR FRED.
WELL, WE CAN'T STAY HERE. WE NEED TO MOVE.
WAIT, WHAT IF DANNY IS STILL HERE?!
IF HE IS, THEN WE ARE TOO LATE TO HELP NOW.
FUCK.
YOU STILL THINK YOU CAN RIDE, DAD?
I'M THE ONE THAT TAUGHT YOU, CLARABELLE. REMEMBER?
YOU GOT ANY BULLETS LEFT IN THAT GUN?
A FEW.

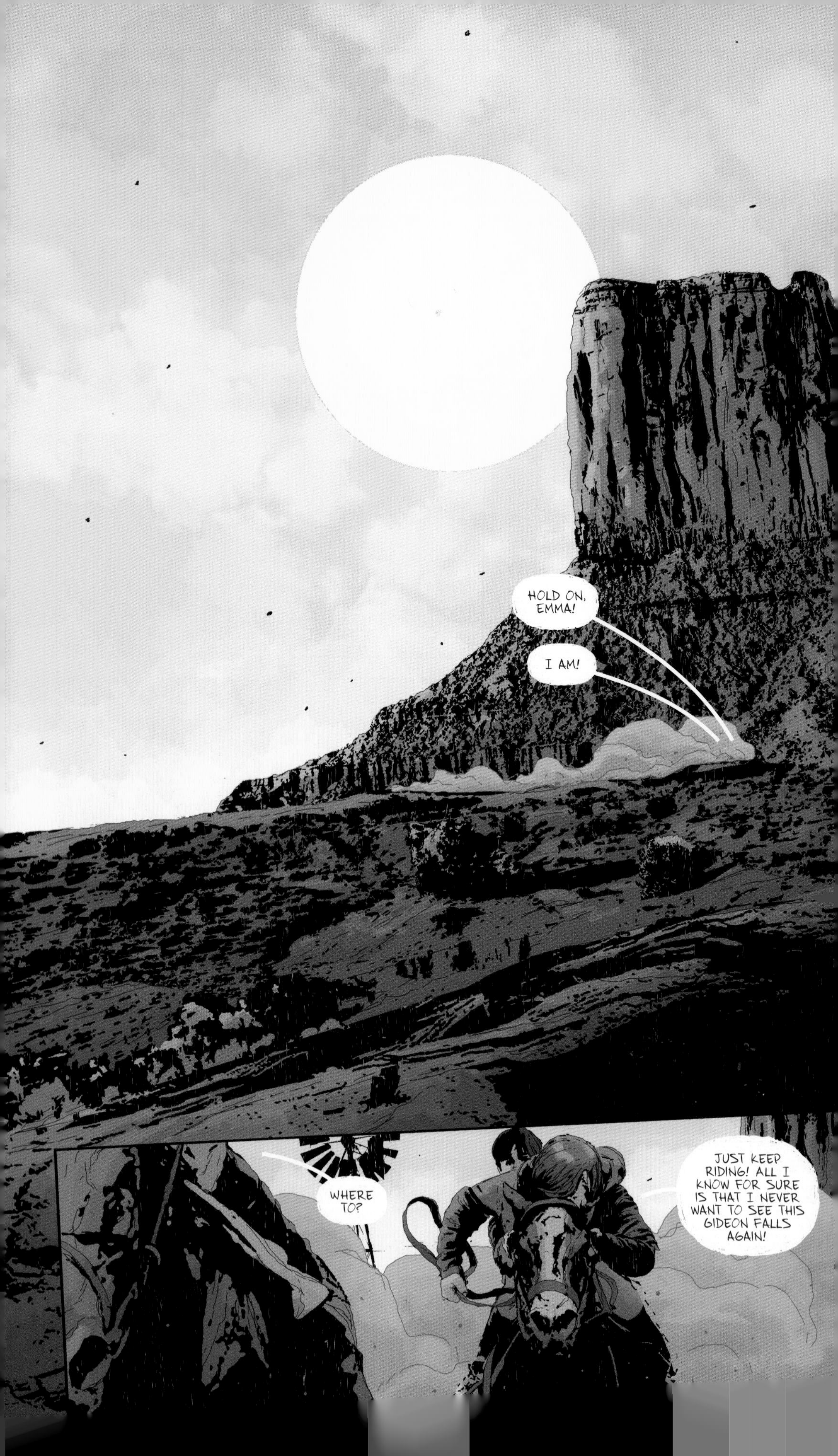
HOLD ON, EMMA!
I AM!
WHERE TO?
JUST KEEP RIDING! ALL I KNOW FOR SURE IS THAT I NEVER WANT TO SEE THIS GIDEON FALLS AGAIN!

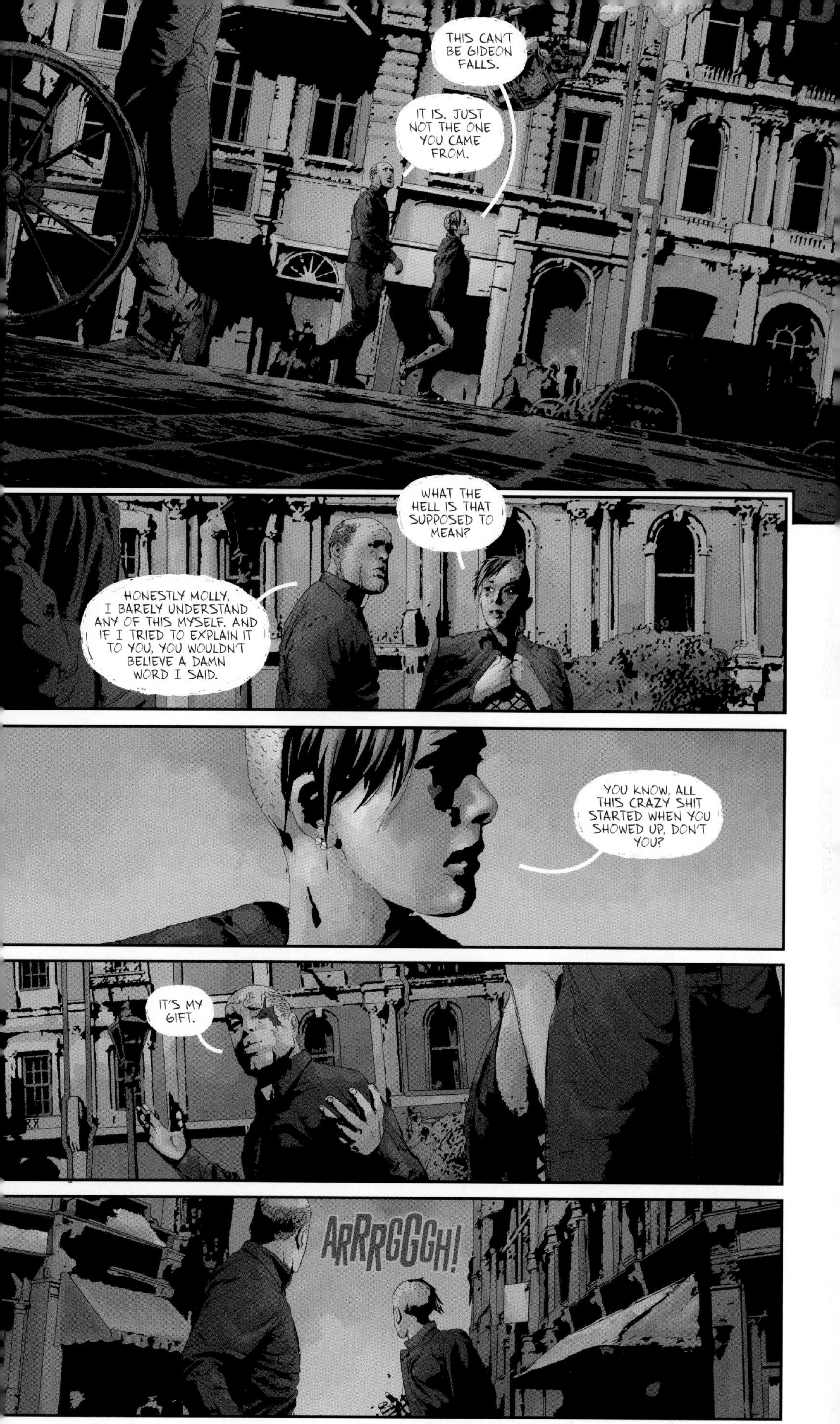

THIS CAN'T BE GIDEON FALLS.
IT IS. JUST NOT THE ONE YOU CAME FROM.
WHAT THE HELL IS THAT SUPPOSED TO MEAN?
HONESTLY MOLLY, I BARELY UNDERSTAND ANY OF THIS MYSELF. AND IF I TRIED TO EXPLAIN IT TO YOU, YOU WOULDN'T BELIEVE A DAMN WORD I SAID.
YOU KNOW, ALL THIS CRAZY SHIT STARTED WHEN YOU SHOWED UP, DON'T YOU?
IT'S MY GIFT.
ARRRGGGH!

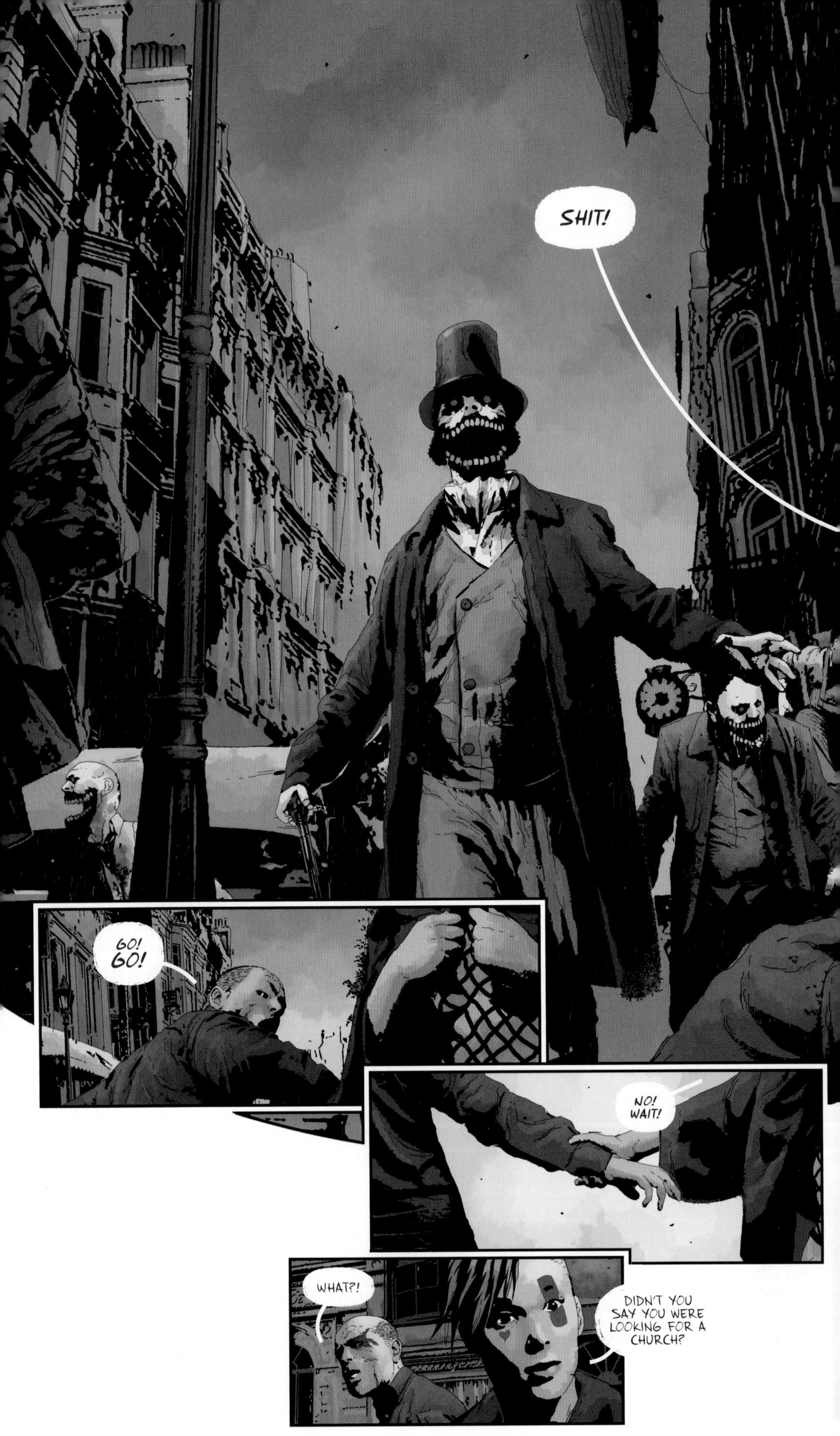
SHIT!
GO! GO!
NO! WAIT!
WHAT?!
DIDN'T YOU SAY YOU WERE LOOKING FOR A CHURCH?

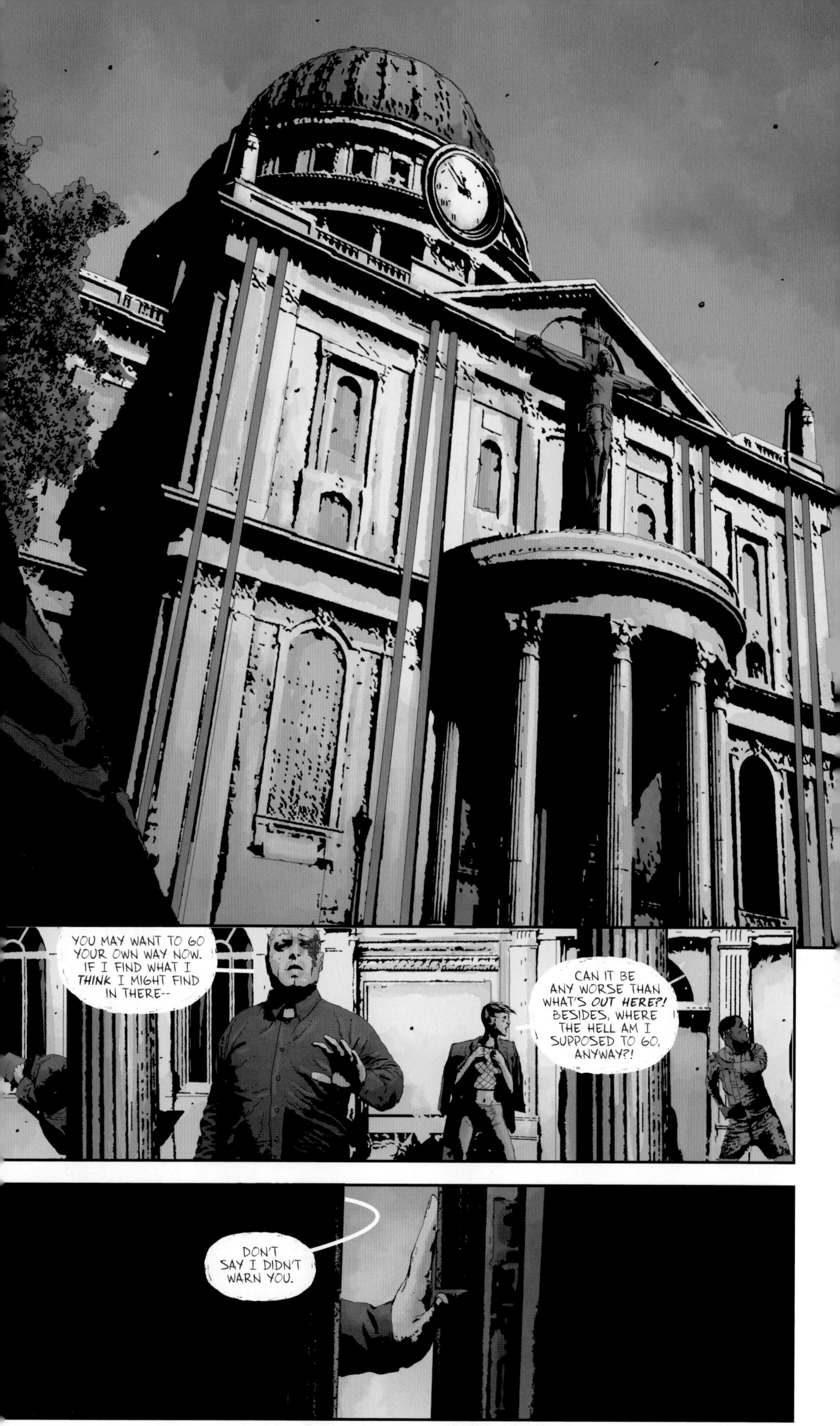

YOU MAY WANT TO GO YOUR OWN WAY NOW. IF I FIND WHAT I *THINK* I MIGHT FIND IN THERE--
CAN IT BE ANY WORSE THAN WHAT'S *OUT HERE?!* BESIDES, WHERE THE HELL AM I SUPPOSED TO GO, ANYWAY?!
DON'T SAY I DIDN'T WARN YOU.

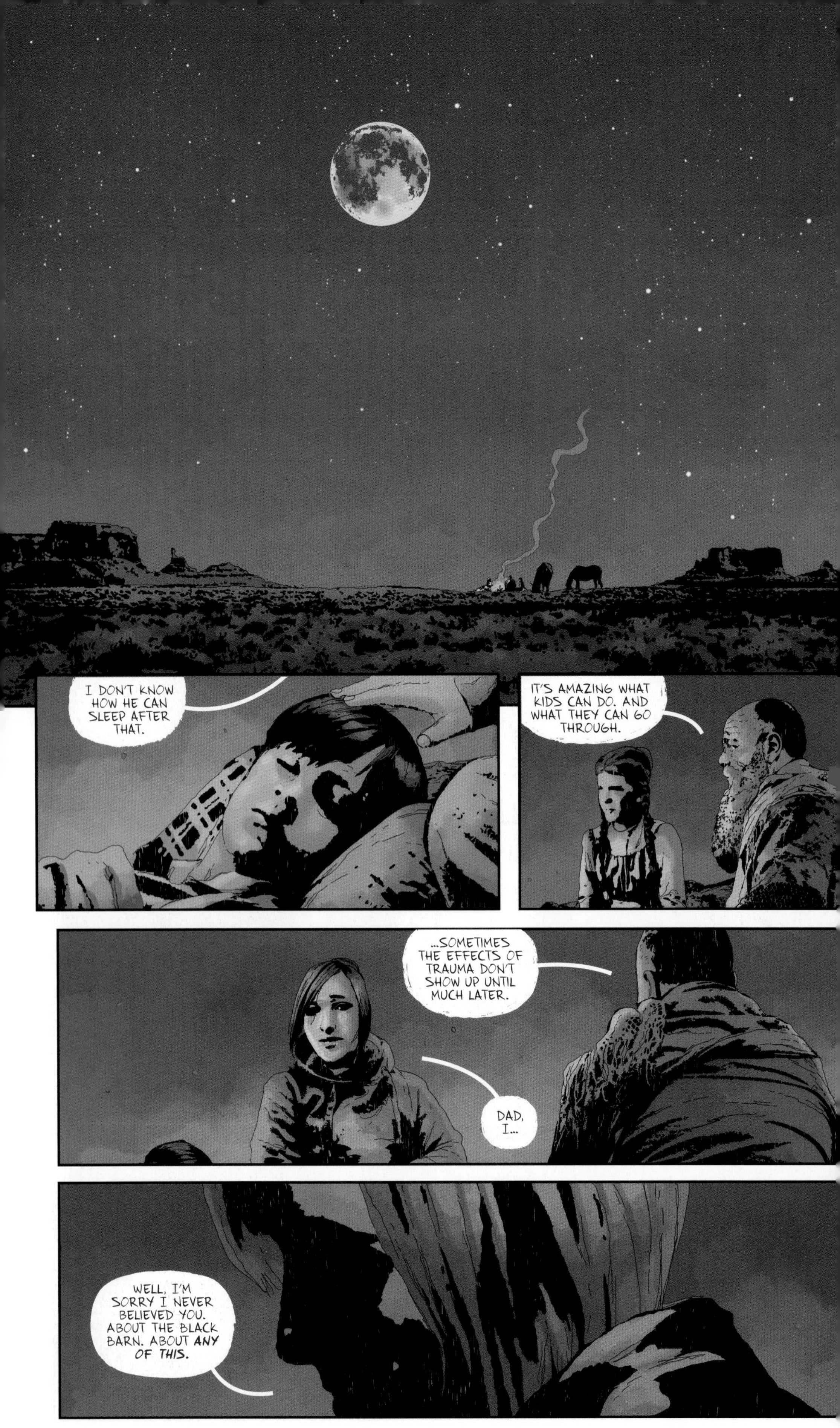
I DON'T KNOW HOW HE CAN SLEEP AFTER THAT.
IT'S AMAZING WHAT KIDS CAN DO. AND WHAT THEY CAN GO THROUGH.
...SOMETIMES THE EFFECTS OF TRAUMA DON'T SHOW UP UNTIL MUCH LATER.
DAD, I...
WELL, I'M SORRY I NEVER BELIEVED YOU. ABOUT THE BLACK BARN. ABOUT ANY OF THIS.

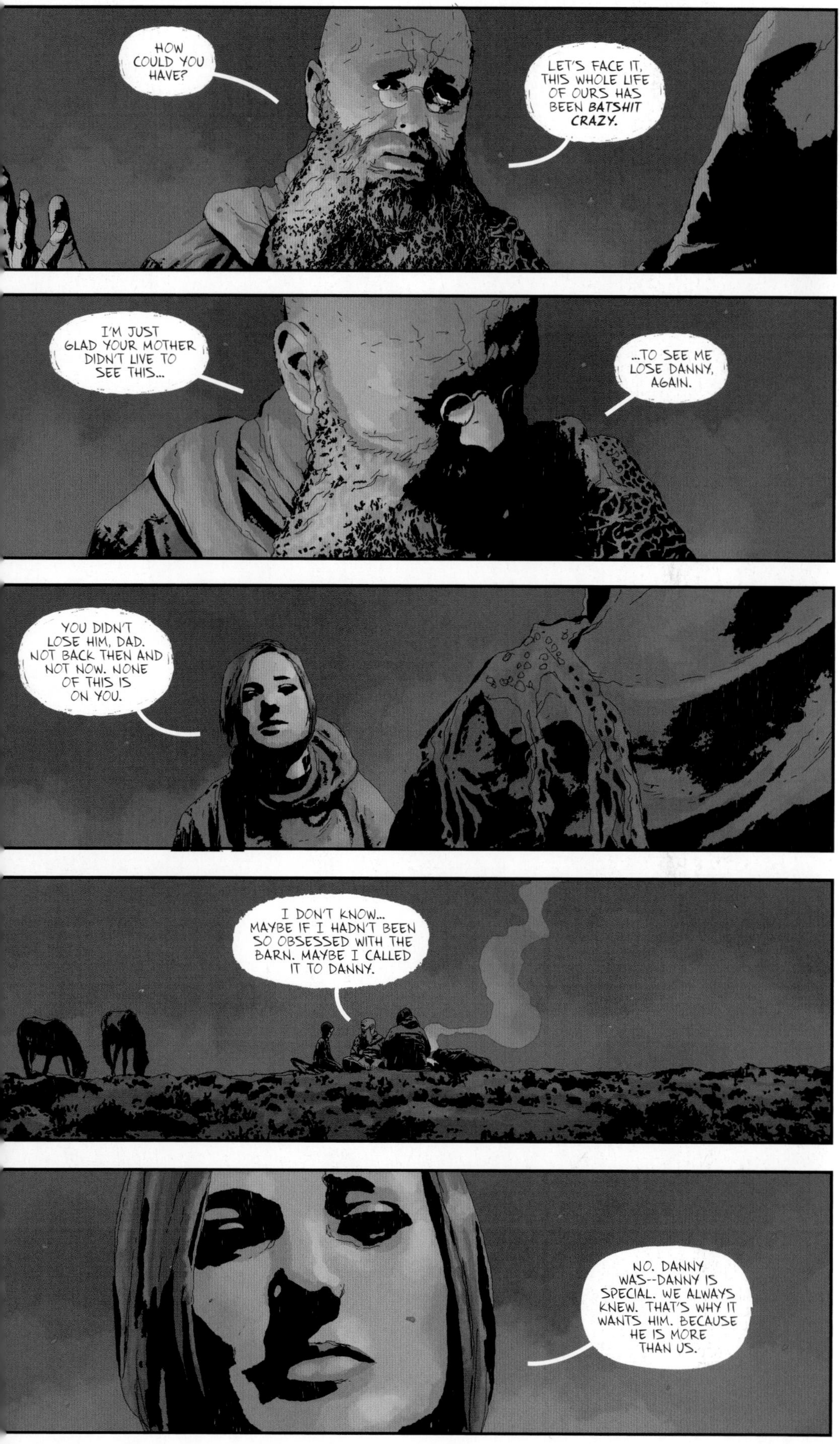
HOW COULD YOU HAVE?
LET'S FACE IT, THIS WHOLE LIFE OF OURS HAS BEEN BATSHIT CRAZY.
I'M JUST GLAD YOUR MOTHER DIDN'T LIVE TO SEE THIS...
...TO SEE ME LOSE DANNY, AGAIN.
YOU DIDN'T LOSE HIM, DAD. NOT BACK THEN AND NOT NOW. NONE OF THIS IS ON YOU.
I DON'T KNOW... MAYBE IF I HADN'T BEEN SO OBSESSED WITH THE BARN. MAYBE I CALLED IT TO DANNY.
NO. DANNY WAS--DANNY IS SPECIAL. WE ALWAYS KNEW. THAT'S WHY IT WANTS HIM. BECAUSE HE IS MORE THAN US.

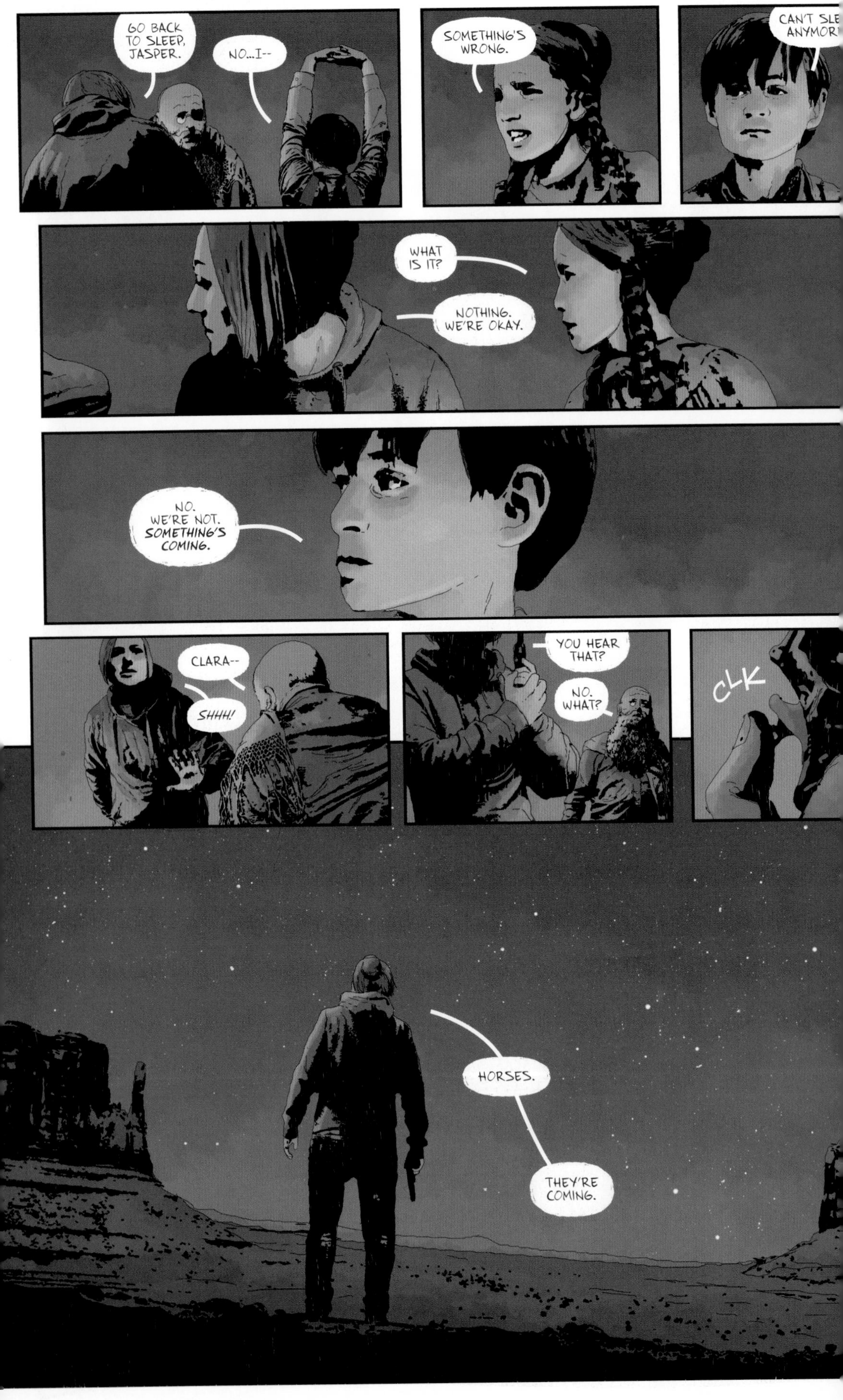
GO BACK TO SLEEP, JASPER.
NO...I--
SOMETHING'S WRONG.
CAN'T SLE ANYMOR
WHAT IS IT?
NOTHING. WE'RE OKAY.
NO. WE'RE NOT. SOMETHING'S COMING.
CLARA--
SHHH!
YOU HEAR THAT?
NO. WHAT?
CLK
HORSES.
THEY'RE COMING.

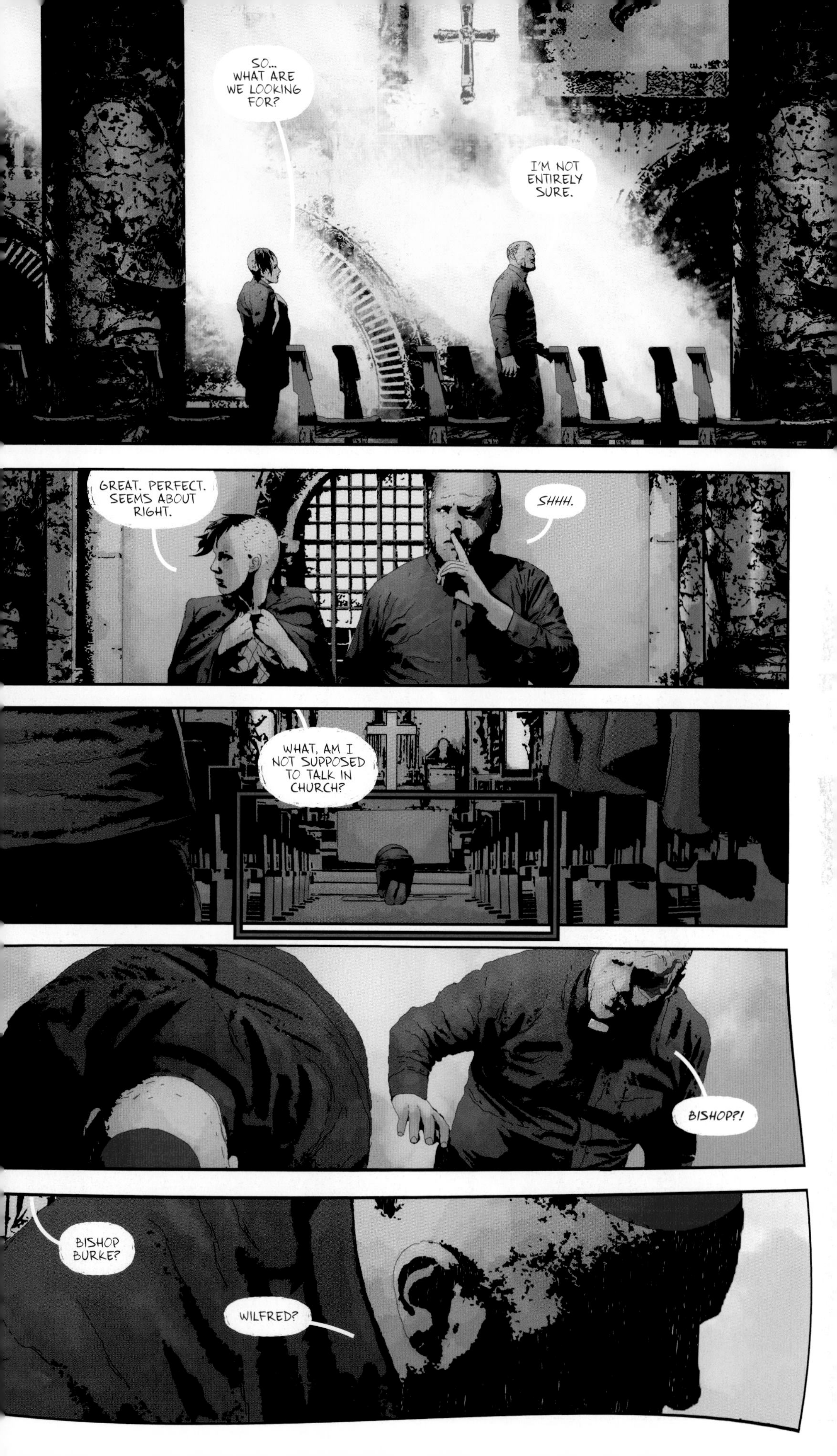
SO... WHAT ARE WE LOOKING FOR?
I'M NOT ENTIRELY SURE.
GREAT. PERFECT. SEEMS ABOUT RIGHT.
SHHH.
WHAT, AM I NOT SUPPOSED TO TALK IN CHURCH?
BISHOP?!
BISHOP BURKE?
WILFRED?

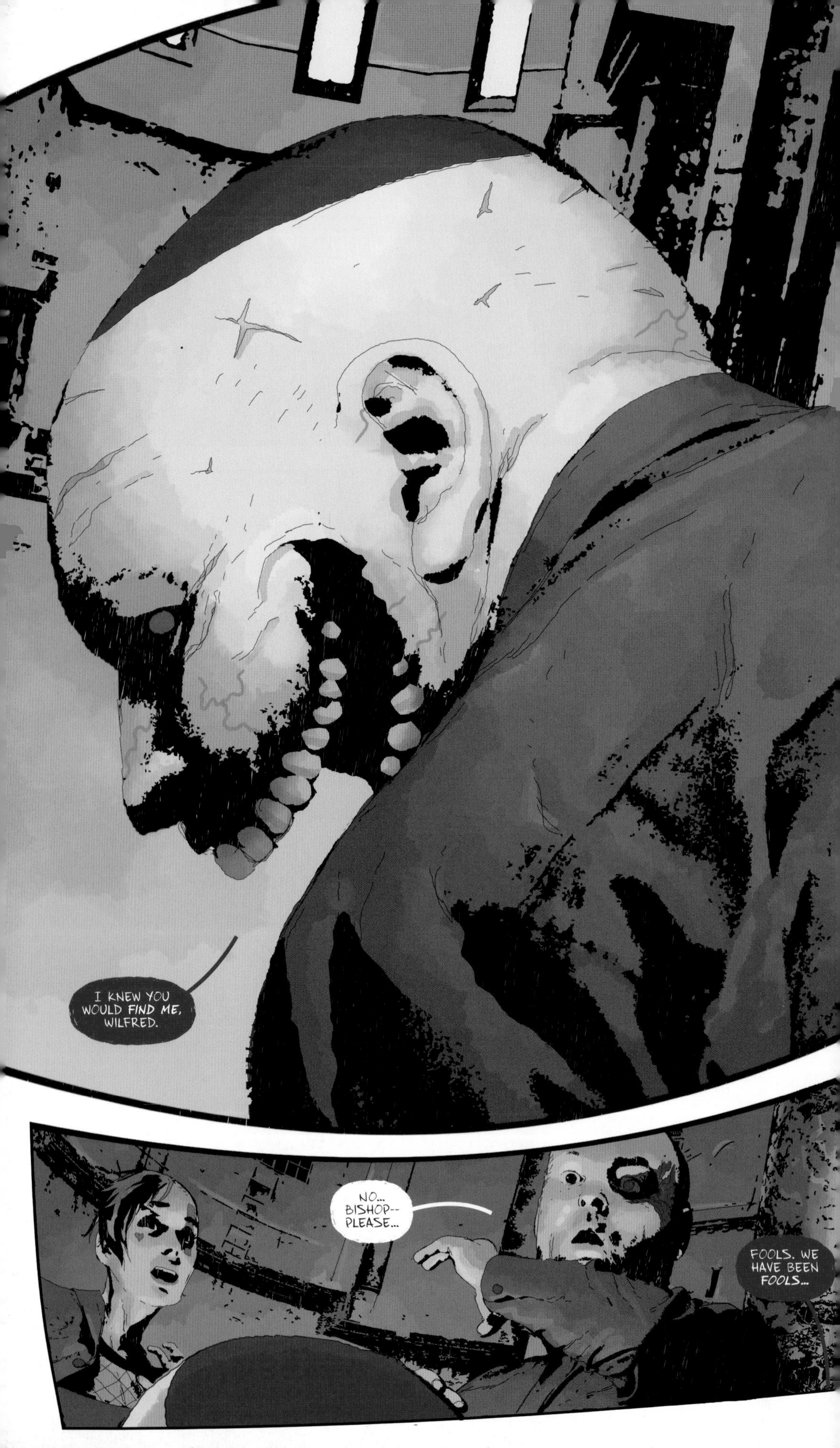
I KNEW YOU WOULD FIND ME, WILFRED.
NO... BISHOP-- PLEASE...
FOOLS. WE HAVE BEEN FOOLS...

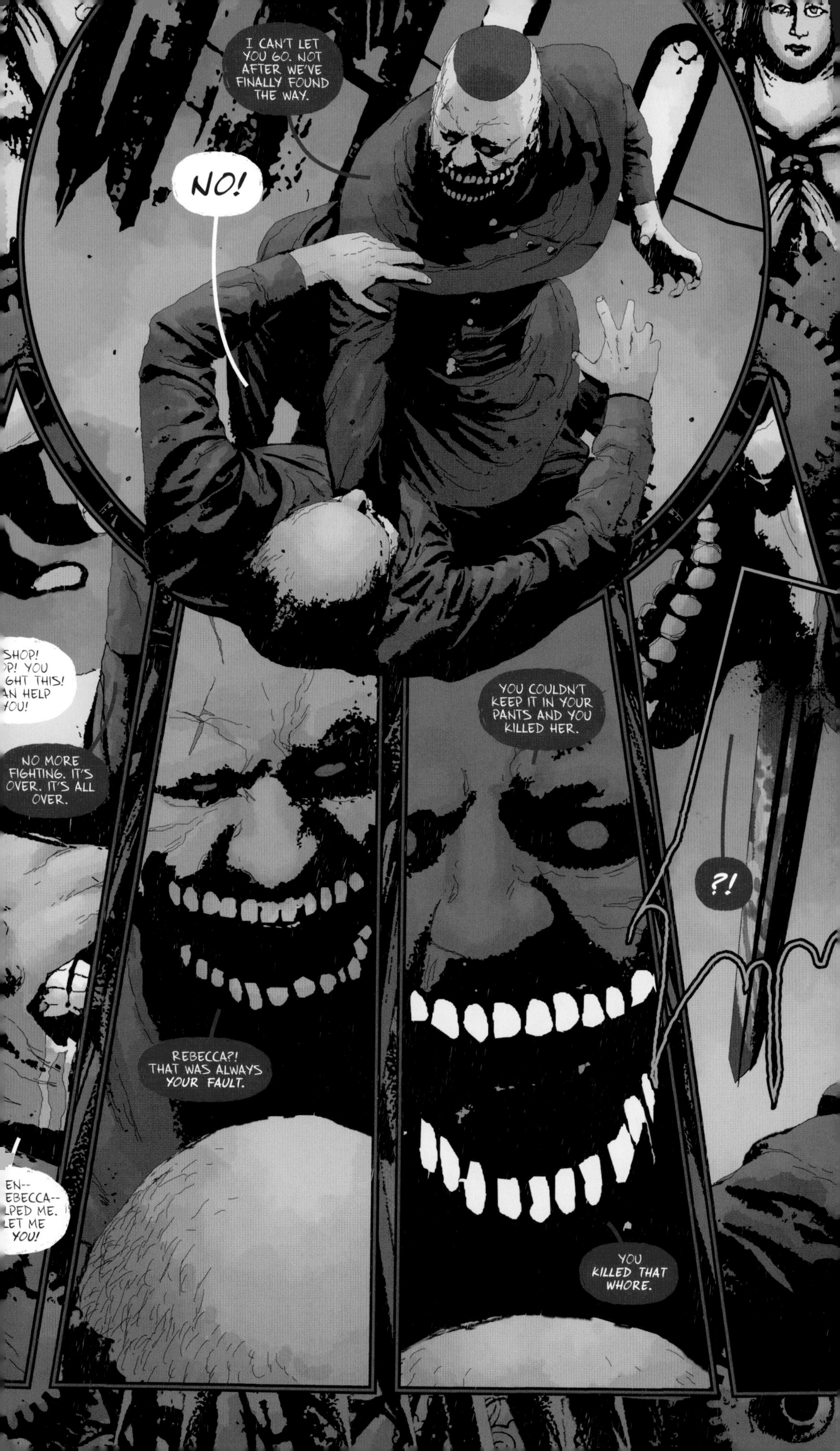
I CAN'T LET YOU GO. NOT AFTER WE'VE FINALLY FOUND THE WAY.
NO!
SHOP! P! YOU GHT THIS! AN HELP YOU!
NO MORE FIGHTING. IT'S OVER. IT'S ALL OVER.
YOU COULDN'T KEEP IT IN YOUR PANTS AND YOU KILLED HER.
REBECCA?! THAT WAS ALWAYS YOUR FAULT.
EN-- EBECCA-- LPED ME. LET ME YOU!
?!
YOU KILLED THAT WHORE.

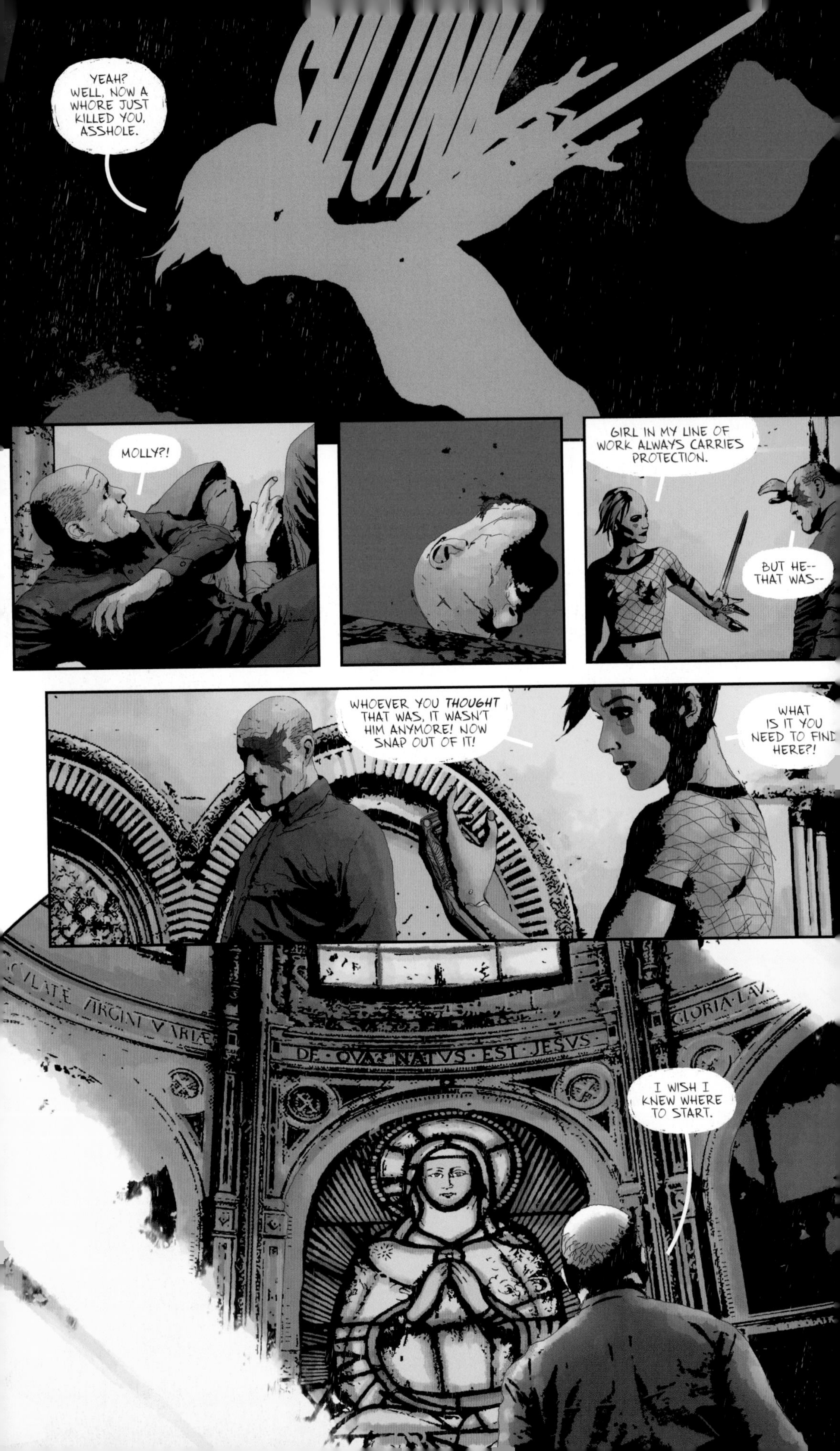
SHUNK
YEAH? WELL, NOW A WHORE JUST KILLED YOU, ASSHOLE.
MOLLY?!
GIRL IN MY LINE OF WORK ALWAYS CARRIES PROTECTION.
BUT HE-- THAT WAS--
WHOEVER YOU THOUGHT THAT WAS, IT WASN'T HIM ANYMORE! NOW SNAP OUT OF IT!
WHAT IS IT YOU NEED TO FIND HERE?!
DE · QVA · NATVS · EST · JESVS
GLORIA · LAV
I WISH I KNEW WHERE TO START.

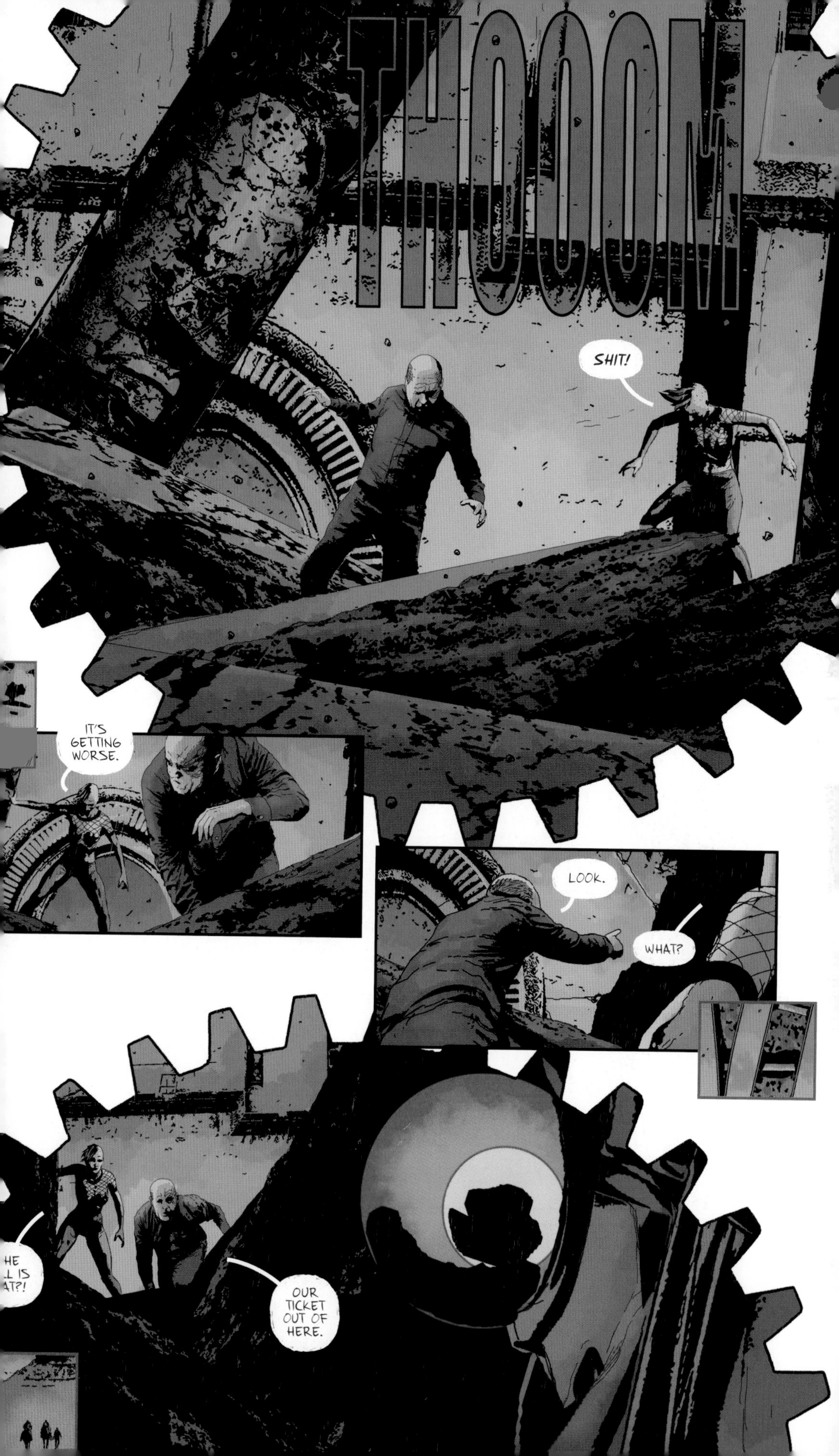
THOOOM!
SHIT!
IT'S GETTING WORSE.
LOOK.
WHAT?
OUR TICKET OUT OF HERE.

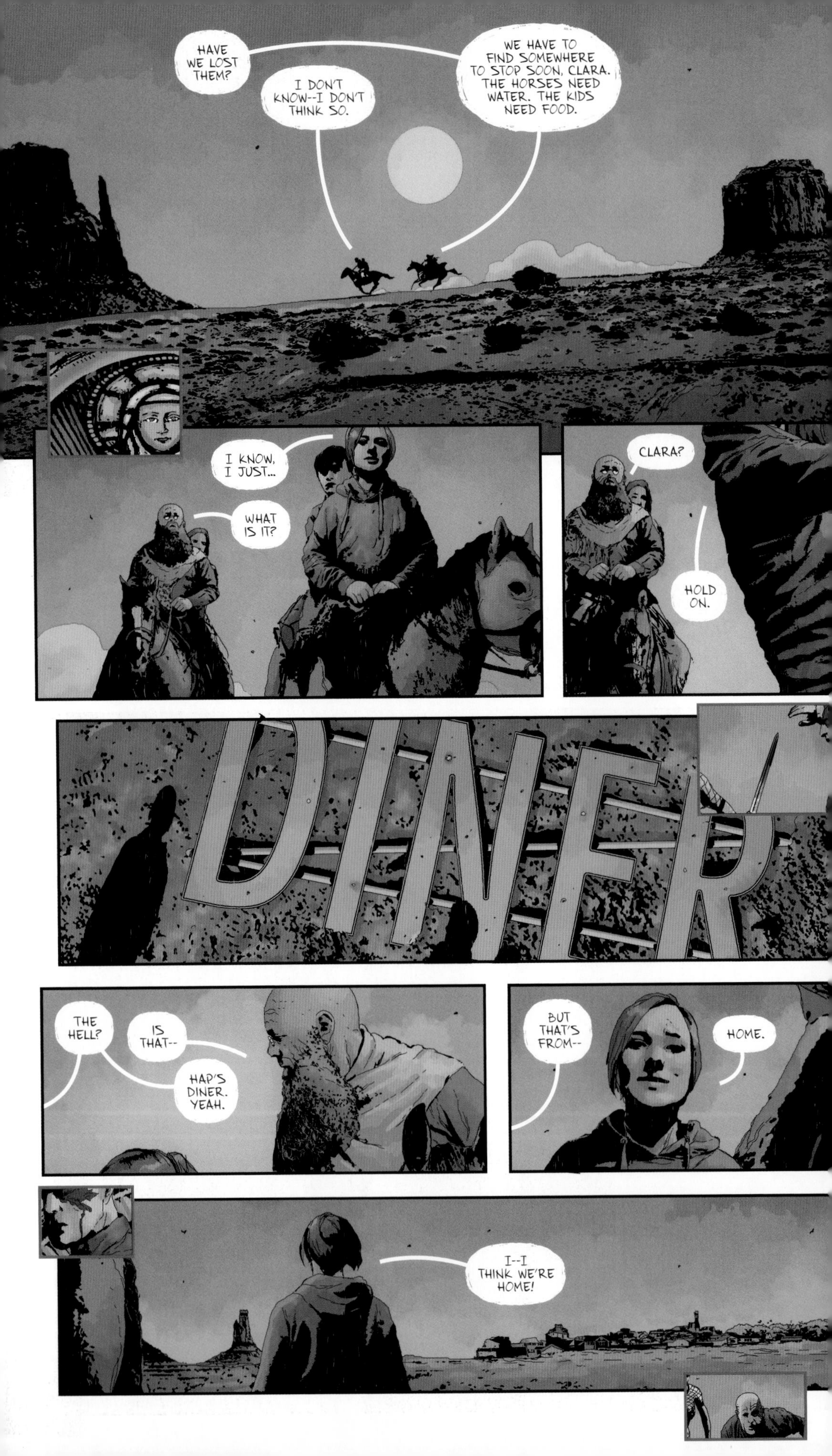
HAVE WE LOST THEM?
I DON'T KNOW--I DON'T THINK SO.
WE HAVE TO FIND SOMEWHERE TO STOP SOON, CLARA. THE HORSES NEED WATER. THE KIDS NEED FOOD.
I KNOW, I JUST...
WHAT IS IT?
CLARA?
HOLD ON.
DINER
THE HELL?
IS THAT--
HAP'S DINER. YEAH.
BUT THAT'S FROM--
HOME.
I--I THINK WE'RE HOME!

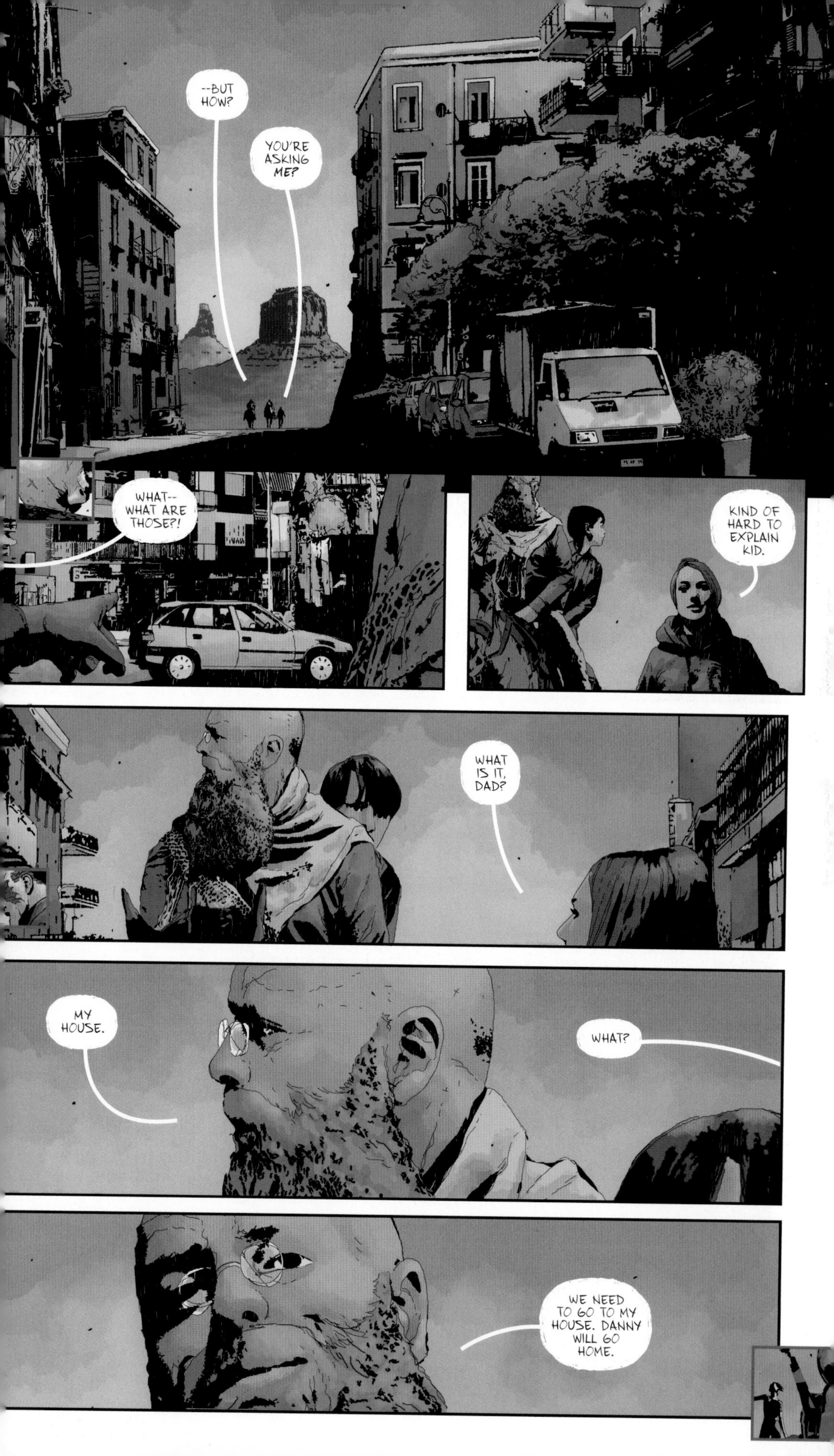
--BUT HOW?
YOU'RE ASKING ME?
WHAT--WHAT ARE THOSE?!
KIND OF HARD TO EXPLAIN KID.
WHAT IS IT, DAD?
MY HOUSE.
WHAT?
WE NEED TO GO TO MY HOUSE. DANNY WILL GO HOME.

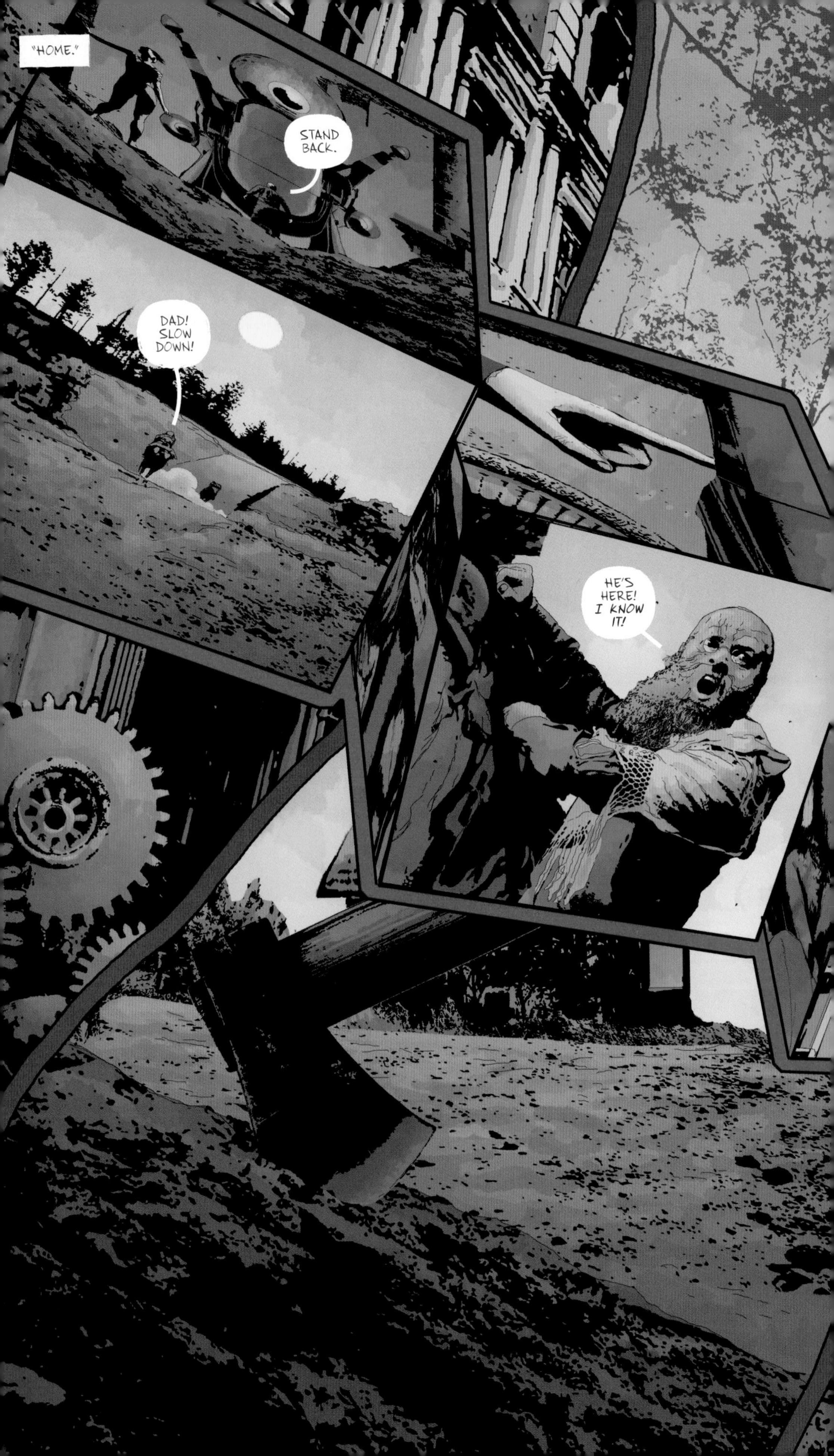
"HOME."
STAND BACK.
DAD! SLOW DOWN!
HE'S HERE! I KNOW IT!

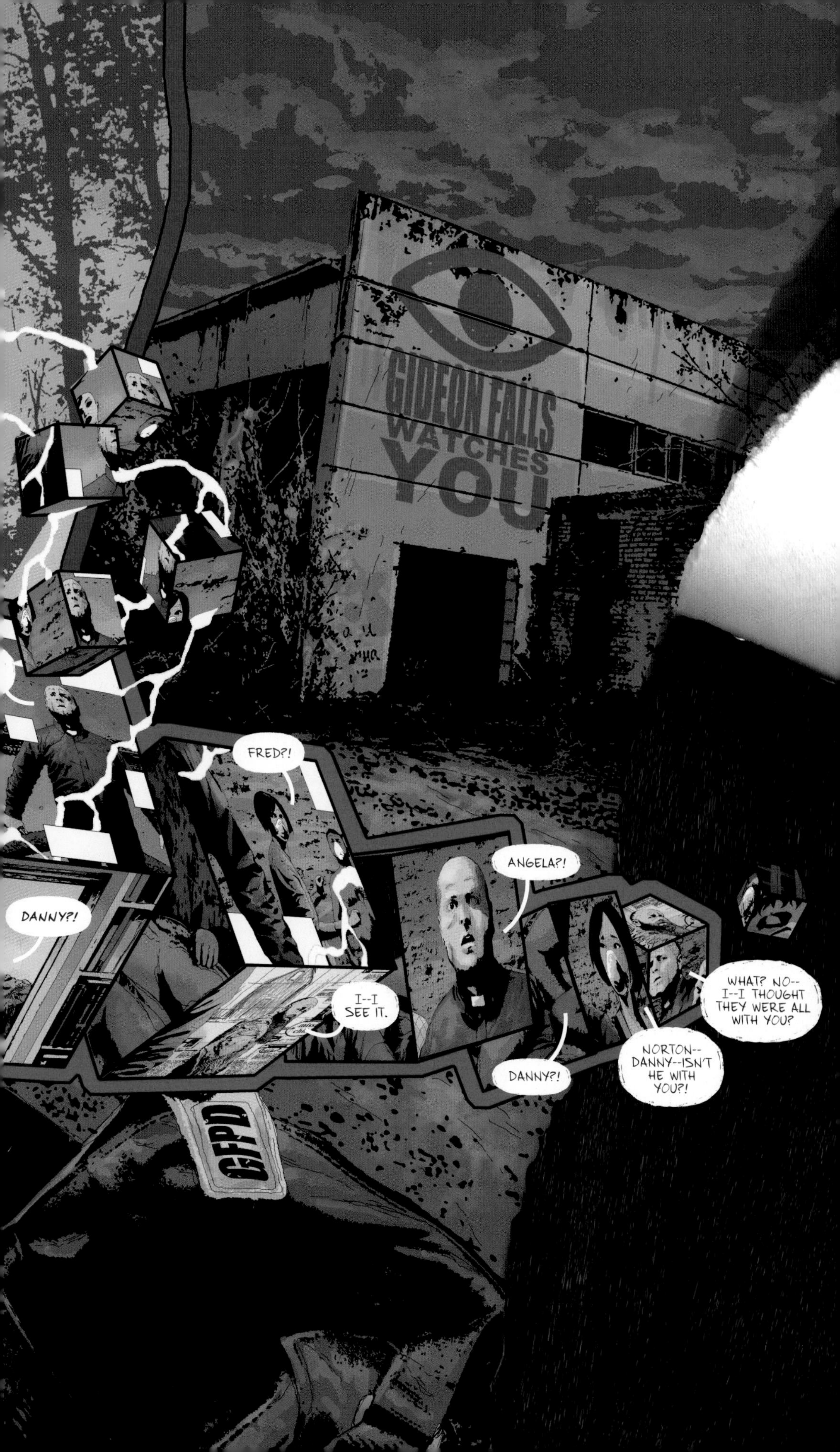
GIDEON FALLS WATCHES YOU
FRED?!
DANNY?!
I--I SEE IT.
ANGELA?!
DANNY?!
NORTON-- DANNY--ISN'T HE WITH YOU?!
WHAT? NO-- I--I THOUGHT THEY WERE ALL WITH YOU?
GFPD

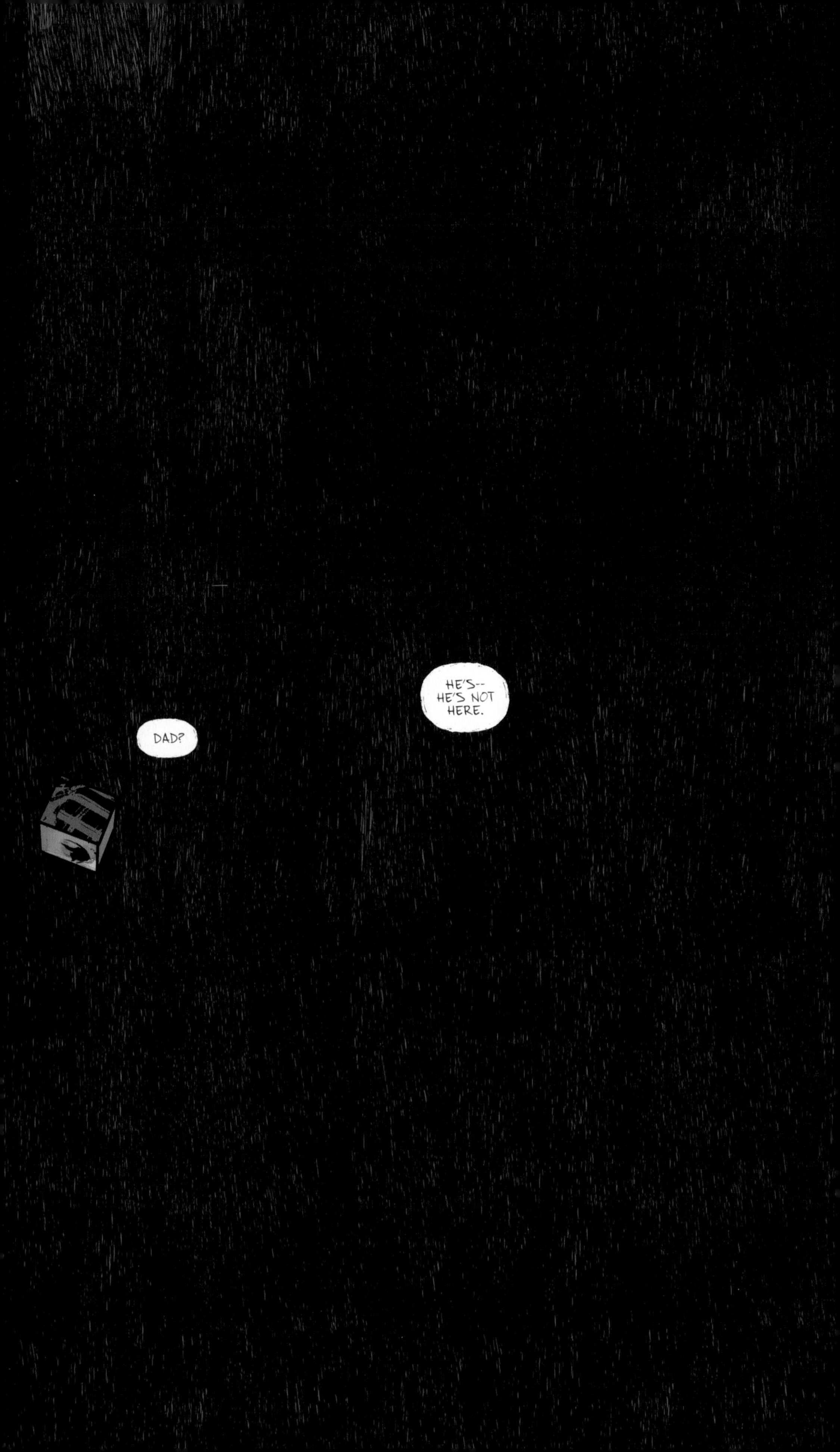
DAD?
HE'S-- HE'S NOT HERE.

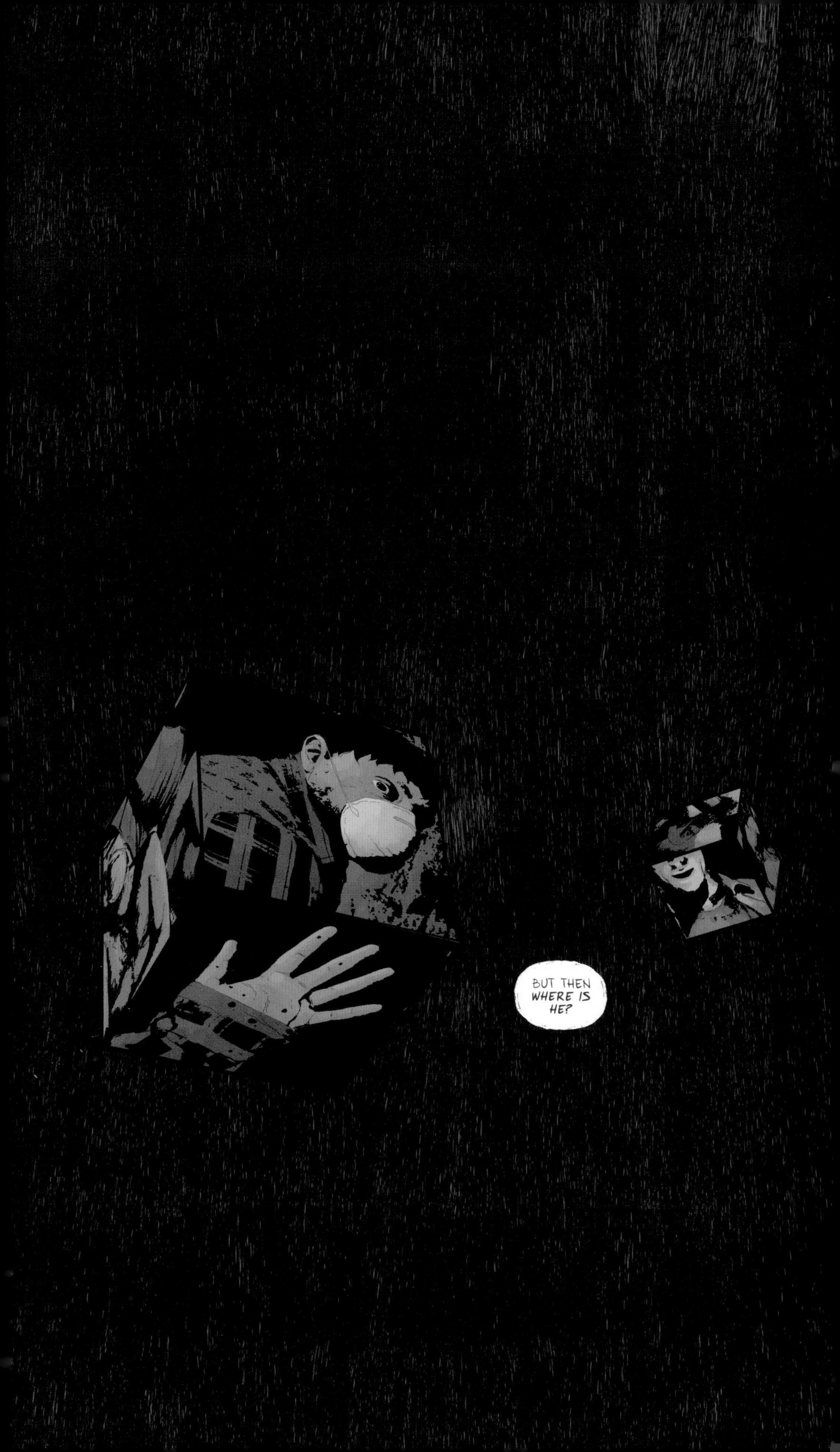
BUT THEN WHERE IS HE?

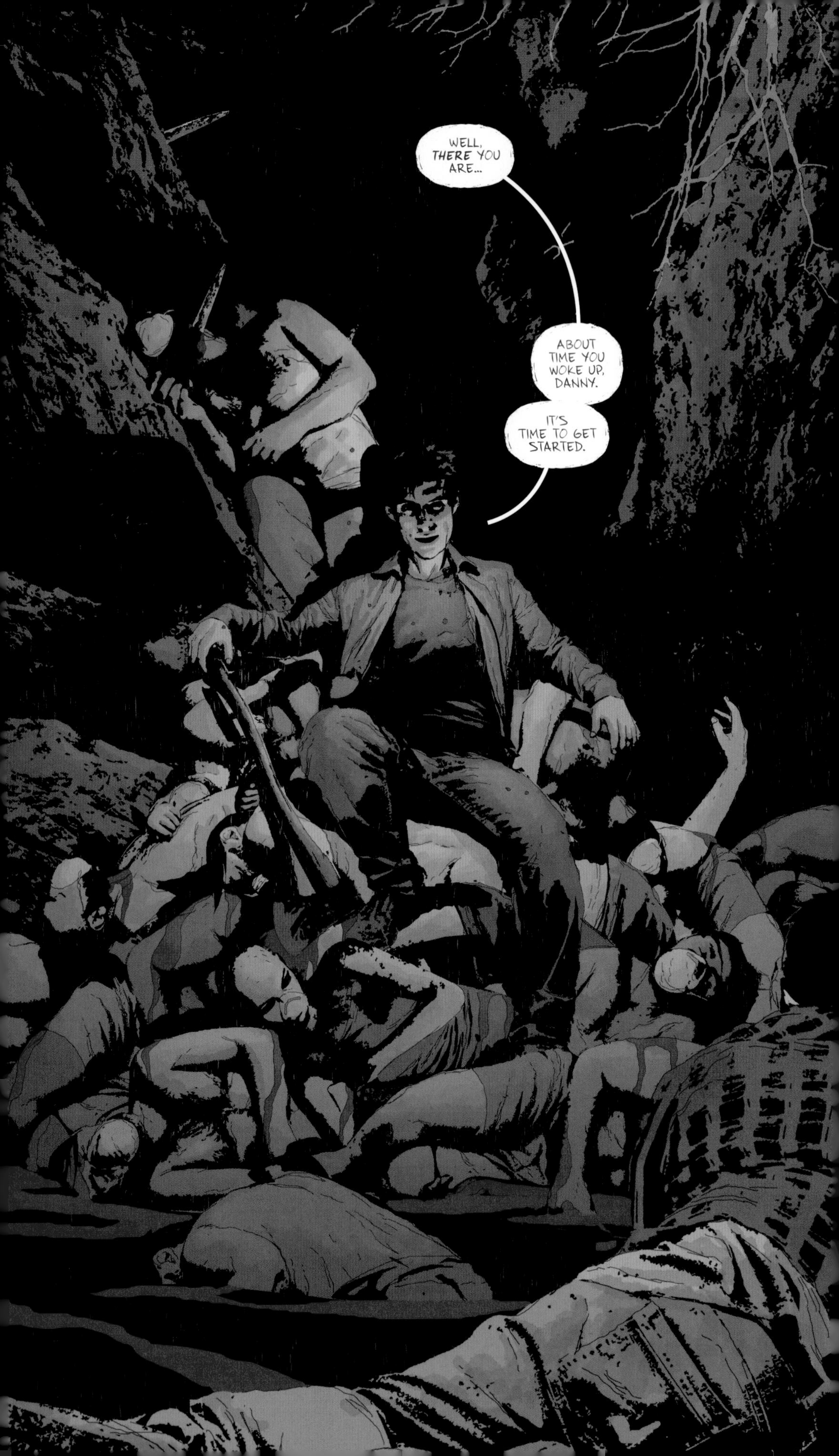
WELL, THERE YOU ARE...
ABOUT TIME YOU WOKE UP, DANNY.
IT'S TIME TO GET STARTED.

COVER GALLERY

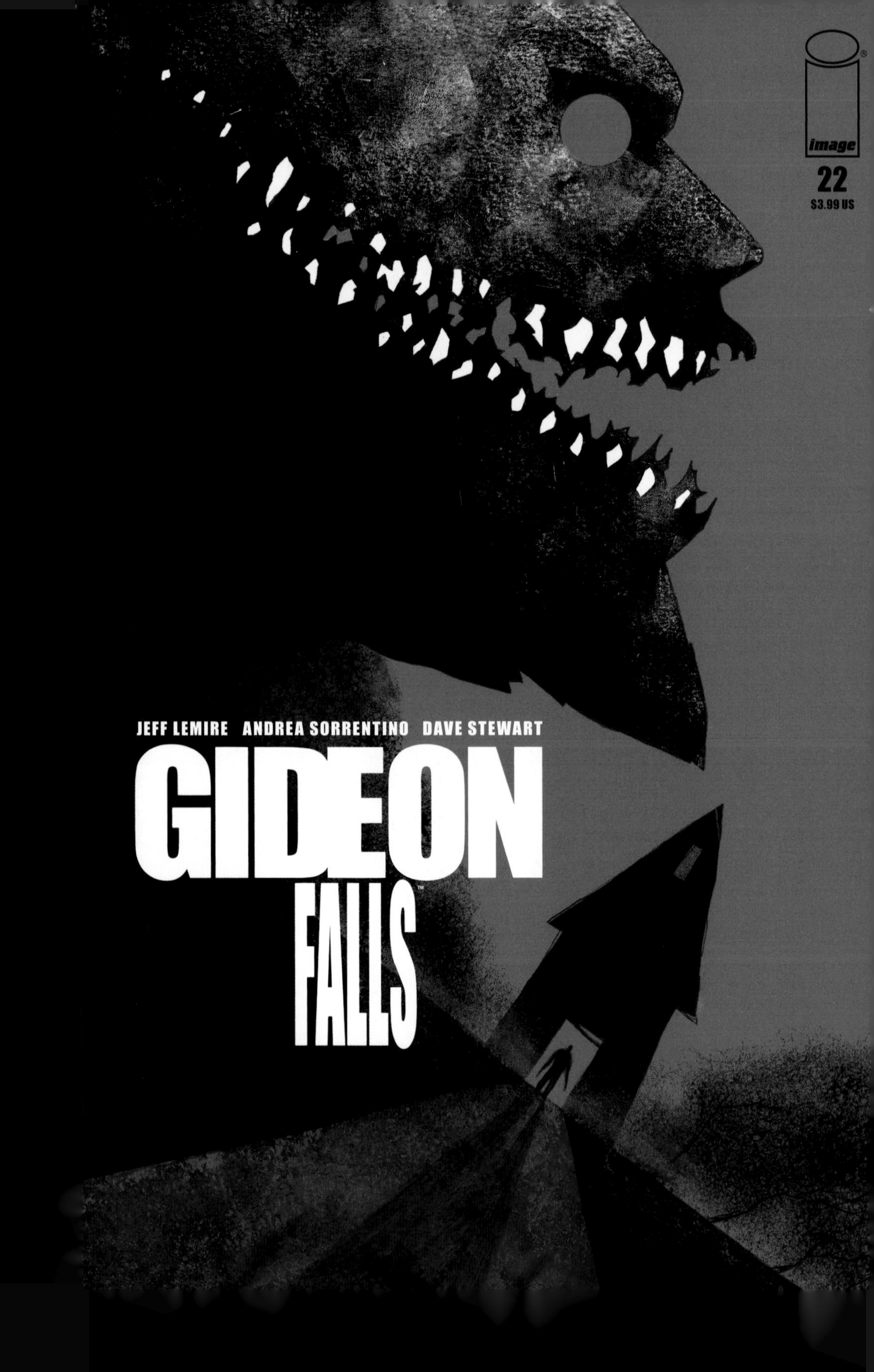
image
22
$3.99 US
JEFF LEMIRE ANDREA SORRENTINO DAVE STEWART
GIDEON FALLS™

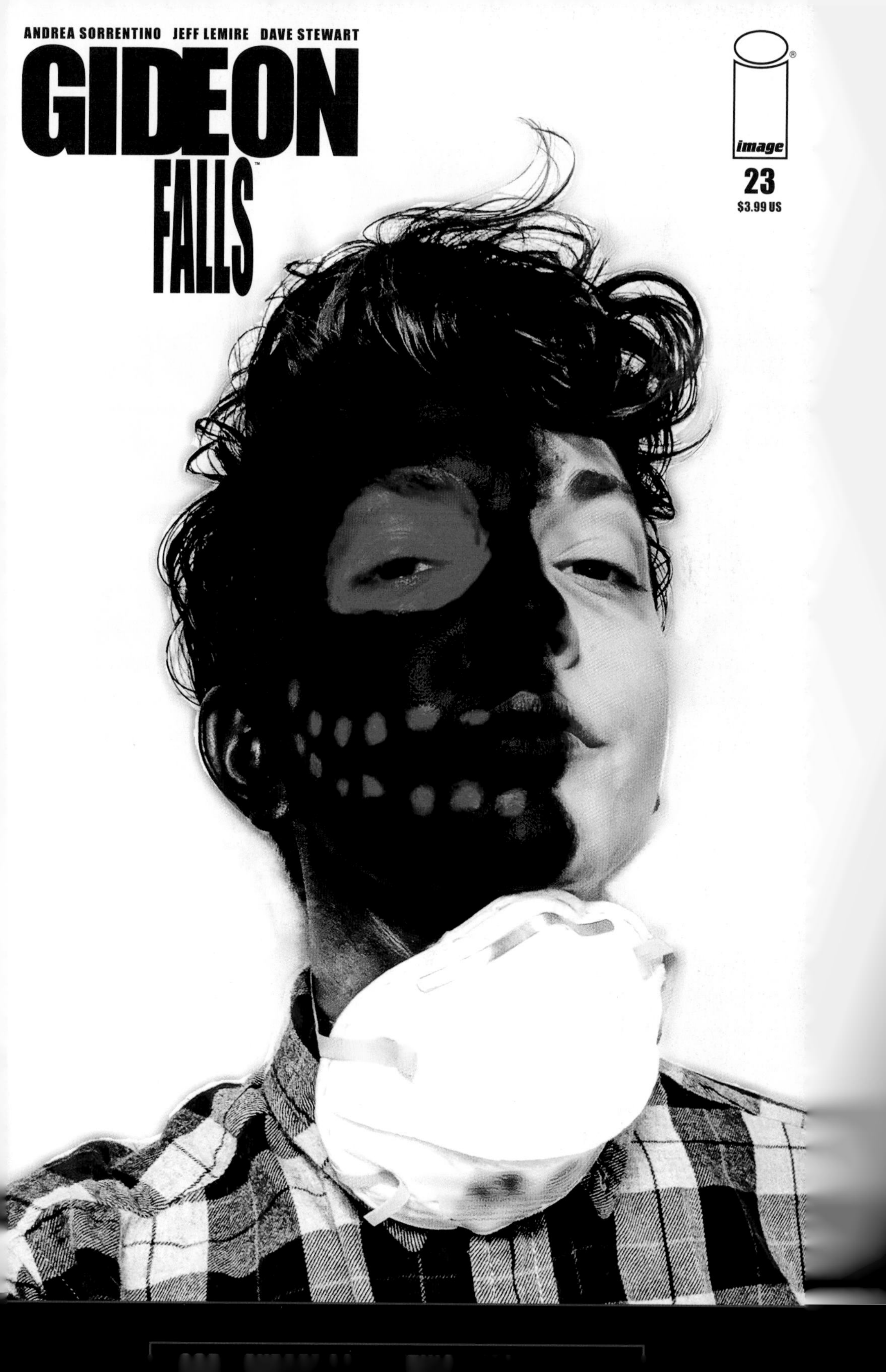
ANDREA SORRENTINO JEFF LEMIRE DAVE STEWART
GIDEON FALLS™
image
23
$3.99 US

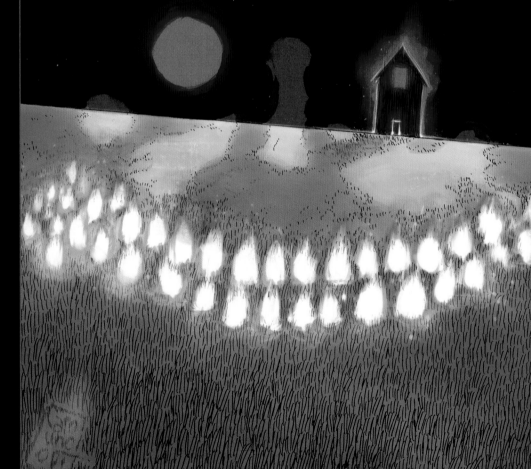